THE TUNNEL RUNNER

Want more thrilling anthologies from Black Beacon Books?

The Black Beacon Books of Mystery
The Black Beacon Book of Ghosts
The Black Beacon Book of Horror
The Black Beacon Book of Pirates
Steampunk Sleuths
Tales from the Ruins
A Hint of Hitchcock
Murder and Machinery
Shelter from the Storm
Lighthouses
Subtropical Suspense

How about a novel or a collection?

Flicker by Cameron Trost
Dark Reflections by Paul Kane
Fortitude by Karen Bayly

www.blackbeaconbooks.com

TUNNEL the RUNNER

cameron TROST

**BLACK
BEACON
BOOKS**

The Tunnel Runner
Published by Black Beacon Books
Cover photography by Emmanuelle Loquet-Trost
Copyright © Black Beacon Books, 2016

Black Beacon Books
www.blackbeaconbooks.blogspot.com

National Library of Australia Cataloguing-in-Publication entry

Creator: Trost, Cameron, 1981- author.

Title: The tunnel runner / Cameron Trost.

ISBN: 9780992321116 (paperback)

Subjects: Families--Fiction.
Suspense fiction, Australian.
Brisbane (Qld.)--Fiction.

Dewey Number: A823.4

Cameron Trost is an author of mystery, suspense, horror, and post-apocalyptic fiction best known for his puzzles featuring Oscar Tremont, Investigator of the Strange and Inexplicable. He has written four novels, *Dead on the Dolmen*, *Flicker*, *Letterbox*, and *The Tunnel Runner*, and three collections, *Oscar Tremont, Investigator of the Strange and Inexplicable*, *Hoffman's Creeper and Other Disturbing Tales*, and *The Animal Inside*. He runs the independent press, Black Beacon Books, and is a lifetime member of the Australian Crime Writers Association. Originally from Brisbane, Australia, Cameron lives with his wife and two sons near Guérande in southern Brittany, between the rugged coast and treacherous marshland.

camerontrost.com

1

The first time Gabriela told Ripley she had seen somebody scale the barbed wire fence separating the railway line from Newmarket Road and dash across the tracks and disappear through the rocky surface of the embankment, he simply assumed her overactive imagination was at work again. The second time, he decided to take her more seriously, without actually admitting he believed her. But the third time, her persistence paid off. She succeeded in convincing him.

It was a few minutes past ten o'clock on a Tuesday evening and Ripley was watching the news on the ABC.

Gabriela walked into the living room and stared at him.

He met her gaze and held it.

She didn't open her mouth. She didn't need to tell him anything. She knew that he understood the silent message.

It had happened again. That it made no sense at all was beside the point. That the fundamental laws of physics dictated that a human being could not traverse solid rock was of absolutely no significance. Gabriela had witnessed the strange occurrence once again and she wanted him to react. That was all there was to it.

He smiled at her.

She frowned back.

He found it irresistibly cute the way her brow creased in the middle and her lips dipped down at the sides, but her words soon put an end to that.

"It's happened again. Why won't you believe me? Don't you understand how hurtful that is?"

He reached for the remote and pressed the mute button.

"I believe you," he said.

Those three words hit her with such impact that she took a step backwards. Her eyes widened and her frown disappeared.

"Really?"

"Yes." It was the truth. Overactive imagination or not, she couldn't possibly have witnessed the same hallucination three times. "I believe you. If you're sure that you've seen somebody disappear through some kind of hole in the embankment three times, then I suppose you must be right. You're not crazy and you're definitely not a compulsive liar. So, yes, I believe you, babe."

She bit her bottom lip and stared at him.

"What do you want me to do? Tell me and I'll do it." He knew she wanted him to say that. "Do you want me to go over there and look for the hole?"

She studied him for a moment, confused. She was trying to work out how it was that he hadn't understood her meaning at all. She would never understand why men had such a hard time comprehending their women. They could read intricate maps and work out how to fix just about any kind of machine by pulling it apart and looking at it, but for some reason, they could never really understand something as simple as how their partners in life interpreted the world.

"No. I just wanted to know that I'm not crazy, and that you believe me."

"Well, you're not, and I do."

She sighed. "It's strange though. There can't be a hole in the embankment. It's solid rock. It doesn't make sense, does it?"

Ripley nodded his head but resisted the temptation to roll his eyes. He was glad she had pointed out what he dared not say. On the other hand, it clearly meant that she wasn't really saying what she wanted from him.

"So, you do want me to take a look after all? Why can't women just say what they want?"

"We shouldn't have to. Men should know."

"Well, we don't. We're stupid."

Ripley got up and marched to the bedroom. He went to his wardrobe and rummaged through it until he found a dark grey hoodie and a pair of black track pants.

"What are you doing?" Gabriela asked, following him into the room.

"What do you mean? I'm hardly going to run along the railway lines in my pyjamas, am I?"

Panicking, she grabbed him by the arm and pulled him towards their bed. She pushed him onto it.

He offered no resistance.

"I don't understand, Gabs. Don't you want me to find out how this person does it?"

"No. Why would I care about that?" She straddled him and rubbed herself against his groin. He could feel her softness through her thin pyjama pants.

"Well, because it's a mystery. It doesn't make sense. It doesn't make any sense at all, and neither do you for that matter. You're the one who kept going on about a strange person going through the wall, and now that I've told you I believe you, you just want me to forget all about it!"

"I don't really care about how whoever it is does it, silly. What I care about is that you believe me. Now that I know you do, I'm satisfied."

She sucked his neck.

Ripley felt the urge to reply, but decided to hold his tongue, or better still, to keep it busy. He pushed Gabriela onto her back, pulled her pyjama bottoms off and tossed them to the floor, and buried his face between her legs.

Now that he had admitted he believed her, she would forget about the hole in the wall. He too would forget all about it, for a while at least.

2

"I'll never understand women," Ripley told his colleague, Harriet, during their mid-afternoon break the next day.

"Don't worry, that's normal," she assured him as she added a dash of light milk to her coffee. "Do you want some kind of advice? This isn't about sex though, is it?"

"No, I think I've got that under control."

"Oh, is that so, Mr I'm-not-half-sure-of-myself?"

"It's a little bit weirder than that, I'm afraid."

Harriet listened intently to Ripley's explanation of the situation.

"That's pretty bloody cool, Rips. Well, you know what you have to do, of course?"

He took a sip of coffee before giving his reply. "Yes, of course, absolutely nothing at all. She doesn't actually want me to *do* anything. She just wanted my emotional support. She wanted me to reassure her that she wasn't a lunatic."

Harriet stared at him blankly for a few seconds.

"Incredible. You really don't get it at all, do you? Men are so thick!" she said, shaking her head.

"What?"

"This whole affair has unsettled her. She's probably scared stiff."

"She didn't seem scared stiff last night."

"I don't need to hear about your bedroom antics," she cut him off. "Anyway, sex just proves my point. It doesn't mean she's not scared. On the contrary, it probably makes her feel safer. It reminds her that you are a potent male capable of protecting her. Every teenage boy knows that. That's why they go for horror movies over romantic comedies. Am I wrong?"

8

"I guess you're right. But that doesn't make sense."

"What has sense got to do with anything?"

"So, what you're saying is that she's as curious about this business as I am?"

"She most definitely is."

"She wants me to solve the mystery, to provide her with an explanation?"

"Of course, she does. Just, be careful, won't you?"

Ripley nodded.

"We'd better get back to work," Harriet suggested, glancing at the clock that hung on the coffee room wall, a metre above the microwave and toaster.

"Yeah, let's go," Ripley agreed.

But his mind was far from being in work mode. He was already mentally preparing his plan of attack for the coming night's surveillance operation. The form that seemed to disappear into the rocky embankment may have been nothing more than a kid taking a risky shortcut home, but Ripley had to consider the possibility that there were more sinister goings-on afoot. Perhaps Gabriela had stumbled onto some kind of drug dealing arrangement.

He stopped himself there. He wasn't going to let his imagination run wild the way she did, but he would need to be ready for any eventuality. He would have to watch his step, and he was definitely going to need to be armed. For over a year, he had been doing regular exercise with Pete, Ben, and Oscar, and now it seemed that all the hard work might be coming to some practical use.

While he walked back to his desk, Ripley rehearsed his plan of attack in his head. He decided he would join Gabriela in watching the railway tracks from the bedroom window so that he could observe the figure for himself. He would make a mental note of where the person seemed to vanish into the earth. Then, he would wait for Gabriela to go to sleep. She was usually in bed before eleven and slept soundly. He would dress himself in dark clothes and a pair of gloves. There would be no need to jump the barbed wire fence. All he would have to do was go down to the station and lower himself onto the tracks. From there, he could walk over to the embankment. He knew the Ferny Grove timetable like the back of his hand, there would be no danger of finding himself in the way of a train.

He frowned as he sat in front of his computer and stared vacantly at the monitor.

No, that was no good. There were cameras everywhere on Wilston station. He didn't want to attract attention, even if he wasn't going to be doing anything especially offensive. He didn't want to find himself being accused of vandalism or attempted burglary.

There was no other option. He was obliged to take the shortest route to the rocky embankment. That meant scaling the barbed wire fence. He had seen that done in action movies, all he needed was a thick bathmat to throw over the barbs while he climbed over.

He would arm himself with a hammer. Nobody would mess with him then, would they?

What if he succeeded in locating the hole? Would he go inside, into the unknown?

He knew there was no way he could plan for that. He could only hope that if the opportunity presented itself, he would know what to do.

———◦———

While Ripley was walking home, he received a text message from Gabriela telling him that she was going out to dinner with some of her colleagues.

"That's perfect," he told himself.

He knew that dinner actually meant a few glasses of sparkling wine, followed by a lengthy meal and hours of chatting.

Gabriela would certainly not arrive home until around midnight. He would be able to get prepared earlier than he had intended. He could even position himself among the bushes that grew on top of the rocky embankment and watch the strange figure approach from just a few metres away. It would be daunting, but it would also be exciting – the thrill of the chase, a feeling he had only read about in books or seen in films.

Then, another idea occurred to him, just as he was walking across the pedestrian bridge that spanned the brown water of Enoggera Creek and its mangrove covered banks. There was no reason he had to wait for his quarry at all. As soon as night fell and the traffic on Newmarket Road had decreased, he would be able to inspect the rocky embankment and find the entrance long before the figure arrived on the scene. That would be the simplest way to go about it.

Ripley went about his usual evening routine, trying not to let his nerves get the better of him. He drank a beer and watched the news on SBS while he prepared dinner. After that, as the sun went down and flying foxes began filing across the sky, he started to prepare himself for the night's outing. He got dressed in his darkest and thickest clothes and took a rusty old hammer from the tool kit in the broom closet. His father had left it there in a futile attempt to encourage him to become more of a handyman. He then went to the bathroom and rolled the bathmat up. It was humid and didn't smell very pleasant, but if deployed correctly, it would prevent him from being shredded by the barbed wire. He hadn't thought to ask Gabriela if the shadowy form had used some kind of protection when climbing the fence. Maybe, with experience, one could learn how to safely straddle barbed wire unaided. It seemed unlikely, but he had to admit that he knew nothing about this person and his abilities. He had no idea at all what he was getting himself mixed up in.

For a fleeting moment, perhaps the most lucid he'd had since his conversation with Harriet, Ripley considered abandoning the undertaking. But he imagined how pleased Gabriela would be when he sat her down and explained everything to her. He would be her hero.

The moment of doubt passed. He had to go ahead. He had to discover what was happening on the other side of the railway line. Gabriela needed him to make her world feel safe. She needed him to satisfy her curiosity.

Once he was ready, Ripley turned the bedroom light off and drew the curtains open. Newmarket Road was growing quiet already. He heard cars passing by only every ten or twelve seconds. It was still a bit too frequent, but soon the gap between cars would be closer to twenty or thirty seconds and that meant, if his guess was correct, he would have enough time to dash across the road and scale the fence undetected. He just had to bide his time a little longer.

Eventually, Ripley decided that the moment had come to make a move. The traffic had died down considerably and the sky was now dark enough. The next train wasn't due for twenty minutes, and the mysterious figure, if it was to follow routine, would arrive within the hour. Now was the perfect time for Ripley to investigate the rocky embankment and, if he was unable to locate an opening himself, to find a spot to hide and wait.

He made sure that he had everything he needed, switched the lights off, and opened the door to his flat just a fraction. He could detect no movement or noise coming from the stairwell, so he slipped outside, pulled the door shut, and hurried downstairs. He walked casually but quickly out to the footpath and looked up and down the length of the road. There were no cars at all.

Nothing but a few metres of bitumen lay between him and the footpath on the opposite side. From there, he would scamper up the fence, tossing the bathmat across the barbs as he did so, and then climb down the other side. As easy as that, he tried to convince himself, but his throbbing pulse betrayed his body's true feelings.

He sprinted across the street and launched himself at the fence.

His senses were pricked and his body felt as though electricity coursed through it. He was both vulnerable and immensely powerful at the same time.

Before dashing across the street, he had worried about how he would be able to get over the fence, but now he found himself standing on the other side of it and he didn't even know how he had done it. Time and reality had skipped a step.

He reminded himself where he was, right beside the train tracks. He couldn't just stand there for too long. He risked drawing attention to himself.

To his right, along the tracks, he could see the distant outline of Wilston Station, and back the way he had come, through the wire fence, was the humble block of flats where he lived. But from this forbidden vantage point, the places that marked his daily existence seemed intrinsically different. It was as though they were warped versions of the world he knew, ones that belonged to a parallel universe.

Ripley looked up at the top of the fence. His bathmat was still there, draped ridiculously over the barbed wire. It proved to him that he had really scaled the fence and defeated its barbs. Those few frantic seconds had actually happened. But it couldn't stay there. He realised that he had to remove it. If the shadowy figure noticed the bathmat, suspicions would be aroused.

Ripley grabbed the chain fence and pulled himself up, but just as his right hand was about to reach out for the bathmat, he was disturbed by the headlights of a car turning left onto Newmarket Road from the rail bridge on Lamont Road.

He let go and dropped to his feet, but they slipped and he fell onto his back, almost hitting his head against the jagged gravel that held the railway sleepers in place.

He remained where he was for a moment.

The car drove past without slowing at all.

Once he was able to force himself to his feet again, he checked for any approaching headlights before climbing up the fence and yanking the bathmat off the top. It came loose easily and fell heavily at his feet.

He wasted no time in picking it up and jogging across the railway tracks to where the rocky embankment stood. It was close to two metres high and stretched along for two hundred metres. As Ripley walked along it, he looked back towards his flat now and then to make sure that he was within the line of sight of his bedroom window.

There was no obvious opening in the embankment, and even after closer inspection, he was unable to locate any subtle crack or hollow that could accommodate a person. He was going to have to wait for the appearance of the mysterious stranger, regardless of how long that might take.

Ripley was starting to nod off, despite his discomfort, when he heard the shrill whirring of a train approaching Wilston station. It must have been about nine forty-five. It wouldn't be much longer before the figure approached, assuming he would come at all that night. He stretched his legs a little, making sure not to let them hang over the edge.

It must have been roughly ten o'clock when the figure came into view. He didn't get a chance to see from which direction it had come. He just saw it sprint up to the fence and swing over the top like a gymnast. The fence rattled for a moment and then the figure was running straight towards him, heading for the embankment. It was wearing a black hoodie, so Ripley couldn't see a face. He wanted to move closer as the shape reached the base of the embankment, but he didn't dare. Whoever it was, he or she, no, definitely he, judging by the build, was very athletic and moved purposefully. It wasn't some child playing around, nor was it a junkie.

As the man reached the foot of the embankment, and was no longer visible from above, Ripley crawled forward, his hand tightly gripping the head of the rusty old hammer hanging from his belt. He peered over the edge and saw him crawling along its base.

The man continued along on his hands and knees until he came to a dislodged manhole cover. He tugged at it and the cover lifted noiselessly, as though it had been kept well-greased and clear of any dirt or gravel. Then, just as he had been a few seconds earlier, Ripley found himself alone.

He had a decision to make; whether to follow the strange figure into the unknown, or to go home and take a hot shower. He had answered the perplexing question of how somebody could disappear through solid rock, but he was no closer to understanding just what was going on.

He tightened his fingers around the shaft of the hammer as he stared at the metal cover.

He drew a deep breath.

Then, he changed his mind. He exhaled and relaxed his grip.

There had been enough adventure for one night.

———————————◦◦———————————

Gabriela crawled into bed just after midnight, smelling of cheap sparkling wine. Ripley hadn't been sleeping soundly, just slipping in and out of an uneasy somnolence. He had been thinking about the manhole and wondering why anybody would crawl into one. He regretted not having followed the man down there but knew that if he had, he might have regretted it even more. At any rate, he was comfortable in bed.

Gabriela snuggled up beside him. Her lips were close to his ear and the smell of alcohol mixed with perspiration and make-up filled his nostrils.

"Are you sleeping?"

"No."

"Did you have a good night?"

"Yeah, I guess I did. I discovered where the man you've noticed jumping over the railway fence goes."

"No way! Where?"

"Down a manhole."

15

"Are you serious?"

"I am indeed."

"That's insane. Did you follow him? You shouldn't have. You could have been hurt, honey."

He knew that she didn't mean it. She was glad he had solved the mystery. The next step was to discover where the manhole led.

Ripley pulled Gabriela towards him and held her in his arms.

"Are you tired?"

"Not really," she answered, kissing him. "Not too tired for my little adventurer."

3

When Ripley woke up, his thoughts immediately turned to the manhole. He could feel it rapidly becoming an obsession. He went to the toilet and found himself staring down into the bowl, to where a hole led from his bathroom into the unknown beyond. Gabriela was carrying out her usual morning routine of drinking a coffee and checking her emails, but as Ripley walked yawning into the living room, her gaze caught his and told him that she too was thinking about the disappearing act.

"Good morning."

"Morning, Gabs. Is the water still hot?"

"Should be," she answered casually.

He made himself a coffee.

"Where do you think the manhole leads to, Rips?"

He shrugged his shoulders as he inhaled the aroma of his coffee.

"You must have some idea. It must go somewhere. There must be some kind of reason he crawls underground."

"Look, I don't know. I really don't know any more about it than you do."

"We should check it out tonight after work. Maybe this person needs help. It could be some kind of political refugee."

More likely a junkie, Ripley thought. But he knew that he didn't really believe that. Whoever it was seemed to have had a clear enough mind and a very strong body.

"He didn't seem to have need of much help. On the contrary, I think he can look after himself very well indeed."

"Then why doesn't he have a job and live in a house or flat like a normal person?"

"I don't know. I suppose not everybody wants to live that kind of life. Anyhow, maybe he does have a job and home, Gabs. We don't know anything about him. We can't assume he sleeps down there."

She gave him a blank look.

"I'll file a report today," he continued. "I'll have Lifeline or some other charity look into it."

"No. We can't do that," Gabriela argued. "We have to find out for ourselves."

"Fine then, I won't call anybody."

"Don't even tell anybody about it, all right?"

He nodded, but of course, it was too late for that. He had already told Harriet.

"We'll go over there again tonight then," Gabriela repeated.

Ripley could hardly believe what he'd just heard.

"Let's talk about it this evening,' was all he said.

That day, walking home from work, Ripley looked intently at every manhole cover he passed. Gabriela would be expecting a decision from him. She would want to know whether he was going to investigate the manhole or not. If he decided not to, she would make life difficult for him and make him feel that he had let her down. She would be right after all. He *would* be letting her down.

When he arrived home, he always went straight to the fridge to get a cold beer. Gabriela knew this, that's why she chose to leave her note wedged under the six pack of Cooper's Celebration Ale.

"I can't bear not knowing any longer, Rips. I know you'll be angry and tell me that I never think things through before acting, but I have thought this through and I need to know. Even though

I'll probably be back before you get home and have a chance to read this note, I thought I'd better leave it just in case."

She had already gone over there, without even bothering to wait for him. She hadn't even given him the chance to make a decision. Worst of all, she had gone over there so early. It wasn't even six-thirty yet. There were cars and pedestrians everywhere. Wasn't she worried she might be arrested for walking on the railway tracks? No, he reminded himself, of course not. The possibility wouldn't have even occurred to her. Her mind didn't work that way.

Ripley rushed across to the bedroom window and looked out.

She was nowhere to be seen.

He tried to spot the metal manhole cover, but because it was in a slight ditch, it was hidden from view. No wonder Gabriela had thought the figure had simply vanished into the rough surface of the embankment.

He rushed out of the flat and across the street.

Had she climbed the barbed wire fence despite the heavy traffic on Newmarket Road or had she found another more discreet access point?

He scanned the scene. On the other side of the bridge leading onto Lamont Road was a house with no front fence and only a very low side fence. From there, it was just a matter of going down the slope and dropping down the embankment. Ripley wondered why the man didn't use this route instead of climbing over the tall barbed wire fence.

He walked across the bridge to Lamont Road and stopped for a moment in front of the run-down old house adjoining the railway line. There was no sign of activity coming from either inside or outside. With its chipped paintwork and unkempt garden, he wouldn't have been surprised if nobody lived in it at all.

Ripley jumped the low fence in one bound and hurried down the embankment, almost landing right on top of the dislodged metal cover. It was easier to see in the early evening light. As he had suspected, it was perfectly clean, no leaves, twigs, gravel or other debris blocked it.

A ladder led down a concrete cylinder which was also very clean, as though somebody did regular housework in there. At the bottom, a narrow tunnel was drowned in darkness.

"Gabriela!" he called.

There was no answer, except for the echo of his own anxious voice.

4

Brand Molekin walked down the tinned food aisle of Coles. He manoeuvred his way around an obese mother who was pushing a trolley ridden by a toddler. Inside the trolley were dozens of bags of frozen wedges, onion rings, and pizzas. Frozen food was not an option for the tunnel folk. They had to stick to tins, pasta, and rice for long term storage, or fresh produce for rapid consumption. Brand had to be selective in what food he took because there was only so much he could hide on him. The more he stole, the greater the chance that one of the security cameras would catch him slipping items into his pockets or that he would arouse suspicion when leaving the shop without making any purchases.

At twenty-three years old, Brand was in the average age range for a tunnel dweller. He hadn't always lived underground. Once he'd lived in a house with a roof over his head. He'd had a normal name, Barry Craig, and a family – the word sent a shiver down his spine. Family was what had driven him onto the streets, and a chance encounter was what had made him aware that life was much better *under* the streets.

He'd been sleeping in a park near Spring Hill one humid summer night when he woke up to find a ghostly shape floating across the Victoria Park golf course at high speed. His street kid instinct kicked in immediately and he raised his left arm, to which he tied his backpack while he slept. But his backpack was no longer there. Somehow, the thief had succeeded in untying it without disturbing him.

He leaped to his feet, felt for the knife he kept in one of his socks, and pursued the shadow across the field. Its speed was remarkable, but despite only just having been woken up, he was even faster.

He was hot on the shadow's heels when it suddenly curved left, darting downhill towards York's Hollow. It crossed the wooden footbridge spanning the ancient aboriginal hunting ground and set the waterfowl squawking in alarm. For a brief instant, the figure's tight black-clad outline was lit up by an overhead lamp. It was a perfect example of the female form, its muscular buttocks rippled with every rapid stride. She wasn't drug-fucked like most of the other girls of the street he had encountered before.

She headed uphill and he suddenly realised that he wouldn't be able to catch her, but then she made what he thought was a big mistake. Instead of taking advantage of her superior fitness and losing him in the parklands, she entered a storm water outlet. She had decided to go to ground.

He followed her inside.

It could have turned out to be foolish on his part, but it didn't. Little did he know, but he had just made a life-changing decision. He was about to come into contact with the tunnel folk.

After stating his case, he was offered the chance to become one of them. A chance he couldn't refuse. The girl's name was Fox Terra and she had broken one of the tunnel folk's most important rules by stealing from a homeless person. Barry was given the opportunity to choose her punishment, either a week of isolation in the Spring Hill sewer cell or three days of personal servitude to him.

He chose neither. He forgave her.

Over time, Brand Molekin managed to assert himself as one of the community's most valued members. Fox had quickly fallen in love with him and together they provided the tunnel folk clan with its most talented shoplifting duo.

As far as Brand was concerned, theft was an art form.

A perfect opportunity was presenting itself, and, true to his nature, he wouldn't fail to take advantage of it.

22

The obese woman had dropped a tin of ravioli and was struggling to bend low enough to pick it up.

He dipped down and retrieved it for her.

"Thank you," she said, huffing as though she had just sprinted a hundred metres.

"It's my pleasure," Brand replied.

He continued his shopping and left the supermarket at a moment when all of the check-out staff was busy and the security guard was giving directions to a Korean tourist who was trying to get to the Post Office.

He walked along the mall, using the reflections in the display window of the hairdressing salon to check that he wasn't being followed. He had to be careful. The others were counting on him for their daily nutrition.

Brand no longer felt safe in the outside world, it was foreign to him now. The tunnels provided him with refuge. He knew his way around them and he knew which tunnels would lead him back to his clan. He also knew which to avoid using. His life depended on that.

Meanwhile, Fox was slipping through the backyards of Alderley in search of specific items of clothing. Collecting apparel from suburban clotheslines was one of the riskiest tasks a tunnel dweller could be given, but it was also one of the most important. Although the temperature was far more predictable underground than on the surface, the lack of sunlight meant that it was never very warm and the rough conditions meant that clothes became worn-out after just a month or two of use. Constant crawling and climbing tested the endurance of even the best quality work trousers and coarse jackets. Although the tunnel dwellers tended to wear tracksuits when they went up to the surface, they found it more convenient to don heavy work clothes underground. However, today Fox had to find some more delicate items of clothing. The community was in need of thick, clean socks and sports bras for the girls.

She hid behind a line of rubbish bins while she scoped out the clothesline at the back of a block of flats. The line was hanging heavy with all kinds of useful items. She identified those that were required from a safe distance. Stealing during the daylight hours was always risky, but it had to be done then, residents seldom left their clothes out at night. Also, most people were at work during the day so there were fewer potential witnesses hanging around. Fox always gave preference to stealing from blocks of flats. Neighbours' suspicions were less likely to be aroused in backyards that were frequented by several people rather than just one family.

She stood up and walked casually over to the clothesline. She wasn't wearing her hood, it wasn't necessary to hide her identity because her shoulder-length mousy hair hid her face from view. Hoods just served to sound alarm bells in people's minds.

She glanced up at the staircase and windows of the block of flats but detected no sign of life.

After unpegging the required items of clothing, she walked back towards the flats, as though about to climb the staircase, just as a resident of the building would do. But instead of walking up the stairs, she slipped out onto the street and jogged away.

She wound her way through quiet suburban streets, carrying the items of clothing she had taken in the least conspicuous way possible. She slipped socks into her track pants, making it look as though she had a few extra kilos of fat on her previously perfect thighs, and she wrapped the sports bras around her waist, under her jumper, making it seem as though she had a flabby belly.

Fox had never been arrested, but she had come awfully close several times. She couldn't bear the thought of being locked up in prison with criminals and butch chicks. She didn't consider herself a criminal. Even though she knew that stealing was wrong, she felt that it was necessary. There was no reasonable alternative to living in the tunnels and there was no way she could survive down there without taking from the surface. As a child and teenager growing up in the surface world in the suburb of Redbank Plains, she had known only abuse and denigration. Living in the tunnels, despite the dangers that had to be faced down there, she was respected. She was one hell of a thief too; that fact couldn't be denied. Theft was her calling, her profession, and she couldn't imagine doing anything else.

She slipped across Shand Street and into Grinstead Park. From there, she would follow Kedron Brook all the way along to Montrose Street and jog her way up to Eildon Hill, the plateau capped with a reservoir that supplied many northern Brisbane suburbs with potable water. Eildon Hill was also one of the tunnel folk's favourite surface locations, providing them with three known access points that allowed them to enter secure stretches of the tunnel system.

She would rendezvous with Brand in the main receptacle under the hill, and from there, they would follow the straight stretch of tunnel that led back to the community.

5

Ripley had no idea what he was doing or where he was going, but if Gabriela had gone down there, he had to follow her. There was no telling what kind of trouble she might find herself in. He tried to force images of the worst case scenario from his mind, but they were too persistent. The only comforting thought that occurred to him was that the shadowy figure was probably still several hours away from coming home for the night.

He clambered down the ladder. The musty smell of the air down there overwhelmed him, and it took him several minutes to get accustomed to the subterranean atmosphere.

The passage led into darkness, but Ripley hadn't brought a torch with him. The possibility that he would need one hadn't even entered his mind. He wondered whether Gabriela had thought of it. There was no turning back now though. He had to find her as quickly as possible, before the man came back.

Maybe walking in darkness was going to be better after all, that way he would be unaware of whatever horrors lay around him. He would pass hordes of rats and the waste washed from suburban streets without knowing anything about it. However, Ripley would have been surprised to know that the passage he was about to stumble along was impeccably clean. He had no idea that it was a regularly maintained thoroughfare and that the darkly-clothed man he had witnessed the previous night was by no means the only person to use it.

Ripley couldn't tell whether the tunnel was leading him downward or horizontally. It was square shaped and low. He had to walk with his head bowed and shoulders stooped. The flat concrete floor beneath his feet seemed to be level and he imagined that he was stumbling forward in a straight line into the rise of land that lay between Newmarket Road and Wilston Village, passing under grand Queenslander houses and gardens delimited by picket fences. Eventually, the tunnel would either have to lead downhill with the fall of the land or come to an end at the surface. He did his best to imagine that he was walking the streets above as he felt his way through the dark because that was the only way to keep from panicking.

"Gabriela!" he called lowly, but in the enclosed space it reverberated like a shout. His voice bounced off invisible walls and he hardly recognised himself. It was a nervous voice.

He regretted his act instantly.

What if somebody else answers my call?

But nobody did. It was met with cold silence.

Ripley stumbled on through the dark until his neck was sore from being bent forward and his shoulders felt as though the weight of the world rested upon them. After a while, the exact length of time was impossible to guess in that featureless world, the passage began leading Ripley down. He could tell that because the pressure on his legs had increased and he could feel his thighs working harder. His apprehension increased as the passage curved, growing so strong that he could swear that the strange taste he detected on his dry tongue was that of fear itself. Although he knew that the passage was just following the lay of the land and that he was only a metre or two below the surface of the streets of Wilston, Ripley felt as though he was walking blindly into the depths of hell, a cold concrete hell that had not been designed by any devil but by a nameless public works engineer.

"Gabriela!" he called out again, no longer concerned about who might hear him. "Where are you?"

Nobody answered. Could he have expected anything different? Did he really think he would find his girlfriend down there? Surely she wouldn't have had the guts to venture so far down into such dauntingly claustrophobic obscurity.

27

She must have, because I've been touching the wall the whole way along and haven't felt any openings. This is the only way she could have come. Do I love her? Yes. No... Do I really love her? Yes! I do!

"Gabriela? I'm not leaving without you!" he shouted. He knew full well that his cry was more for his benefit than hers, but perhaps she could hear him, even faintly, somewhere down there.

The pressure on his thighs lessened as the passage became level again. He tried to imagine where he was in terms of the streets above. Could he have reached Kedron Brook Road? Was he lurking beneath the corner where the old grocery shop that was now a trendy café stood or was he closer to the Cold Rock ice cream parlour? There was no way of knowing, but he had to imagine where he was in reference to the world above. His sanity depended on it. If he was indeed where he thought he was, then his anxious subterranean trek was the surface equivalent of a leisurely three-minute stroll past purple jacaranda trees and immaculate flower beds.

The passage began heading uphill and Ripley's spirits rose with it. There was no longer a shadow of a doubt about it. He knew where he was, between Kedron Brook Road and Eildon Hill. The uphill walk in such cramped conditions was going to be difficult, but where Gabriela had gone he would follow. His legs strained as they pushed him up the ascent. There was bound to be an exit somewhere on Eildon Hill. She would have taken advantage of it to leave the tunnel.

Ripley crossed his fingers.

His thighs started burning as he forced himself to continue up the hill and more than once he wondered if he would collapse from exhaustion and a lack of oxygen. He was fitter than Gabriela. He exercised regularly while she slept in every morning, only getting out of bed just before it was time to leave for work. The idea that he might pass out from exertion where she had been able to press on seemed ridiculous to him. But

28

perhaps her smaller frame had been an advantage in the underground passage. She wouldn't have had to stoop as much as him. Or maybe... the mere thought of it sent a chill down his spine... maybe she *had* collapsed and been helped along by somebody. Or maybe... he could feel his pulse accelerating... she had been intercepted – kidnapped!

"Gabriela!"

"Hello?" a female voice replied.

Ripley froze and dropped to his knees, partly out of shock, partly out of fatigue, but mostly out of relief.

"Who's that?" the voice came again, and with it his momentary sense of relief vanished.

"Gabriela?" His single-worded question was timid and disappointed.

"No, who's Gabriela? Who are *you*? Don't move. I'm coming."

Ripley didn't have any intention of moving. He was too stunned, too confused. The voice was that of a young woman, but it wasn't Gabriela's. What was she doing down there in an underground passage? How could she find her way around in the absolute darkness that reigned in that subterranean realm?

His last question was answered immediately. An eerie glow formed somewhere in front of him, slightly to his left. It grew brighter and brighter, chasing his sense of isolation and stifling claustrophobia away, but not affecting his fear.

The walls of the passage he had been stumbling along for what seemed like an hour, but was really only a matter of minutes, became visible. The soft orange glow of the torchlight made the cold grey of concrete recede behind him. Only then did he notice how remarkably clean the passage was.

The passage veered sharply to the left just in front of him. The light was coming from that direction – and then, all of a sudden, it was right in his face and Ripley felt like a kangaroo caught in the headlights of a road train.

There was no knowing what would come next, what his fate

would be. He wondered how he could explain why he was down there. As absurd as it seemed, he felt as though he had broken into her house and invaded her privacy.

What happened next was the last thing he could have expected. She started laughing, a deliciously sweet laugh.

"Hello?" he addressed the light shining on his face. He felt like laughing too, but his body obviously didn't feel the same way.

"You look petrified!"

He smiled. "Well, I'm not used to being in such confined conditions."

"You're not kidding."

"I'm a bit of a fish out of water."

"You can say that again, or a surface walker out of his comfort zone."

"A surface walker?"

The torch was lowered, surely a sign that she had decided he was not a threat to her. The beam of light flooded the passage floor and Ripley noticed that there were lines and numbers painted on it, as though somebody had marked out distances from one place to another. Then, his gaze moved upward to the form standing in front of him – a figure that seemed strangely out of place but at the same time somehow in keeping with the singular world around it. She was wearing a tracksuit that hugged her chubby body and Ripley found it hard to imagine what such an unfit looking girl was doing in such a physically demanding environment. Her glowing face was attractive and angular, in stark contrast with her body.

"Yes, surface walkers, that's what we call people who don't live underground."

"You mean to tell me that you live down here?"

"That's right. There is a whole..." she cut herself off. "The real question is, what are *you* doing down here? You obviously don't work for the city council."

"No, I don't," Ripley hesitated, unsure of just how much he should tell her, but his hesitation was fleeting. He needed her more than she needed him. He was a stranger in her world.

"I'm looking for my girlfriend."

She laughed.

"It's not a joke. I'm worried about her. She could be in serious danger."

"Sorry, it's just that this is a strange place to lose your girlfriend. Why did she come down here?"

"She saw somebody enter this passage via a manhole and wanted to find out where he was going."

She frowned. "Do you mean the one on the Ferny Grove railway line, near Wilston Station?"

"Yes, that's it."

"Can you tell me what time she saw this person?"

Ripley didn't know what to say. He didn't want to get himself or Gabriela into trouble, perhaps he had stumbled across some kind of criminal activity.

"Don't worry. I'm just trying to work out who she saw."

"Well, it must have been around ten o'clock at night."

"Ah yes, that's all right then."

"You know who it is?"

"Yes."

Ripley looked at her blankly.

"Can you tell me who?"

She thought for a moment. "I don't think I can. No, I've told you enough already."

They stood in silence for a long instant, two shadows in the darkness linked by a mere beam of light. He wanted to ask her why she lived underground. Surely she would be better off living in the city above, with a job and a normal life. He wanted to ask her, but didn't.

She was the first to speak again, changing the subject back to the pressing matter of the surface walker's girlfriend.

"I'm afraid I haven't come across your Gabriela."

Ripley couldn't hide his surprise. "How do you know her name?"

She laughed at him again, ensuring that he continued to feel ridiculous.

"Because we tunnel dwellers are psychic, of course."

"Tunnel dwellers?"

She sighed. "You were calling her name. *Gabriela! Gabriela!*"

"Oh, so I was. Sorry, I can't think straight down here."

She nodded sympathetically. "That's normal. It's a very different environment. It must make you feel trapped, just as it makes me feel sheltered."

"I have to find her. Will you help me?"

"Of course, I'll help you, surface walker."

"You can call me Ripley if you like."

"Fox is what they call me."

"That's a strange name."

"I'm a strange girl," she smiled. "Listen Ripley, if your girlfriend came through the Ferny Grove line access point, she must have come the same way you've come. Since I didn't run into her from the way I've come, then she must have reached the Eildon Hill junction before me."

"Which means what exactly?" Ripley was struggling to understand the thoroughfares and locations of an unknown world.

"It means that either Gabriela exited the passage and returned to the outside world at Eildon Hill or she took one of several turn-offs leading into different tunnels."

"So, if the former is the case, she's probably waiting for me at home, but if she took the latter option?"

"Then she could be just about anywhere under Brisbane."

Ripley put his head in his hands.

"On the up side, if you'll pardon the pun, most surface walkers would have taken the opportunity to climb back out of the passage. Therefore, she's probably at home, waiting for you."

Ripley sighed.

"Where do you live?"

He hesitated. As nice as she seemed, he didn't feel comfortable giving her his address.

"I have to be able to get in touch with you so I can let you know if I hear anything."

"I'm not leaving without her," Ripley said firmly.

"You have to check whether she's back home. There's no point wandering around down here if she's at home cooking you dinner and wondering where you are."

She had a point.

"I need to be able to get in touch with you at any time of the day or night, and since I don't have a telephone, that means I need your address."

"All right," Ripley gave in. He told her where he lived and she led him to the Eildon Hill junction.

"There's just one more thing, Ripley." Her tone of voice warned that what she was about to say was very serious.

"Yes?" he asked.

"You mustn't mention us to anybody on the surface. Our survival as a community depends on it."

Ripley frowned and hesitated a moment before nodding once.

"Do you promise?"

He nodded again, more resolutely this time. "Yes, Fox, I promise. And do you promise to bring Gabriela back to the surface?"

She looked at him with eyes full of sympathy. "I won't rest until I find her."

"Thank you."

She indicated the rusty but still solid ladder that would deliver Ripley to the surface world and watched as he climbed his way up through the concrete shaft.

Once at the top, Ripley pushed a grate open and found himself in a clearing. He looked back into the dim junction below, but Fox had already vanished.

The sun was setting and flying foxes were already flapping across the evening sky. Ripley was lost for a moment, until childhood memories of after-school bike rides came rushing

33

back. He was about halfway down Eildon Hill. A dirt track led up from the clearing to the flat top of the hill and a stretch of grass led downward to the houses that stood at its foot. Ripley was just an easy eight-minute walk from home. If he ran, it would only take two or three. He stretched his neck, shook his sore legs, and took a deep breath. He wanted to get home as quickly as possible. All he could do was hope that Gabriela would be there, waiting for him.

6

"You'll never guess what's just happened!" Fox said when Brand finally met up with her at the meeting point.

"What then?" he asked indifferently, as though expecting his partner's story to be nothing out of the ordinary. On this occasion, he was wrong.

"I met a surface walker. That's what."

His brow furrowed, forming a deep crease of concern across his nose and making him look more menacing than he naturally did. "You were caught stealing?"

"No. I met him down here."

"Here! A surface walker was down *here*?" Brand shook his head. "This is bad, Fox, very bad."

"I don't think so. He was just looking for his girlfriend."

Brand's alarm grew.

"What was his girlfriend doing down here?"

"She saw Dart coming into the system and decided to try to work out where he was going."

"A curious surface walker on the loose. This isn't good, Fox. Is she still down here?"

"I don't know, probably not. I hope not. He was so worried about her."

"We have to tell Cooper about this."

Fox nodded.

Cooper Caverna, the founder and elected leader of the tunnel dwellers, had helped them through some rough patches and never ceased to remind them that if they had chosen to live below the surface, it was because, whatever trials they may face, they preferred life underground to an existence up top, where those who had grown up in their biological families had known only abuse, neglect, or complete disinterest. Cooper had gone to university before moving underground. He had studied history and sociology and become so fascinated with one particular area of academic thought; that of the concept of utopian society, that he had decided to experiment with the idea of building one. That silly pursuit, surely the misguided dream of just another naïve student who refused to accept the unwritten law of consumerism and the holy doctrine of the market system, slowly became a reality as an increasing number of his friends spent more and more time in disused tunnels.

Within a year, there were eleven dedicated tunnel dwellers who were spending so much time underground they eventually left their share houses and began sleeping below the city. At first, they occupied a dirty section of tunnel in Auchenflower, the entrance to which was conveniently located in a public park close to toilets. However, as numbers increased, the need to supply an ever larger community with the means of leading a healthy lifestyle grew. Cooper and his group of eighteen tunnel dwellers launched an ambitious plan to explore and accurately record the subterranean systems of Brisbane while, at the same time, moving their settlement closer towards the centre of the city, where they would be near a high concentration of surface infrastructure.

The project was a massive success, and, within a couple of days, the settlement had been shifted to a cluster of abandoned and surprisingly spacious chambers, the original purpose of which was unclear. The Chambers were cleaned, and furnished with goods collected from the surface.

The tunnel dwellers took unwanted beds, tables, chairs, and wardrobes that had been left at the kerb outside suburban homes, or stole lighting equipment and domestic appliances from the homes of the rich.

Within no time at all, the Chambers had been transformed from a handful of gloomy, interconnected box-like rooms into communal lodgings the likes of which many surface walkers could never even dream of inhabiting.

It was towards these Chambers that Fox and Brand were making their way without the slightest hesitation. They knew the tunnels as well as anybody.

Shortly after establishing the Chambers, Cooper had surprised his eighteen followers by calling an election. He didn't want the new community to be controlled by an autocrat, even if its very existence was due to that individual's initiative. As far as he was concerned, the future of the colony and the strength of its social fabric depended on the energetic pursuit of the values that they held in common, values that included the strong belief that equality and respect lay at the heart of the society they wanted to build. Every member would work according to his or her abilities and would share the fruit of their work with each other. There would be no room for special treatment or exceptions, all would follow the same rules. An elected leader would be necessary as an arbitrator on the occasions, which would hopefully be rare, when general discussion failed to lead to consensus.

Cooper decided that the ballot should be secret. All that would be needed was an urn, one that symbolised the birth of a new, true democracy beneath the streets of the city's unequal society. He suggested that a letterbox would be ideal.

Brand and Dart, two of Cooper's original followers from university, were given the honour of acquiring the urn. Their task was simple but not without its risks. They were to go to Hamilton, one of the city's wealthiest suburbs, and identify a letterbox that met two criteria. Firstly, it had to belong to a sickeningly extravagant house, and secondly, it had to be one that could be removed without making too much noise or spending too much time working it free. Removing a symbol of wealth and injustice and using it as the foundation of an egalitarian society was a delicious idea, the kind Cooper adored. On the surface, such an act would be considered a theft, but for

37

the tunnel dwellers, the possession of an excessive tract of land and a house big enough to support four or five families was the act of a truly callous criminal. Taking the letterbox and putting it to good use was merely poetic justice on a derisible scale.

A shiny red letterbox adorned with the number 60 in big brass digits was discreetly removed from outside an oversized abode on Hillside Crescent one night and brought back to the Chambers. It was clearly out of place, sitting conspicuously in the middle of a huge, dimly lit hall in a tunnel world where not even the most adventurous postman would dream of going on his rounds. The strange symbol of their new society gave the tunnel dwellers a sense of hope. It was a reminder of their ability to initiate a fair and endurable community.

However, after five years of annual elections, a time during which the population had increased to twenty-six members, the ballot box had been a mere formality. Cooper Caverna was elected with a vast majority every time, and the Charter of Communal Values and Rules that he had drawn up in collaboration with the entire underground population never failed to be ratified. One of the rules, and one which had never yet been put into practice, was that the location of the Chamber must remain a closely guarded secret and that the arrival of any surface dwellers in the system be signalled to the community as a whole as promptly as possible.

Brand and Fox listened for any unexpected noises as they strode through the tunnels, turning here and there, and crawling up inclines or sliding down into lower sections where necessary. They were hoping to hear uncertain footsteps ringing out or the whimpering of a lost soul drifting through the damp atmosphere, but they detected nothing out of the ordinary.

"I hope she has the good sense and enough luck to crawl up a ladder and find a trap she's strong enough to push open," Brand said, more to himself than to Fox, as he ducked under a copper pipe that spanned the passage.

"So do I. She could get trapped and starve down here if she

ventures too far along the wrong branch. Or she might fall and hurt herself."

Brand nodded. "The rats would make short work of her if she got too exhausted to keep moving. Do you remember the time Jake tripped over and sprained his ankle during one of the westward explorations? He was lucky that day. If we hadn't found him—"

"Stop! I don't want to think about that, Brand. Anyway, it's not rats I'm worried about, not the animal kind at least."

"What are you talking about? No tunnel dweller would do her harm."

"That's what we like to tell ourselves, but I'm not so sure. There are hundreds of kilometres of tunnel down here and more storage area than we even know about." Fox lowered her voice. "And there is at least one of us who I'm sure gets up to more than he lets on. I wouldn't like *him* to find the surface dweller."

Brand didn't reply, but he quickened his pace. He knew that she was right. They had to let Cooper know about the situation as soon as possible.

7

Ripley opened the door to his flat and stepped inside. There were no lights on and there was no noise at all. His stomach churned as though he had eaten something rotten, and he felt a sudden and overbearing weight push down on his shoulders as though the ceiling had collapsed on him. Gabriela was not at home. She was still down there. His skin crawled as he imagined her stumbling through the dark passages of an unknown world, one that was so very close, just a few metres below the sunlit surface of Brisbane's streets, and yet somehow so very distant.

Fox had seemed like a girl who knew how to look after herself in that subterranean world, and her assurances that she would find Gabriela had been sincere. Ripley didn't like to admit it but he was going to have to rely on that strange – what had she called herself? A tunnel dweller? – to rescue his girlfriend and bring her back to the surface.

He walked into the living room, where the blank screen of the television and the empty couch only made his loneliness worse. At this time of the evening, Gabriela would usually be watching the news or checking her emails. After that, she would go into the kitchen. Tonight would have been her turn to cook and Ripley's turn to do the washing-up. He sighed as he realised that she would not be eating tonight, and neither would he. He couldn't while she was wandering the damp, rat-infested tunnels beneath the streets.

Why hadn't she found her way out? Surely it wasn't that hard to climb a ladder and open a manhole the way he had. He started feeling angry at her. He wanted to tell her to stop being so stupid and to just go up. All she had to do was go up, up to where the stars were winking at her from their celestial home. How could she be so bloody stupid! But he had to stop himself. He had to try to think clearly. She needed him to be strong, and to be smart. He had promised Fox he wouldn't tell anybody about the tunnel dwellers and now he had to make a difficult decision, whether to break or honour that oath. If he told the emergency services about what had happened, he would be condemning the tunnel dwellers to exposure, and, even though Fox seemed to be a friendly girl, he had no idea how the others might react to such an infringement. It might make them angry at him, and that anger might be taken out on Gabriela. It was too risky. On the other hand, depending on strangers to rescue her was also a risky bet to make. Should he go back down and join the search? Fox had told him to stay at home so that she could contact him if – no, when – she found Gabriela. But how could he just sit back and do nothing?

Ripley walked to the bedroom window and looked across Newmarket Road to where he knew the entrance to the tunnel system was; just an inconspicuous manhole cover by the side of the Ferny Grove railway line. He hoped to see Gabriela crawl out of it.

If only he could tell her about the Eildon Hill junction, he could lead her out of the underground maze. Then, he had an idea. Maybe, just maybe, she had her mobile with her! He almost kicked himself. He should have thought of that earlier. In all his excitement and panic and his desire to find her and hold her in his arms, he had overlooked the simplest way of getting in touch. He grabbed his mobile phone and searched for her name in the contacts list. He pressed the dial button and held his breath. *Please answer, please, please, please!* Then, he heard the last thing he wanted to hear, the sound of her mobile phone ringing. It was echoing a tauntingly happy tune from the kitchen or living room.

Fuck!

He threw his mobile on the bed with such force that it bounced off again and hit the wall, scratching the paintwork. He wanted to shout at her, to ask her what the hell she thought she was doing. The least she could have done was take her bloody mobile phone with her. She took it everywhere else she went, much to his annoyance, but she hadn't thought about taking it with her into the tunnels. Perhaps she had assumed there would be no reception underground. Or maybe she just hadn't thought much about what she was doing at all.

Ripley put his hands over his mouth and measured his breathing. He looked towards the railway line, still hoping that his dark-haired angel would appear from beneath the ground. The sun had disappeared behind the earth and the sky was growing darker by the minute. Flying foxes crossed the sky and the stars twinkled brighter, both rejoicing in the absence of the mighty sun. They were happy that night was falling, but not Ripley, he would not be able to sleep, not while Gabriela was down there in the damp and the cold, lost in a land of rats and spiders and whatever else hid in those dark passages.

Fox was his only hope.

He stumbled into the silent living room, where Gabriela should have been. Something buzzed over by the pot plants. It was her mobile, sitting inside her handbag, announcing that she had a missed call. He sighed. He had to wait for Fox. He had to sit at home imagining all kinds of horrible fates and possibilities until Fox returned his girlfriend to him – but what if she didn't? Ripley told himself that she would, that she knew the tunnels like a pickpocket knows back alleys. Fox would bring her back. He had to believe that.

He went to the fridge to get a beer.

There were two full six packs of Cricketers Arms Lager.

He grabbed a bottle and opened it, took a gulp, and then went back to the living room.

He sat down on the couch and drank the beer while he stared from the blank television screen to Gabriela's handbag and back again, over and over. She was lost down in the tunnels. He too was lost, right there in his familiar living room.

Once he'd finished his beer, Ripley thought about grabbing another one, but resisted the temptation. He didn't want to get drunk. What if Fox and Gabriela turned up and he was sleeping on the couch with a forest of empty beer bottles standing around him? Gabriela would never forgive him.

He had to distract himself, so he reached for the remote and switched the television on, but after channel surfing for a couple of minutes, the pretence became too much to bear.

He turned the television off and stood up. Waiting was not going to be an option. He had to help Gabriela. He had to go back down there. But this time he would be better prepared.

He went back to the bedroom and picked his mobile phone up off the floor. Reception or no reception, he was taking it with him. He left his flat and went to the shopping centre at the corner of Newmarket and Enoggera Roads. The walk only took him about five minutes. It wasn't very busy as the shop was about to close for the night and most customers had already bought their evening groceries. Ripley had a handful of very specific items to purchase. He zipped through the aisles, weaving past trolleys and wayward children, until he found what he was looking for. He took a torch and three six volt torch batteries. He also noticed some car care products nearby and decided to take a can of red spray paint. Then, he went to the aisle where cereals were stocked and took a few packets of muesli bars and some dried fruit. He would need some spring water, but just one bottle, he didn't want to have too much weight to carry.

After paying for his purchases, Ripley hurried up to Eildon Hill. He had no idea whereabouts in the tunnel system Gabriela might be, but at least from the Eildon Hill junction, he would be able to keep track of his location to some degree and thus have a better chance of not getting completely lost.

He made his way back to where he had left the tunnels just a couple of hours earlier and pushed the manhole cover aside.

The darkness below was deep and daunting.

Gabriela was down there, and despite Fox's reassurances, he couldn't help but feel that she was in danger.

8

When Brand and Fox arrived in the Chambers, they found Cooper in conference with Shock and Pierce. The community had always done its best to provide itself with all the modern equipment that surface walkers were accustomed to having in their homes. However, a reliable and secure internet connection was one mod-con that they had long been planning on installing in the heart of the Chambers but had continually proved unable to set up.

Shock was the tunnel dwellers' expert on all such matters. He had been a student of electrical engineering on the surface and had been planning on pursuing a career in the field when he met Cooper and was introduced to life under the surface. The opportunity to install the entire electrical infrastructure of a new society was far more tempting than any job he could have landed with an engineering firm, even if there was no money to be made from it. There was also the other reason for leaving the surface world, the real reason, but nobody spoke about that in his presence.

Pierce was the handyman. He was by no means the only one in the tunnel community, but he was the man everybody turned to when something needed fixing or hooking up. Growing up in a home where the only thing his father had left him before running off into the sunset with a seventeen-year-old girl was a fine collection of tools, Pierce had taught himself DIY. While his mother allowed herself to be dominated by a series of abusive boyfriends, he would lock himself in the backyard shed and try to forget the world. All that, however, came to an end when one of her boyfriends decided to ban him from the shed.

Pierce had told his mother that she needed to tell the man to leave them and to never set foot on their property ever again, but she wouldn't. She kept her boyfriend and lost her son.

The three young men sat at a wooden table near the red letterbox at the centre of the dimly lit main chamber. They looked up as Brand and Fox arrived and could tell by the expression on their faces that there was a problem.

"What's wrong?" Cooper asked.

They sat themselves down at the table and looked at each other as though deciding who would start.

"Fox encountered a surface walker," Brand said.

Cooper looked at her. "Where was this? Down here?"

She nodded. "It was near the Eildon Hill Junction."

"Well, at least it's not too close to here," Pierce replied.

"Perhaps not, but a surface walker down here can only mean bad news. We can't afford to take any risks. Tell me about him, Fox."

"It's not a man, it's a woman. I met her boyfriend. He was looking for her…"

"Wait, wait… slow down. You met a man and he told you that he was looking for his girlfriend, is that right?"

"That's it, exactly."

"Did he tell you why he thought his girlfriend was underground?"

"Yes, it's a long story. Well, they noticed Dart entering the tunnel through the manhole near Wilston Station and that made them curious."

"Oh no, this is sounding worse by the second," Shock said.

"Do they think Dart noticed them?"

"I don't think so."

Cooper seemed relieved. He stood up and walked away from the table. He needed a moment to let the news sink in. The main chamber was mostly empty. The majority of the tunnel dwellers were still away, pursuing their daily tasks. A handful even worked normal jobs on the surface, providing the community with a small but useful cash income. Low-wattage lamps were attached to the walls, near the corners. They hung above bookshelves, desks and work benches. Cooper strolled towards an elevated platform at one end of the chamber. A flight of concrete stairs which numbered six steps led up to the flat deck where several large dining tables were lined up. He placed a foot on the first step and then turned around and walked back towards the others.

"Is the young man still down here?"

"No, I got his address from him and told him that I'll look for his girlfriend and take her back to him when I find her."

"That's good thinking, Fox. So we just need to find her. She entered the system using the Wilston Station manhole?"

"Apparently so."

"And her boyfriend walked all the way along to the Eildon Hill Junction."

"Yes. Without a torch."

Cooper nodded. "That's not bad going for a surface walker."

"She could be anywhere by now," Brand pointed out.

"I know," Cooper agreed, "but we need to find her before she finds us here."

"Or gets herself killed," Fox said.

Cooper sat down at the table again and pushed the papers pertaining to the internet project aside.

"We need to organise a search plan that will cover as much of the tunnel network as possible in a short time."

"This is the first time we've had to launch a search, isn't it, Cooper?" Brand asked.

"Yes, it is. We haven't even done a practice drill before," he admitted in a self-critical tone.

"Who do we have available?" Fox asked as she started removing stolen clothes from her tracksuit and placing them on the table. Brand removed the food from his person as well.

"There is just the five of us for the moment."

"We might have to wait for everybody else to get back," Pierce suggested.

The others groaned.

"We don't know exactly when they will be back though. I think we should leave a note explaining the situation and telling them where we have gone and where they should search," Fox said.

Brand hummed in agreement.

"We don't have much choice," Cooper admitted. "We need to sort this problem out as quickly as possible."

"We need to do this methodically," Shock pointed out. His mind was always pre-set for attacking any problem from a logical perspective. As far as he was concerned, the world was a circuit board and obstacles were just gaps waiting to be bridged. "Before we start planning the search, we need to decide what we will do when... or rather if, we find her. Oh yeah, what's her name, Fox?"

"Gabriela."

"And her boyfriend?"

"Um... Riley, no, Ripley."

"Like in *The Talented Mr Ripley*?"

"Or that crazy bitch in *Aliens*?"

"That's right."

"So, if we succeed in finding Gabriela?"

Cooper thought for a moment. Shock had posed a very good question. What would they do if they found her?

"If we find her, we'll take her back to where she belongs. We'll lead her to Wilston Railway Station."

Pierce opened his mouth to say something, but the words didn't come. All the same, everybody had noticed his hesitation and knew what was on his mind. They looked at him, waiting for him to speak up. He had no choice but to articulate his thoughts.

"I think that... well, I don't know what we should do exactly, but we have to be careful. Having surface walkers down here doesn't bode well. It could herald the end of our community if

48

this girl, Gabriela, tells everybody about our existence."

"I know," Fox cut in, "but before Ripley left the tunnel, he promised that he wouldn't mention us to anybody. I think he would make his girlfriend keep her mouth shut as well."

"Maybe, but we should plan to hold some kind of debriefing all the same," Pierce insisted.

"What do you think, Cooper?" Brand asked.

"Well, I don't think that bringing her here is a good idea. Having a surface walker know of our existence is one thing but having her know about the Chambers is another altogether. I agree with Pierce that we would need to debrief her before returning her to the surface. The best place for the debriefing would be at a large junction a safe distance from here. I suppose the exact location will depend on where we find her... assuming we do."

"Very well," Brand said. "So, where should we search?"

Cooper walked over to the bookshelf closest to the elevated platform where the dining tables stood. Dinner was going to have to be postponed that night. He withdrew a map of the tunnel system and was returning to the centre of the chamber when a voice boomed out from the darkness near one of the chamber's entrances.

"You're all as weak as piss!"

Everybody turned towards where the voice had come from, and even though they couldn't see who was there, they recognised it.

"Shit," Fox muttered under her breath.

"Dart?" Cooper asked.

The form stepped out and strode across the large concrete chamber towards the group.

"A surface walker has discovered us and you're all chatting about debriefings and gossip over afternoon tea. We can't afford to be exposed. If the surface finds out about us, we will be flushed out like turds in a toilet and end up living on the streets or, even worse, as slaves to the surface world's unjust

49

society."

They looked at Dart and saw the sinister smile that tickled his lips. They knew what he was thinking but they hoped that they were wrong.

Then, he spoke, and confirmed their suspicions.

"You all know we can't allow this girl to return to the surface."

"Are you saying we have to persuade her to join us?" Shock asked, even though he knew all too well that that was not what Dart had meant.

They waited for the tunnel runner to explain himself.

"We have to be strong. We have to do what is right for the community. There is a time to be gentle lambs, but there is also a time to be vicious wolves. Otherwise, we'll end up like sheep on the surface."

"Dart, we do not kill. We came down here to make a better society, one where every man and woman is respected and protected."

"It must be done, Cooper. We can't risk being exposed. You are our leader and you have responsibilities."

Cooper glared at Dart. They had never been friends. Cooper had always disliked him and felt that there was something unsavoury about the tunnel runner. He had tried to put his feelings aside for the sake of the community and because Dart was an important member of the group. He was strong, fast, and good at what he did. He was a great tunnel runner. This was not the first time they had exchanged words but it was the first time Cooper had heard Dart suggest murder. Everybody had suspected he was a maniac, now he had declared it loud and clear.

"We are not going to murder anybody, Dart," Brand stated firmly. His voice was final and left no room for negotiation.

"We have to protect our community!" he growled.

"Not through killing, Dart. Our community is worthless if we abandon our values. Killing is against our code. The code we all voted for and ratified."

"Cooper has failed us as a leader. He is weak!" Dart declared to the others. His intention was obvious. He wanted to instigate a coup.

Cooper stared at him.

"Cooper is our elected leader and our code was written by all of us. If you want to remain with us, you need to respect the code," Brand said sternly.

"I don't give a fuck about the code! Codes are for cowards and fools. Moral certitude and a sense of purpose are the forces that rule my conscience. If I find this girl, I will execute her in the name of the tunnel dweller community!"

"You don't have the authority to do anything on behalf of the community, Dart!" Cooper shouted.

Once the angry echo of their leader's voice had dissipated, a heavy silence filled the chamber.

Dart's face turned as cold and hard as stone. There was no love lost between him and his fellow tunnel dwellers. His vision of how the community should be didn't match that of the others. They sought to create a subterranean utopia based on equality and social values whereas his idea of the perfect society was one in which they did whatever they had to do to make their lives better and those of the surface walkers worse. He hated the people who lived in the houses and flats of the city of Brisbane, and he placed no value at all on their lives. There was no common ground. The space between Dart and the others was a no man's land.

"Cooper, it's as simple as this. If I find that girl, I will kill her. I know what's best for the tunnel dwellers even if their elected leader doesn't."

"Dart! I forbid you to leave the Chambers until further notice!"

"Fuck you, Cooper!"

The others were speechless as Dart stormed out of the main chamber and disappeared. This was the first time they had faced such a situation. Many people had become disenchanted with life underground and broken all ties with the tunnel dwellers before, and, quite naturally, there had been many disputes about all kinds of matters from the timing of meetings to the adjustment of internal regulations. Dart was recognised as a weird puppy and he was no stranger to causing trouble and attempting to provoke dissent, but this time it was much worse. The moment he left the chamber, it was clear to Cooper, Brand, Fox, Shock, and Pierce that he had become a rogue element. Dart would no longer accept any instructions from Cooper and it would no longer be possible to trust him. One way or another, he was going to have to leave the community.

"What are we going to do about him?" Brand asked.

Cooper said nothing.

"Let's not waste any more time on him," Fox suggested. "We need to plan our search."

Dart strode back into the main chamber and walked across it, heading towards the exit to the northbound passage. He was carrying a hatchet in one hand and a heavy chain in the other.

"What's he doing?" Fox whispered to herself in disbelief.

"Dart! You can't be serious!" Cooper pleaded.

The tunnel runner ignored them.

Brand moved to follow him.

"Don't even think about it, Brand. If you mess with me, I will kill you!"

"Dart, you can't do this. If you leave this chamber, you'll be expelled from the community for good."

"Fuck you, Cooper! Fuck you and fuck the community! Is that clear enough? I live down here and I won't have any surface walkers ruining my realm. If any of you try to stop me–" Dart finished his warning by lifting his hatchet high above his head.

He vanished into the passage.

Pierce left the chamber without a word.

"Cooper!" Fox pleaded.

"We have to find her before he does," Cooper said, staring at the exit through which Dart had vanished.

Pierce came back carrying torches, dried food, and an

assortment of weapons including rusty metal bars, pick handles, and hammers.

"What's all that for?" Brand asked.

"I'm not going into the tunnels with that psychopath hanging around unless I've got a fair chance of defending myself. He wants that girl dead and he won't hesitate to kill us too if we get in his way. Take my advice and arm yourselves!"

Pierce handed the supplies and weapons out.

Cooper stepped forward. He was looking pale, not just from a lack of sunshine. He held a few copies of the tunnel system map out to the others and started indicating where each should look.

"Fox and Brand, you stay together and search the western tunnels. Pierce, I want you to go east towards the river. Shock and I will go north and meet up at the Eildon Hill junction. Follow?"

They nodded.

"And if we come across Dart?" Brand asked.

"Avoid him if you can."

"But if we can't?"

Cooper paused. "Well, if you can't, do whatever you have to. Just be careful – *very* careful."

They looked at each other. Fear was engraved on their faces.

"Let's move!" Cooper yelled, switching his torch on and gripping a hammer so tight that his knuckles turned white.

They rushed out of the chamber and into the tunnels.

9

Ripley found that negotiating his way around was much easier with a torch. The passage that had led him under Wilston and up to the Eildon Hill junction seemed far shorter now that he could see where he was going, but it still made his legs work hard. The beam of light flashed up and down as he strode, making the tunnel floor and the ceiling light up alternately. As his thighs pushed ever harder against the steepening gradient, he kept telling himself how completely stupid he was being. The idea that he could wander around the city's subterranean passages and somehow stumble across Gabriela was absurd. Then again, he would have thought the notion that people could actually live down there fantastic before his meeting with Fox. If only he could happen to cross paths with her again.

As he drew closer to the junction, Ripley could feel a subtle hint of a breeze reaching him from the grate he had used to leave the tunnel earlier that evening. The fresh air had two distinctly opposing effects on him. It enticed him to abandon his futile pursuit and to return to the surface where he belonged while also reinvigorating him and filling him with optimism. He decided to let the latter effect sway him.

He switched his torch off for a moment and looked up at the grate. The breeze caressed his face and starlight reminded him that there was an expanse above that was even more unfathomable than the labyrinthine confines into which he had ventured. All was silent, except for the hollow breathing caused by air getting caught in the shaft.

He turned his attention back to his immediate surrounds and switched the torch back on. There was no telling where Gabriela had gone. He knew no more than he had known when he met Fox, except that his girlfriend was not alone down there, and he was hardly sure whether that was a comforting piece of information or a disturbing one. He scanned the junction with his torch and watched as shadows fled along the cold concrete walls until the beam hit the entrance to the passage Fox had taken. The darkness swallowed the light. It was a long tunnel. This was new territory. Once he had set foot in that passage, he would be stepping into an unknown world, even if the streets above were familiar. He hesitated for a moment, but Gabriela's smiling face, warm voice, and familiar scent quickly filled his mind. She was in there somewhere, and just as he would have been prepared to walk the city's streets looking for her, so would he explore its underground streets.

At the first fork, Ripley pulled his can of red spray paint out. He was about to mark an arrow pointing back towards the Eildon Hill junction when he noticed that there was already one there. The coincidence sent a shiver down his spine. It was as though somebody had read his thoughts.

He found himself looking over his shoulder into the empty obscurity before he could get a hold of his reason. The arrow drawn on the wall had been there for a long time already, parts of it had flaked off.

He turned back to the two branches of the tunnel network that lay in front of him. He had to guess which one Gabriela would have taken, but it seemed such a ridiculous choice to make. As curious as she was, he could not for one moment imagine her having roamed this far into the tunnels. She would surely have left at the junction.

Only, it was clear that she hadn't.

Ripley chose the right-hand branch.

He continued along it for what seemed like hours, choosing which direction to take whenever he came to a fork and checking that there was an arrow to indicate the way back to the Eildon Hill junction. After a while, the arrows stopped and he had to spray his own onto the wall.

He had no way of knowing where he was in relation to the city above and he came across nothing that indicated that Gabriela had passed that way. The only thing of note was that the passages were increasingly dirty, but surprisingly dry. From time to time, his feet kicked up dust and made him sneeze. The sound boomed throughout the tunnels like thunder.

The further he walked, the more he had the feeling he was venturing into tunnels that had not heard the echo of a human footstep in many years. He wanted to turn back but didn't want to retrace his footsteps, and reminded himself that he wouldn't find Gabriela by walking back the way he had come. He had to keep pushing forward.

The grime became thicker beneath his feet until every step demanded effort that Ripley's legs could no longer make. He was tired and knew that he couldn't stay awake much longer, but the need to find Gabriela and the dread that the idea of sleeping in the tunnel inspired in him made him keep walking.

Fox and Brand worked their way through the western tunnels quickly but cautiously. In all the years that they had lived below ground, they had never really felt afraid. All tunnel dwellers held the belief that life in the tunnels was safer than life in the city above. This was the first time they were aware of a distinct danger lurking through the multitudinous passages they called home. The comfortable, if sometimes vaguely ominous, lengths of enclosed obscurity they lived in now took on a sinister allure. Dart was out there somewhere, armed with an axe and the conviction that it was his duty to kill any surface walker he might come across, as well as any tunnel dweller who tried to stop him.

The light from their torches brushed the walls and floor of the passages in practised unison so that they could simultaneously see where they were placing their rapidly moving feet and plan where they were going. Brand had a copy of the tunnel system map in his back pocket, ready to be pulled out if ever they got lost.

For the moment, they knew precisely where they were. The smell of roasted barley told them that they were close to the Castlemaine Perkins Brewery in Milton. But it didn't tell them where Gabriela might be. There was no way of knowing where she had passed. If they had moved slowly, they might have been able to look for clues indicating whether she had gone the way they were heading, but any decrease in speed would have prevented them from being able to cover all the western section of the tunnels and would have reduced their chances of finding her before Dart.

"How far could she have gone?" Fox asked breathlessly. As fit as she was, her legs were tiring and her feet were beginning to hurt. She couldn't imagine the soft surface walker having come so far from Wilston.

"I don't know," Brand admitted.

He stopped jogging.

Fox came to a halt just in front of him.

Their panting filled the otherwise quiet tunnel. The only other sound they could detect was that of cars accelerating up a long stretch of bitumen, probably where Milton Road climbed into Auchenflower.

"Can I see the map?" Fox asked.

She shone her torch in the direction of his back pocket.

Brand pulled it out and opened it. The details were not very clear and the plain white lines and numbers bore little resemblance to the reality of shadowy tunnels and grimy floors.

Fox let her finger trace a path along the map.

"We must be here."

"I would say so," Brand agreed. "How much further do you think we should we go?"

Fox studied the subterranean network. The passages continued west towards Mount Coot-tha and south until they reached the river. Shock and Cooper were searching the northern zone, but there were more kilometres of tunnels up there than could be covered in a year. The whole undertaking was utterly futile.

"Somebody is covering all of the tunnels on the north side of the city. Assuming we keep looking for an indeterminate length of time, we are sure to find her sooner or later."

Brand nodded in agreement. "We're also sure to stumble across Dart."

Fox shone her torch up and down the length of the tunnel.

"There is one place she might be and where nobody is looking at the moment."

"Where's that?"

"Her home. For all we know, she might have gone back there by now."

"She might have. She told you the address, didn't she?"

"Yeah, she did. Shall we go?"

Brand scanned the tunnel floor in front of them but couldn't find any trace of recent movement.

"I think you're right. It's probably the best bet."

"Let's go then," Fox said, already spinning around, ready to start running back the way they had come.

10

The crisp beam of light from Ripley's torch was beginning to falter just as he found himself wandering into a stretch of tunnel unlike any he had come across yet. It was filthy and the air was fouler. He knew that he would have to change the battery within a few minutes. He was also increasingly aware of his fatigue, both mental and physical. His legs hurt and his neck was sore from where he had to stoop to make progress through low passages. His thinking was becoming confused and he had already started to forget to spray red crosses on the wall whenever he came to an intersection or chamber.

He could feel a smouldering anger gaining force within him where previously there had only been a sense of desperation and a stubborn glimmer of hope. Fox had promised that she would find Gabriela and return her home, but he had found no sign of any human activity during all the hours he had been scouring the network of underground thoroughfares. He had to admit to himself that there must have been hundreds of kilometres of tunnel to search and that they could have been looking for her elsewhere. Nevertheless, the possibility that the tunnel dwellers were not doing their utmost to find Gabriela could not be shaken from his mind.

The beam of light from his torch made a noticeable change from white to weak yellow. Ripley was holding off changing the battery because he wanted to get as much light out of each one as he possibly could. At any rate, he wouldn't need light much longer. His eyelids were refusing to stay open and his knees were starting to buckle like the legs of a plastic chair under the summer sun.

As he dropped to his knees, a timid voice told him that he couldn't fall asleep on the tunnel floor. But his fatigue was stronger than his sense of disgust at where he was about to settle in for the night.

He placed his backpack under his head and cradled his torch against him as though he were a child with a teddy bear. Then, he switched it off and found himself in a darkness that was so perfect he couldn't even see his own nose. He imagined being woken up a few hours later and switching his torch on to find Gabriela's grimy face smiling down at him. He wanted to imagine that moment a little longer and to pretend that it was real, but he fell asleep.

Fox pushed the metal cover near Wilston Station open and raised her head so she could check that the coast was clear. There were no trains approaching from either direction and Newmarket Road was empty. She placed her small, strong hands on the concrete edge and pushed herself up. Brand clambered out behind her.

There was no movement under the bright light that illuminated the railway station or the softer light of the streetlamps. It was late at night and the surface walkers were all fast asleep.

They left their weapons near the cover and ran across the railway tracks, leaping effortlessly over steel, wood, and gravel as though it were a flat surface.

Fox crouched down at the wire fence and prepared to leap, and at the very moment she pushed up with her muscular legs, Brand placed his hands under her buttocks and boosted her with all his strength. It was a perfectly synchronised manoeuvre. She twisted her lithe body so that the sole of the shoe on her right foot crushed the barbed wire running across the top of the fence. Almost simultaneously, with the agility that had earned her the name the tunnel dwellers had bestowed upon her, she pulled herself over the barbed wire so that the tips of her breasts, which were protected beneath her thick T-shirt, were the only part of her body that so much as brushed the metal spikes.

She clambered sideways down the far side of the fence before letting herself drop to the ground.

Looking up and down Newmarket Road, she verified that there was still no sign of traffic.

Brand copied her method and succeeded in getting over the fence, but with less grace and ease than his partner.

"Where is it?" he asked.

"I don't know. I can't see the numbers from here. We need to cross the road first."

They dashed over and approached a row of letterboxes that belonged to a block of flats.

"You wouldn't believe it!" she whispered to Brand.

"What? This is it?"

"Too easy."

Brand looked up at the flats. Every light was out except for one. A dim glow like that of a bedside lamp emanated from one of the windows facing the street. They wondered if it was Ripley and Gabriela's flat.

"Follow me," Fox said. She walked up the stairs until she found the door to their flat.

She knocked gently, not wanting to make too much noise.

"You won't wake them up like that," Brand told her.

He reached out to knock more loudly, but didn't get the chance. The door was already swinging open.

It was Gabriela. Her expression changed instantly from one of desperate hope to one of apprehension.

"Who are you?" she asked, backing away from the open door.

"Gabriela?"

Her mouth opened, and after a moment, she said, "Yes?"

"My name is Fox. This is Brand. We met your boyfriend, Ripley, in the tunnels."

Hope returned to Gabriela's face.

"You've found him!"

"You mean he's not here?" Fox asked.

The hope disappeared.

"No. He's in the tunnels, like you said. I don't understand what's happening."

"He went looking for you, but I found him and told him to come back here and that we would come and tell him when we found you."

"Oh no, it's all my fault! Now he's lost down there!" She started crying. "I'm such an idiot!"

Brand frowned. Everything had changed so quickly. One minute, it was Gabriela who was lost down there, and the next, it was Ripley.

"Fox, stay here with her, and whatever you do, don't let her go back into the tunnels. I'll go back and keep looking for Ripley before Dart..." He stopped himself. Gabriela didn't know about Dart yet. At least she was safe from his clutches. "I'll go back to looking for him."

Fox nodded and grabbed his arm before he could run away. She pulled him close and kissed him. She whispered in his ear, begging him to be careful.

Brand drew a deep breath and then disappeared.

"Are you going to be all right, Gabriela?"

"I don't know. I'm confused."

She tried to stop crying.

"Aren't we all? Can I come inside so we can talk about what's going on?"

Gabriela nodded rapidly, as though she were shivering. "Of course, yes, do come inside."

Fox could tell that Gabriela was distraught as soon as she had stepped inside. Even though she had been living underground for many years and almost never set foot in the homes of surface walkers, she recognised the signs of a deeply concerned young woman. The faint light that came from Gabriela's bedroom was that of a bedside lamp, it was the only light switched on in the flat. The rest of Gabriela's abode was hidden in darkness. Through the open bedroom door, Fox could see the window that she had noticed from the outside. One of the curtains had been tied back while the other hung unrestrained. Gabriela had clearly resisted the habit of keeping her curtains drawn closed that night in order to be able to watch the railway line in anticipation of the moment Ripley would crawl out from the subterranean passage. Fox knew what it was like to be worried about the man in her life. Brand would occasionally disappear for a day or two without explanation. The difference between them was that she was more nervous about him when he was on the surface for too long whereas Gabriela was concerned about her boyfriend being lost down in the tunnels.

Gabriela told Fox to take a seat in the lounge.

"Would you like me to turn the light on?" Gabriela asked.

Her guest could sense she preferred darkness. Perhaps it was so Fox couldn't see her tears.

"No, I don't mind the dark. I'm used to it. I feel naked under bright light."

Gabriela sat next to her visitor.

"You spoke to Ripley down there?"

"Yes," Fox answered, trying to offer a comforting smile. "He was searching for you. He told me you went down there out of curiosity because you saw a dark figure enter the tunnels through a manhole next to the railway line."

"That's right. I just wanted to know where he was going, that's all."

"Ripley must have got worried because you were in the tunnels for such a long time and decided to go after you. Why were you down there so long?"

"I really don't know. I suppose I let curiosity get the better of me. I wanted to discover where the man I'd seen entering the tunnels was going every night. I got carried away, and by the time I'd made my way back here, he was gone. He went to try

63

to find me, but now he's the one who's lost."

Fox put her arm around Gabriela.

"We'll find him. There are several of us looking and we know the tunnels inside out." She paused. "But I have to tell you something."

"Tell me what?" Gabriela asked warily.

"One of the tunnel dwellers – that's what we call ourselves – is angry at you and Ripley for having entered our domain. He thinks you'll tell others and that the authorities will come looking for us and force us to abandon our home."

"Well, we won't. I don't understand why you live down there, but I don't want to cause you any trouble."

Fox hummed as she thought about what to say next. She didn't want to make Gabriela feel more afraid for her boyfriend than she already did, but the truth had to be told.

"I understand that, Gabriela, but Dart doesn't."

"Dart... he's the one who's angry?"

"Yes, he's the person you noticed disappearing through the manhole near the railway tracks."

Gabriela remembered how agile and strong he had seemed and felt a shiver tingle on the nape of her neck.

"Should I talk to him?" she asked, even though she cringed at the very thought of encountering him.

"No!" Fox almost shouted, making Gabriela jump a little. "I'm sorry. Listen, you can't talk to him. I hate to scare you like this, but you have a right to know."

She hesitated.

"What?" Gabriela urged.

"Well, there's no other way of putting it." She took a deep breath. "He wants to kill you."

Gabriela gulped and looked towards the door of the flat as though expecting Dart to burst through it and launch himself at her.

"Take it easy, Gabriela. You're safe here," Fox reassured her.

"Maybe I am, but what about Ripley?"

Fox sighed. She didn't know how to reply to that. She was worried about Ripley too. She was even more concerned for Brand.

"This can't be happening again, can it?"

"What do mean by that?"

"I think I'm cursed. I've already lost one person I love because of my stupidity, and now I might be losing Ripley."

"Who did you lose?" Fox winced as soon as she had mouthed the question. The tunnel dwellers knew pretty much everything about each other's personal backgrounds, but she could remember that on the surface, people often kept secrets and didn't appreciate being asked to talk about delicate matters.

But Gabriela wasn't offended. On the contrary, she seemed glad that Fox was there with her and ready to listen to what was on her mind. She closed her eyes while she thought about where to start. What she was going to share with Fox wasn't easy for her to discuss.

"I lost my little brother. It was a long time ago, so long ago that I can barely remember what happened. My parents would tell me about it occasionally and now I'm not sure whether my memories are real or merely scenes that I imagined as a result of their explanation of the events."

Fox held Gabriela tighter. Even though the girls had only just met and Gabriela was still coming to grips with the idea that a whole community lived beneath the streets of Brisbane, they already felt close to each other.

"Don't talk about it if it's going to make you upset."

Gabriela shook her head. "No, I want to talk about it. You don't mind, do you?"

Fox shook her head. "Of course, I don't. It's important to talk about what's on our minds. We all need to share our burdens from time to time."

"I've been thinking about it all night. I would rather talk with you than just continue tormenting myself alone. It's very nice of you to have come here, Fox."

"Not at all. I'm just glad you got out of the tunnels. We'll find Ripley and bring him back here as soon as possible."

"I hope so. I can't bear the thought of him, well, you know, not coming back from down there. I can't believe I could have been so stupid. I'm the one who started all this. I noticed, what did you say his name was?"

"Dart," Fox spat the name out like a bad taste.

Gabriela shook her head, trying not to think about the possibility that Dart would find her boyfriend before Brand or the others did.

"I got him into this mess with my damned curiosity."

"We'll get him back to you, Gabriela."

"You don't know that, Fox. I know you're trying to comfort me, but you just don't know that. I don't want to lose him too. My brother disappeared when I was just a little girl, maybe seven years old, and he was just three or so. We were at the Ekka and had just bought some sample bags. I remember – or was told by my parents – that they had bought my little brother a sample bag that contained spooky toys and costumes including some fake cobwebs and blood make-up. They had dressed him up like a monster and he wanted to go to the Haunted House because he thought he looked scarier than the 'real' monsters there. He wanted to try to frighten them.

"So, we went to Side Show Alley and made our way through the crowds that were weaving around between the roller coasters, dodgem cars, and shooting galleries. It was the Ekka public holiday and the show grounds were absolutely packed. Mum had told me to hold my little brother's hand because he had a habit of running off the moment he was given the chance.

"Anyway, I don't know exactly how it happened. I don't know what I really remember. The fact is that I messed up. We weren't walking fast enough for his tastes because we were trying to navigate our way through the crowd. Because he was so little, he must have thought he could get to the Haunted House faster by weaving through the legs of the people in his way. He managed to pull his hand free from mine, and, before I could react, he'd run off into the crowd.

"I tried to chase after him, and my parents tried to keep up with me, but we couldn't. He ran past the ticket counter, the howling Wolfman, and the growling ghouls, and straight into the Haunted House."

Fox could see through the dim light that teased the obscurity in Gabriela's flat that tears had started welling in her eyes again.

"That was the last time you saw him?"

Gabriela nodded.

"Did security try to find him?"

"Yes, of course. They followed procedure. They put a message out across the PA system, over and over again, but nothing came of it. Nobody took him to the lost children's desk."

"Do you think he was kidnapped?" Fox asked, her question an apologetic whisper.

"I don't know. He just ran into the Haunted House and vanished from our lives, and whatever attempts I'm sure my parents and authorities made to find him were unsuccessful."

"Listen, Gabriela. We are going to do everything we can to find Ripley. You have my oath."

Gabriela smiled sadly.

"Thank you. I'm sorry for the trouble that I've caused."

"There's no need to be sorry. Just stay here and don't go back into the tunnels. Do you promise?"

She paused for a moment, and Fox was almost expecting her to refuse, but she said, "Yes, I promise."

"Good. I'm going to go back down and join the search team. You should try to get some rest."

"Do you have to go back? There are others looking for him, aren't there?"

"Yes, probably dozens by now."

"Dozens? How many people live in the tunnels?"

"Quite a few," she replied in a mischievous tone.

"Stay here with me. Please, don't leave me alone now. I beg of you."

There was no way Fox could possibly deny such a heartfelt request.

"I'll stay."

"Thank you so much."

Gabriela breathed a sigh of relief and tried to calm down. Now that she had shared her troubles, she wanted to change the topic of conversation, and, despite all the turmoil it had caused, she couldn't help but give in to her curiosity once again.

"Now that I've told you something about my life, can I ask you some questions?"

"Sure. Go ahead."

She leaned closer.

"Tell me, when did you give up living a normal life? Why on Earth did you decide to go underground?"

It was Fox's turn to draw a deep breath. It was clear to Gabriela that she had quite a tale to tell.

"Before I get started, can I take the liberty of making us a pot of tea?"

11

Cooper and Shock were exhausted and sore when they arrived back in the Chambers. Scouring dozens of kilometres of tunnels and storm water drains from Spring Hill all the way up to Kedron and back again through Stafford and Newmarket had been a mental and physical ordeal. Neither of them could remember having covered so much distance in such a short length of time ever before. The worst part of it was that it had all been for nothing. They had found no trace of unexpected activity and had certainly not come across a female surface walker fumbling around.

As they entered the dimly lit main chamber, they dared to hope that somebody had succeeded in finding the young woman; somebody other than Dart. However, as they walked across the spacious room, greeting the other members of their community, who were preparing to settle in for the night, it became perfectly clear that no news of the evening's strange events had reached their ears. The tunnel dwellers' routine had not been disrupted.

Wyrm, a relative newcomer who had come in contact with the tunnel folk through their University of Queensland branch, was sitting comfortably in one of the armchairs that hugged the wall near the short passage leading to the library. He was reading a sociology textbook with the help of a hand-held solar lamp. Bella and Spirit, who both worked at a West End café during the day and never failed to supply the community with pilfered coffee beans and left-over muffins, were reclined on bean bags and talking quietly together. Even though the sleeping quarters were not in the main chamber, everybody had to speak in a reasonably hushed tone late at night because voices were amplified and travelled a long way in their subterranean concrete habitat.

"Most people have gone to sleep," Cooper observed. "They don't seem to know about what has happened, wouldn't you say?"

Shock nodded. "It doesn't appear so. Didn't you leave a note?"

"Did I?" Cooper asked himself. Then, he remembered. "No, I didn't. I was going to but got distracted by Dart's outburst."

"That's understandable. Speaking of Dart, I wonder if anybody has run into him."

"Where have you two been all night?" It was Zak, one of the community's amateur chefs. "We were getting worried that our leader might have decided to leave us for a life on the surface."

"There's no chance of that, Zak. On the contrary, we've been dragging our sorry selves through some of the network's least frequented passages."

"You weren't attacked by hordes of giant rodents or mutated sewage monsters?"

"Nothing like that – just endless tunnels."

"Why were you doing that?"

"It's a long story and I don't want to tell you the full version just now, but to keep it short, we've been trying to find a surface walker who made the silly mistake of entering the system and getting herself lost."

"That sounds like a challenge."

"It is, and so far we're failing miserably," Shock answered.

"Zak, you haven't heard any talk about a stranger being spotted down here?"

"I haven't. None at all. The only news of the day that has been going around is that Burrow and that new girl are an item."

"I had a feeling they were going to get along well. Our first lesbian couple in the community. That's news indeed!"

"So, is this outsider still down here?"

"We don't know. We've been looking for her all evening, but to no avail. Brand, Fox, and Pierce have also been searching for her."

"Oh yeah, now you mention it, I haven't seen any of them this evening. I usually cook for Pierce. Are they coming back here to sleep?"

"I hope so. I don't like the idea of them sleeping in isolated tunnels."

Cooper surveyed the main chamber. It was becoming emptier by the minute. He would have to wait until morning to make an announcement.

"Do you know if anybody has spoken to Dart?"

"I don't think so. He hasn't come back yet. I certainly hope he doesn't come across the surface walker girl though, for her sake. You know how much he hates them."

"That's exactly what I'm afraid might happen. I'm going to make an announcement tomorrow. We have to find this girl as quickly as possible. Not only because it's the honourable course of action to take, but also because our anonymity could ultimately depend on it."

Cooper refrained from telling Zak about the confrontation with Dart. It would only risk spreading panic when everybody needed to get some sleep.

"All right, have a good night. You both look like you could do with some rest."

Just as the chef headed towards the chamber that contained his bed, Brand came stumbling into the main chamber. After looking around, he came to the same conclusion as Cooper had; that the community remained unaware of just what had happened.

"Cooper," Brand cut in, still panting. "I have to tell you something."

"What is it?"

"We're no longer trying to find the girl, Gabriela. She's back at her home with Fox. But her boyfriend doesn't know this and is somewhere in the tunnels trying to rescue her."

"I hope Fox keeps her there."

71

"Don't worry. She will."

"With a bit of luck, her boyfriend will make his own way out of the tunnels and back home."

"That would put an end to the problem."

Cooper nodded. "It would put an end to having to find them, but it wouldn't resolve the matter of Dart. Regardless of what happens to the surface walkers, he has excluded himself from the community and has declared himself our enemy. We've never been in such a situation before. We don't know what he might do next."

"Have you called a meeting yet?" Brand asked.

"No, not yet. Everybody has settled in for the night and I don't intend to wake them up. They're going to need a good night's sleep."

"You don't think he'll do something completely crazy, like attacking us in our beds?"

The three men fell uncomfortably silent as they considered the prospect of being hacked apart with an axe while they slept. Cooper looked towards the main entrance to the Chambers, imagining that Dart might be observing them from the shadows.

"Maybe we ought to set up a watch."

"I'm so tired though," Shock admitted. "I don't know if I could stay awake."

"Do you really think Dart is so angry he would risk coming after us all single-handedly?" Cooper asked Brand.

"I don't know. I've never really trusted him. I don't think he would, but I'd sleep a whole lot better knowing that somebody was standing guard."

"All right," Cooper said. "Let's take turns then, just the three of us. I'll force myself to stay awake for three hours while you two get some sleep."

"I'll do the second watch," Brand offered. "That'll give you six hours of solid sleep, Shock."

"Thanks, mate. All right, let's do it then."

"I used to live on the surface," Fox explained. "We all did. None of us were born underground and none of us have given birth underground. I grew up in Redbank Plains, between Brisbane and Ipswich. Do you know the area?"

Gabriela knew where Redbank Plains was, along the Brisbane River to the west of the city, and she knew that it was considered a rather unpleasant place to grow up. It was the kind of suburb you lived in because your family couldn't afford to live anywhere else.

"I know where it is."

"Well, I can tell you it's a real shithole of a place, and there are some pretty pathetic excuses for families that live there."

"Can I ask what your family was like?"

Fox's face went blank. She stared at the cup of tea steaming on the coffee table in front of her. Gabriela could tell that she was watching the way the threads of steam rose up from inside the cup, twirling and swirling, but it was also clear that Fox's thoughts were elsewhere and that the memories running through her mind were far from rosy.

"I don't want to talk about my family. My father was a disgusting pig and my mother was a weak slut."

Gabriela looked uncomfortably at the ground. Her parents had treated her well, and, learning that Fox hadn't been so fortunate, she couldn't help but feel ashamed of herself for some strange reason. Perhaps a psychologist could explain the phenomenon, but Gabriela certainly didn't understand it.

Fox took her cup of tea and sipped at it thoughtfully.

"How old were you when you left?"

"I was nineteen."

"A friend told you about the people living in the tunnels?"

"No, not at all. I discovered them by chance. I'd been trying to find a job and had an interview for a position as a receptionist in the city. I was unsuccessful. My old man went completely nuts. He'd yelled at me and hit me because I was unemployed many times before, but this time he completely lost control. Mum didn't dare try to calm him down. She knew better than to try that. After he had hit me a few times, he made threats." Fox paused and Gabriela could distinguish the latent rage that twisted her lips. "He threatened to punish me the way he knew hurt me most. He hadn't done that in several months, and I wasn't about to let him start again. So, I ran away. I just ran out the front door with nothing but the clothes on my back. I didn't go to a friend's house because I knew he would come looking for me and that their fathers would give in to him and turn me in."

"Where did you go?"

"To a nearby park. I stretched out under a picnic table. There was nobody else around and the park was in complete darkness. I felt safe. It wasn't the first time I had run away from home, but I knew right then and there that I would never go back. I can remember the very moment, as I watched a flying fox cross the overcast night sky, that I told myself I would never see my parents ever again. In that very instant, a smile formed on my lips and a shiver of hope chilled my body. I couldn't have been happier. I tried to fall asleep but was unable to drift off. The discomfort, the excitement, the apprehension, the anger – it all made sleep an impossible dream. I just lay there for hours and brushed insects off my face, arms, and legs."

Gabriela was speechless. She had never ever imagined running away from home before. Her adventure in the tunnel was the most daring escapade she had ever had.

"This was in January and the weather had been scorching hot and disgustingly humid all day long. So, do you know what happened next?"

Gabriela thought for a moment. "Don't tell me a thunderstorm broke out?"

Fox lifted her teacup to her lips and nodded before taking a sip.

74

"That's right," she continued. "Lightning started flashing all around and peals of thunder echoed. Then, the smell of wet bitumen reached my nostrils, and before I knew it, rain was pounding down on me. Two thoughts crossed my mind, one after the other."

"I've got to find some shelter?" Gabriela ventured.

"That was the second. The first was that there was no way my father would come looking for me. That was my very first thought, and it was such an unbelievably reassuring one."

"I can't begin to imagine," Gabriela whispered. "Where did you find shelter?"

"Well, I had no idea where to go, so I just ran across the park. After a few seconds, I found a great black hole gaping in front of me. Thinking back now, considering what I know about the tunnels, I shouldn't have gone in there during a thunderstorm. I could have ended up being washed away in a torrent."

"And somebody else was in there. That's how you met Brand," Gabriela guessed.

"No," Fox laughed. "I didn't meet Brand until later. Nobody else was there. I slept in the pipe and then got a train to Brisbane the next morning. I started living in the streets in the city and tried to avoid undesirable types. I'd had enough of unpleasant people for a lifetime. I stayed away from everybody because I was afraid some sleazebag would try to get me on drugs and turn me into his sex wench. I started shoplifting during the day and sleeping in tunnels at night."

"You must have been lonely?"

"I was," Fox admitted. "But I wasn't sad. I think I learned more about myself during those few weeks than I ever had before."

"What did you learn?"

"What did I learn? That's a good question."

Fox finished her tea while she thought.

"One thing I learned was that there was a job for me."

Gabriela shook her head to show that she had no idea what Fox meant.

"I'm a thief, and I'm very good at it."

Gabriela laughed. "Really? Have you stolen anything since you've been in my flat?"

Fox didn't seem to be offended by the suggestion. She took it for what it was, a joke. "I don't steal from friends."

"Keep going. I'll make some more tea."

"That's how I met the leader of the tunnel dwellers. His name is Cooper Caverna."

"Wow, you make our names sound boring! How did you meet him?"

"I was shoplifting and I noticed him stealing some tinned food. But he was doing it all wrong. He stood in front of the shelf, up close, and checked for cameras or security guards before quickly taking a tin from the shelf and stuffing it in his jacket pocket where it bulged like a fake tit. I wanted to tell him how to shoplift properly but could hardly give him a lesson right there in the supermarket."

"Are you serious?"

"Absolutely! I followed him when he left the shop and decided to keep shadowing him so I could see where he went. He went underground, a hell of a long way underground. I followed him all the way, for what seemed like hours. You know what it's like when you first go down. Time slows to a crawl and distances stretch out. That's how I discovered the community. There were only three or four of them back then."

"You spoke to them?"

"Yes, I wasn't afraid. I could tell they were decent people and I knew before we'd even spoken a word that they were there because life on the surface had let them down."

"What did you say?"

"I told Cooper that he was a pathetic shoplifter."

"Was he angry?"

"No, not at all. He gave me a job."

"Excellent! Just what your dad wanted!"

They laughed.

"Was Brand one of the tunnel dwellers?"

"No, he joined later, after I stole from him one night and he chased me."

"No way! You have to tell me all about it."

"You sure are one curious cat!"

"I know. That's what gets me into trouble all the time, but I can't help it."

"Let's make a deal. If I tell you about how we met, will you let me sleep here tonight? I haven't slept above ground in a long time."

"Deal," Gabriela agreed without hesitation.

12

Ripley's sleep was tormented. He didn't dream about Gabriela or tunnels. Instead, he was in a strange old house full of ornate decorations and antique furniture. He seemed to be alone and felt completely at ease, as though he were the owner. He strolled over to a mahogany liquor cabinet to serve himself a dram of whisky from a crystal decanter. He had just taken a glass and was about to start pouring when he suddenly noticed a movement behind him. To be more precise, there were countless individual movements. He turned around quickly and what he saw made him drop both the empty glass and the decanter. They shattered on the Persian rug, narrowly missing his feet, which were clad in red slippers.

Ripley woke up in total darkness and felt the backpack that was serving as a pillow moving under his head. He could hear an orchestra of nauseating sounds. They were soft but very close.

It quickly became clear that whatever was making these sounds was also causing his backpack to squirm.

He felt for his torch and switched it on.

"Shit!" His voice echoed through the tunnel.

Rats were swarming around him. There were a hundred or more of the ravenous little scavengers. Their beady eyes gleamed mischievously as the beam of light exposed them in the middle of their thieving antics.

It didn't take Ripley long to realise they must have somehow caught scent of the muesli bars in his backpack; even though the bars were sealed in plastic wrappers. They were gnawing at the synthetic material, trying to force their way into the bag. Worst of all, the sudden brightness from Ripley's torch had made almost no effect on the little beasts. They continued struggling with his backpack and gnashing at each other in their selfish race to get to the muesli bars. It reminded him of the evening rush to get onto a train at Central Station.

Ripley wasn't usually bothered by the sight of a rat, but he was overwhelmed by the sheer mass that surrounded him. They covered the tunnel floor, throbbing disgustingly and squealing like little banshees. He wanted to lash out at the critters but hated the idea of touching them. Then, he remembered he had taken a hammer with him just in case he needed to protect himself. The only problem was that it was inside his backpack.

There was nothing else to be done. He had to get it out somehow.

He snatched his backpack up. A dozen rats stuck stubbornly to it, holding on with their rodent teeth and clasping with their tiny clawed toes. He shook the backpack, but they wouldn't be removed so easily. He had to admire the determined little buggers. They were as hell-bent on getting his muesli bars as he was on finding his girlfriend.

He managed to open it up and pull the hammer out, holding it in the same hand as the torch.

Ripley couldn't remember the last time he'd killed anything bigger than a cockroach, but shaking his backpack as though he were trying to strangle it and kicking frenetically at the rodents swirling around his feet, he soon resigned himself to the fact that he would have to ignore his kind-hearted nature and beat the rats away.

He raised the hammer above his head and heard it scratch against the tunnel ceiling. Then, he brought it down in an arc and knocked one of the crazed vermin off.

The blow didn't kill it. The tough little bugger hit the ground running and scurried away, pushing against the incoming tide.

Ripley kept swinging, holding his backpack up high but at arm's length, until every foul rodent had been sent tumbling to the tunnel floor. They were still climbing up his trousers though, clinging to his legs with their clutching paws and gnawing incisors. The rats that he kicked scampered away as quickly as they could, but dozens of others, unable to learn from the treatment dealt to their comrades, took their place on Ripley's trousers.

It was clear he wouldn't be able to beat all of the rodents off. They were too numerous for him to strike each and every one, and either too stupid or too stubborn to be scared away. He would have to kick his way through them and try to find an exit from the tunnels. Going back to sleep down there was impossible and continuing the search without a few more hours of slumber had become unthinkable, no matter how desperately he needed to find his little angel.

Ripley flashed his torch up and down the length of the tunnel, trying to find a rusty ladder or steep concrete staircase that would lead him to the fresh air and starry night of the outside world. But there was no exit to be seen, just endless rats and darkness. He would have to kick his way back through the tunnel until he came to the last ladder he could remember passing before he had dropped to his knees and gone to sleep. He felt sure that it wasn't very far, if his fatigued mind remembered correctly, so he started kicking his way through the horde.

He didn't have to push for long. All of a sudden, and for a reason that was unfathomable at first, they disappeared. The tunnel floor became visible, and, apart from the foul odour and the droppings that they had excreted in their excitement, there was no evidence that the rats had ever been there at all.

Just as Ripley was about to allow himself a sigh of relief, he realised why the rats had beat a hasty retreat. They hadn't caught wind of a morsel more tempting than his muesli bars, nor had they had some kind of silent, communal reunion and instantly decided to surrender to him. The incomprehensible but obvious truth was that another person had entered that stretch of the tunnel network. Somebody far more menacing to their primitive yet keen minds than Ripley could ever be. There was something about this other person that their instincts told them to fear.

Did they know that he was capable of greater violence than the lost surface walker? Could they sense the angst in his heart? Questions fired through Ripley's mind in machine gun succession.

His hand shook as he raised his torch, and the walls of the tunnel vibrated with his nervousness.

"Who are you?" the voice asked from around a bend in the tunnel. The tone was openly hostile.

"My name is Ripley. I'm trying to find my girlfriend," he answered frankly, trying not to sound too fearful.

There was no reply. Ripley held his torch fixed as steadily as he could on the bend in the tunnel. Concrete curved back into obscurity.

Then, the obscurity was gone and a bright light stunned him. The hand that aimed it was much steadier than his.

"You shouldn't be down here."

"I know that, but I have to find my girlfriend."

"She shouldn't have come down here in the first place." There wasn't the slightest hint of compassion in those words.

"Have you seen her?"

The light came closer. Ripley could hear the man's footsteps on the rough surface. He couldn't see who was behind the light though. The tunnel dweller's torch seemed to be more powerful than his.

"You're the first surface walker I've seen down here in a long time and hopefully you'll be the last I'll ever come across."

"I don't want to cause you any bother," Ripley's voice betrayed his fear. "I just want to find my girlfriend and go back to the surface."

"Of course, you do. But then what? It's all very well for you, but what will happen to us when you tell everybody about our community? The authorities won't understand, they'll come down and try to haul us out. They'll make us go back to your world of mindless consumerism and individualism."

"I won't tell a soul."

"Don't lie to me, surface boy! I wouldn't trust one of your kind as far as I could throw your corpse!"

That was the moment Ripley knew he had to flee.

He turned on his heels and ran as fast as his tired legs would carry him. But it wasn't fast enough. He felt a heavy blow on his left shoulder and yelled so loudly that he thought the tunnel might cave in. He spun around and stumbled onto his back, somehow managing to keep his torch, hammer, and backpack within his grasp.

As he stumbled, his torch lit up his attacker. He caught a glimpse of the face, but it was too brief to notice anything other than the hatred in its scowl. He recognised the dark clothes. This was surely the man that Gabriela had witnessed disappearing through the manhole by the railway tracks.

"You want to kill me just because I entered the tunnels?" Ripley asked with a tremulous voice.

"It's not that I want to hurt you, surface walker, but I have an obligation to protect our community down here. We have values. We look after each other and help those who need a hand. We came down here to get away from the dog-eat-dog world above and our survival depends on our ability to remain invisible. So, you understand," his voice become ominously apologetic. "I *have to* kill you."

Ripley wanted to reply. He felt the need to convince the tunnel dweller that he would never tell anybody about what he'd discovered down here. He understood his hatred of the selfish, money-hungry society on the surface, but Ripley still wanted to find Gabriela and go back there. All he wanted was to return to his flat and his normal life.

Yet Ripley couldn't bring himself to respond to his attacker. The words just wouldn't come out.

He knew that he had to get up and run. He had to get himself out of there as quickly as possible, but his attacker was looming over him and would just push him back down onto the dirty tunnel floor.

He dropped his torch but kept a firm grip on his hammer with his right hand while his backpack was clutched desperately in his left. It was at that moment that Ripley noticed the object that had caused the terrible pain in his shoulder. It was a hatchet. Dart was holding it above his head. He was going to do what he believed to be his obligation. He intended to plant the hatchet in Ripley's skull and bring the surface walker's days to an end right there in the bowels of Brisbane. Ripley would never know what had happened to his girlfriend. He was going to be slain without ever knowing whether she had made her way back to the safety of their flat or was still wandering through the tunnels like a dead soul lost in the ether.

Dart whispered what sounded like an apology and then released a howl of anger as he brought the hatchet swinging down.

13

"I could never live in the tunnels," Gabriela admitted to Fox as they shared another pot of tea. "I can't understand what it must have been like to grow up with parents who didn't treat their children right, so I won't pretend to know how you feel, but I just can't imagine hating life up here so much that I'd want to live underground."

"That's good then. I'm glad for you. I wish I felt the same way. All I know is that when I compare the way my life was here to what it's like living with the tunnel dwellers, well, I know where I belong."

Gabriela was lost with her thoughts for a moment. She was remembering what she had felt down there. Then, as though a bell had rung and summoned her back to the present, she snapped out of it. She shook her head and frowned.

"It's so dark down there."

"I love the darkness," Fox replied, and the warmth and calm in her voice told Gabriela that obscurity must have been as reassuring to Fox as daylight was to her. "There's something about it that is comforting, like a loving embrace. I know that sounds corny, but that's the effect it has on me. Many surface walkers think darkness is evil's environment, but I don't feel that way at all. So many of mankind's atrocities have been committed in broad daylight, and so many of the world's most wonderful animals only come out at night. I will never understand why darkness is considered to be less pure than light."

Gabriela didn't know how to reply at first. "Well, I suppose I've never really given it all that much thought. Isn't it dirty down there though? There must be toads and rats and horrible insects everywhere."

"There can be in some parts of the tunnels, but not where we live, not in the Chambers."

"The Chambers?"

Fox took a sip of tea, swallowed, and then kept her lips sealed.

"What are the Chambers?"

"I'm sorry. I shouldn't have even mentioned that. I can't tell you about them, for your sake."

Gabriela nodded. She understood. At least, she thought she did.

"So, you never think about coming back up to the surface with Brand? You don't want to get a normal job and live in a normal house or flat?"

"Not really. I don't even know if we could, to tell the truth. I expect that thieves aren't really in high demand in the workplace."

"What about if you want to have children?"

"In that case, yes, we would have to leave the tunnel community. Falling pregnant down there would be impossible."

Gabriela frowned as she poured them some more tea.

"It's going to be fine, Gabriela. Brand will find Ripley. I don't know how long it'll take, but he'll do it."

Gabriela tried to smile, but it just slipped back into a frown. She looked at the clock. It was already the early hours of Monday morning. She would have to call Ripley's boss in a few hours' time to tell him that he wouldn't be coming in to work. She'd have to think up some kind of excuse for him. Worse than that, if he wasn't found soon, she would have to call the police, whether Fox and her tunnel dwellers liked it or not.

"Fox, I am going to lie down in bed. I don't think I'll be able to sleep, but I'll try. How about you?"

Fox nodded wearily. The prospect of a few hours of rest sounded great.

14

Ripley thrust his hammer up just as Dart's hatchet was about to come crashing into his head. He wasn't able to stop the blow or even fully deflect it, but as the blunt edge of the hatchet struck the handle of the hammer just a couple of centimetres away from Ripley's fingers, he ducked his head to one side and the hatchet and hammer pushed down menacingly towards his shoulder, but failed to connect.

Ripley looked up, desperation in his eyes. He was hoping to find some glimmer of pity written on his aggressor's face but couldn't see the features of the man looming above him. His torch was shining straight into Ripley's petrified eyes.

The hatchet was jerked back and the sudden release of weight on Ripley's hammer almost made him lose his grip on it. That would have been a fatal mistake.

He couldn't see where the hatchet was through the glaring torchlight, but he knew that if he hesitated, he would find out the hard way. He had to move and he had to move fast. One of the exercises he had done with Pete, Ben, and Oscar just a week ago suddenly flashed into his mind. He didn't have time to think about whether it would work or not, so he just did it.

Ripley dropped to one side and rolled backwards along the tunnel floor, his clothes and skin picking up grime and rat shit as he did so, then he pushed himself to his feet.

Dart was just behind him and had his hatchet held over his head in one hand while the other kept the beam of light from his torch fixed on his quarry.

A spark flared as Dart swung the hatchet and it scratched the tunnel ceiling before coming swooping down again. At the same time, Ripley got to his knees and stumbled off. He heard a *swish* as the hatchet missed the back of his head by a whisker. If there had been any doubt in his mind as to the fact that Dart really did mean to kill him, it was now well and truly gone.

Ripley managed to get to his feet and almost tripped over as he ran forward.

At some point in time, probably during the roll, Ripley had let go of his backpack and torch. The rats would get their filthy little paws on his muesli bars after all. He held his hammer tight with white-knuckled urgency. It had already saved his hide once, and he could only hope that it would do so again if necessary.

"There's no point running, surface walker! You can't get away from me. Nobody knows these passages better than I do. I'm the tunnel runner."

The tunnel runner, those words echoed.

Ripley thought to himself. He didn't know what it meant, but he had seen him run, climb, and jump before. He knew that he was physically superior. Ripley's workout sessions with his mates may have helped keep him in shape and taught him a few nifty moves, but they were a walk in the park compared to this man's daily routine.

Ripley was running in the dark. He had to rely on his assailant's torchlight to guide him along the tunnel, but his own body was blocking most of the beam. He could tell the light was aimed at the back of his head – focused on the exact spot where the tunnel runner wanted to plant his blunt hatchet. It was only a matter of time before he received the deathblow.

Ripley would have screamed in terror if he hadn't needed every breath he could suck in to fuel his fleeing body.

The urge to scream was not the only reaction to the situation that Ripley was experiencing. A sense of shame was added to his fear as he felt tears welling in his eyes. He was going to cry. It was as though his subconscious had decided to start mourning his death in anticipation of the inevitable outcome of the encounter. The worst thing wasn't the shame itself. It was the impracticability of weeping. As the tears formed, they made it even more difficult for him to see where he was going.

"The nearest ladder is only twenty metres away. Do you think you can make it there before I get to you, surface walker?" the tunnel runner taunted.

Ripley felt like giving up. He knew that he couldn't escape. The tunnel runner was going to kill him, and he would leave this world alone, having failed Gabriela. He could have been angry at her for having drawn him into the affair in the first place, but he knew it was pointless to feel that way. He had fallen in love with her the way she was – her curiosity included. He just hoped she wouldn't suffer the same fate as him. He hoped she would, or that she already had, left the tunnel system.

Of course, he would never know.

It was time to give up, to stop running – so Ripley did just that.

Dart skidded to a halt. He hadn't been expecting his prey to just pack it all in and turn around to face him like that. He didn't seem impressed.

"Crying are you? You surface walkers are so soft! You have no honour and you have no valour!" He was shining the torch straight at Ripley's face as he raised his hatchet. Ripley dropped to his knees in what Dart took to be a sign of capitulation. Maybe the surface walker had a tiny hint of honour in him after all. But before the hatchet could come crashing down onto the intruder's skull, Ripley lashed out with his hammer and struck Dart's left shin.

A howl of pain reverberated through the tunnels as Dart dropped to his knees.

For a moment, they were kneeling together as though in some kind of unholy communion.

For an instant, the tunnel runner was defenceless.

Through teary eyes, Ripley saw his attacker's face. It was the relatively normal face of a young man who couldn't have been much more than twenty years old, not that of a monster. Ripley's grip on his hammer tightened even more. He could have sunk an imaginary nail into the tunnel runner's forehead – but he didn't.

The instant passed, and Dart, ignoring the pain in his shin, pushed himself tentatively to his feet, checking to see whether he could still stand up.

But that instant had been long enough for Ripley. He was no longer there.

Dart raised his torch, pointed it towards the top of the nearby ladder, and realised that the intruder had got away.

The manhole cover slid back into place with a deafening clang.

Ripley wiped the tears from his eyes and tried to pretend that he hadn't been crying at all. His body was shaking with a combination of fear and fatigue, and he watched the manhole cover with dread. If the tunnel runner followed him up, he knew that he had it in him to hammer him back down again – even if it meant killing him. He kept his gaze fixed on the cover, letting it hypnotise him. He could hear the tunnel runner groaning and listened for any sound that resembled the shaking of the old ladder being climbed, but instead he just heard the groans grow fainter.

The sense of relief that Ripley felt at having escaped with his life was smothered by his concern for Gabriela. Prior to his encounter with the tunnel runner, Ripley had only had his imagination to make him feel worried about what might happen to her down there. Now he knew for certain that she was in grave danger.

He looked up at the night sky for a moment and drew a deep breath of clean air. He had no idea what the time was or how long he had been in the tunnels. He was only aware that it was already Monday morning. He couldn't go to work the next morning while Gabriela was stuck down there with a madman stalking around. He couldn't just crawl into bed and leave her for dead. Then, the possibility that he had forgotten occurred to him once more. What if she'd made her way home? What if the whole absurd adventure had come to an end? It was a possibility

89

that he had to check.

There was only one slight problem that had to be solved first. He had no idea which part of Brisbane he had landed in.

He turned his attention away from the manhole cover. In an instant, it had changed from being the entrance to a vast and nightmarish subterranean world back to being an unassuming feature of the urban landscape, the likes of which he walked past by the hundreds every day on his way to work or down to Alcove, his favourite café.

Ripley surveyed the street that he now found himself in. There was nobody about, which was not surprising considering the time. The only light that exposed his presence came from the waxing moon and the orange-tinted streetlamps lining the suburban street. He was relieved to be out in the open air. It was mindboggling to think that such a strange world lay so close to this one, just a few metres beneath his feet. Yet, as much as the adventure had intrigued him, it had almost got him killed. If Gabriela was back at home, he would make her promise that she'd never go back down there. They would make a solemn oath to each other.

He hoped, with all the energy he could muster, that she was at home. He yearned to find her there, snuggled up in bed, waiting for him, worried about him, so that he could put her mind at rest.

He walked along the street towards what seemed to be a main road at the far end. He looked everywhere as he made his way. His relief at being back under an eternal sky and feeling fresh air caress his filthy face had not yet suppressed the nervousness that had taken hold of him.

He shook his legs as he walked, just like he did after jogging with his mates, in order to stop them from buckling under the pressure of fear and fatigue. He walked in the middle of the street and peered behind parked cars as he passed them. He had been infected with the tunnel runner's paranoia. Perhaps they were not so different after all. Ripley was afraid that the tunnel dweller might have crawled up into his world just as he had intruded on his subterranean home.

The menace of the blunt hatchet continued to spook Ripley and he ducked several times as flying foxes flew low from tree to tree, their leathery wings whooshing like tiny cyclones just behind his head. There were also cats lurking behind fence posts and possums scurrying along power lines, all completely normal things for a Brisbane street in the early hours of the morning, but each subtle movement made Ripley's right hand twitch.

It wasn't until a cat dashed out from under a blue Barina and he almost brought his hammer crashing down that Ripley realised he was still carrying the makeshift weapon. It sent a chill through his body as he wondered what an onlooker would think. When the cover had fallen into place, it had made a thunderous clang that could easily have woken any number of the street's inhabitants. If they had caught sight of this darkly clothed, grimy man swinging a hammer around and shaking like he had a huge dose of some kind of narcotic pumping through his veins, he could only assume they would have immediately called the police. Ripley didn't know what law, if any, he had broken, but he didn't want to have to explain his actions to anybody in authority. He held the hammer as discreetly against his forearm as he could so that the head was in his hand and the end of the handle was tucked into the fold of his arm. He looked around at the houses lining either side of the street, suddenly feeling like an actor in the spotlight despite the silence and darkness of the scene.

He quickened his pace.

As he reached the main road, Ripley looked up at the street sign. He was at Waterworks Road. It was quite a long walk to Wilston, and one that he wanted to complete undetected. The best way would be to follow the bicycle path along Enoggera Creek.

He pushed himself, walking as quickly as he could without collapsing, and as he trekked back to Wilston, his mind was concerned with two desperate tasks; watching out for any movements in the dark and hoping with all his might that Gabriela would be waiting for him.

15

Ripley's shoulder wasn't the only part of his body that was sore. His legs ached more and more as he drew closer to Wilston, as though the promise of home accentuated their fatigue. He watched his filthy shoes as he walked along a softly lit stretch of walkway snaking along the mangrove-covered banks of the creek.

He imagined a tunnel just below his feet, and he imagined Gabriela being down there. Then, as he passed into darkness and his shoes disappeared, he forced himself to imagine her back home in their humble but secure flat.

He would soon know. He was only five minutes away, assuming his legs didn't collapse under his weary weight.

Ripley eventually made it home.

He looked up from where he stood in the front garden and saw that there was a light on in his bedroom.

A chill of hope swept through him.

He was pretty sure he hadn't left any lights on earlier that night. This surely meant that Gabriela was home. The tunnel runner hadn't got his murderous clutches on her. He hadn't chopped her down with his hatchet.

The endless tunnels and hordes of rats belonged to a world whose existence seemed impossible now that he was back at home. The starry sky watching over the sleeping suburb of Wilston filled him with a sense of peace and security. But the pain in Ripley's shoulder reminded him that there really had been a madman and that the hatchet hadn't been a figment of his imagination.

Ripley turned around and looked across the street to where he knew there was a dislodged manhole cover lying inconspicuously between the railway line and the embankment. The nightmarish world he had managed to escape was still close after all – very close indeed.

He hurried up the stairs and unlocked the door to his flat. He had never been so happy to be home. He would never understand why the tunnel dwellers had given up the comforts of normal life for a claustrophobic existence below the streets.

The bedroom door was closed, but he could see the faint glow of Gabriela's reading lamp through the gap between the door and the floor. He asked himself again whether he could have left it on before setting off to find his angel, but he never left lights on when he wasn't at home.

He reached out for the doorknob and realised that he was holding his breath. If the bedroom was empty, he would lose his mind, and he would have to go back into the tunnels at once.

He didn't want to drag the moment out any longer than necessary. He pushed the door open as gently as he could and fell to his knees, crying with relief for the second time that night.

Gabriela was fast asleep in bed, curled up tightly next to Fox Terra. If Ripley hadn't known better, he might have thought that they'd been friends for years.

He longed to wake them up, to know what had happened to her down there, but they both seemed to be sleeping soundly and peacefully. That was surely a good sign, an indication that she hadn't suffered any great trauma. The tunnel runner hadn't chased her with his hatchet. He hadn't touched a solitary hair on her gorgeous head. She was safe and sound.

Ripley crept out of the room and pulled the door closed. He would sleep on the couch. It would be like a cloud compared to his disastrous attempt at getting some rest in the tunnel. In the morning, he would call in sick. Going to work after everything he'd been through would be intolerable, and, at any rate, he had a lot of catching up to do, as well as some important decisions to make.

First things first though, Ripley was going to pour himself a double scotch and have a bath, and it would be the longest he'd ever had.

———◦———

Ripley didn't end up making it to the couch after all. He woke up in the bathtub, his body as sore as ever. The chill of the water and the eerie yet reassuring pink glow of the rising sun that caressed the pane of the bathroom's small window told him he had been sleeping there for at least three hours. The water that covered him was dark with grime and smelled faintly of rat shit and scotch but more prominently of a cocktail of soap, shampoo, and shower gel. His neck was stiff and his skin was swollen and wrinkled.

He admired the hint of light that was ever so slowly growing stronger in the world beyond the window. Never before had he been so happy to be awake at dawn. As he watched the window and tried to come to terms with the fact that he had slept in the bathtub, he struggled to remember what nightmares had been haunting his mind after the previous day's ordeal. But he couldn't remember anything. Perhaps he hadn't had any nightmares at all. For some reason, that possibility disturbed him even more. How could he have so narrowly survived such an adventure and not had a nightmare about it? He remembered the hatchet-wielding maniac and reminded himself that he had come within a hairsbreadth of being chopped up and turned into rodent feed.

He groaned as he sat up, feeling his neck and back creak like hinges in need of a good oiling. He felt something sticking into his bottom, and, reaching down, removed his whisky glass from the murky water. He looked around for the bottle that had accompanied it and saw it standing on the tile floor just beside the purple bathmat. He could have sworn it had been only two thirds empty when he'd removed it from on top of the cupboard, but now it was as dry as he was wet. He leaned forward and pulled the plug, eager to send the filthy water rushing down the drain and into the pipes that would send it flowing away to wherever it went beneath the city. He pushed the water towards the end of the bathtub with his hands as the level went down so that any loud gurgling sound would be minimised. He didn't want to risk waking the girls up just yet. Gabriela needed to recover from what had happened. As much as he wanted to hold her in his arms and tell her how much he loved her and how much he'd been scared that he'd lost her and how bloody angry he was with her for getting them into this whole debacle in the first place, he forced himself to bide his time. He was still filthy and he still reeked of sewer scum. He was cold too. He would need another hot bath.

He got out of the tub, being careful not to knock the empty bottle over, and put the plug back in before turning the hot and cold water taps on.

He stepped over to the bathroom mirror and looked at himself. He looked tired and confused, but considering everything he'd been through, he wasn't in too bad a state. He was even a little proud of himself. Sure, he'd shaken with fear and run away like a hunted animal when the tunnel runner had attacked him, but at the same time, he had beaten off a superior foe and escaped. He had risked everything and given every bit of energy he had to save his girlfriend, and, even though it seemed obvious that Fox had to be given the credit for finding her, the result had been one of success. The adventure was now over.

As Ripley stared at himself in the mirror and tried to smile, something dawned on him. For the first time since he had arrived home and discovered that Gabriela was safe, he felt a sentiment other than just relief. I was satisfaction. He realised that the interruption to his routine hadn't been so unwelcome after all. The adventure in the tunnels had given him more excitement than a thousand workout sessions with his mates ever could.

Ripley turned his sore shoulder to the mirror and inspected it. There was a big black bruise, but the skin hadn't been broken by the hatchet. He hadn't been too badly injured after all.

He thought about the tunnel runner's shin and decided that his opponent had surely come off second best.

He climbed back into the bathtub and slid down into the clean water, letting its warmth seep into him as he watched the pink glow at the bathroom window gradually turn to orange.

16

Ripley woke up in the bathtub again, but this time the water was still warm and he had a strange notion that there was some kind of movement behind him. Before he could clearly form his thoughts, he heard somebody speak.

"Oh, I'm sorry! I didn't know you were here." The voice made him jump like a fish in a net.

He turned his head, but Fox had already left the bathroom.

An instant later, he heard Gabriela laugh, and then, she gleefully called his name as she burst into the bathroom.

"Ripley! You're back! I was so scared. I was worried sick about you."

She crawled into the tub and kissed him.

"*You* were worried? What about *me*? I went into the tunnels looking for you. When did you get back?"

"I don't know what time it was. It was so strange."

"Fox told me she would find you and she didn't let me down. I don't know how we can repay her."

"No, Rips. She didn't find me down there. She found me here. She came here with Brand, then he went back to try to find you. He might still be looking for you. Fox told me all about the tunnel dwellers and explained that one of them is so angry we stumbled into the tunnels and discovered their community that he was prepared to kill us!"

"I know," Ripley said. He turned his shoulder so she could see the bruise.

"What happened? He attacked you?"

"Yes, and almost killed me."

"Are you serious, Ripley? We must never ever go back down

97

there."

Ripley smiled and pulled her closer. Her wet pyjamas stuck to him.

"I'm so glad to hear you say that, Gabs. It was a hell of an adventure, but it's over now. You really need to keep a lid on your curiosity sometimes."

She nodded. "Let's get some breakfast. I'm not going to go to work today. I'm going to call in sick."

"Me too," Ripley agreed. "We both need some rest."

They dried each other off and got dressed while Fox put the kettle on. Then, Ripley put some bread in the toaster while Gabriela set the coffee table.

"I'm sorry, Fox. We've caused a rift in your community and put Brand at risk. If we'd known all this was going to happen, we wouldn't have gone anywhere near the manhole to start with."

Fox sighed. "It's not your fault Dart has reacted this way. You haven't done anything to hurt us. The problem's that he assumes you will. When I joined the tunnel dwellers, it wasn't to declare war on society. It was to find a place where I could feel part of a real family. He doesn't think that way. He doesn't share our values and he doesn't respect Cooper's authority as our elected leader. You were just the catalyst. Sooner or later he was bound to provoke a confrontation with the rest of us."

Fox poured them some coffee.

"What are you going to do now?" Gabriela asked.

"What do you mean?"

"Well, I mean, you can't just pretend that everything will be like it was before. It's dangerous down there now."

"It's just him against the rest of us. He can't pose much of a threat. He'll either have to beg us to let him come back, live all alone in the tunnels – which would be an unbearably miserable existence, or leave the tunnels altogether."

"In any case, we're sorry, aren't we, Gabs?"

She nodded. "You can come and stay with us whenever you

want, and if you and Brand decide to have kids one day and want to live on the surface, we will help you make the transition."

"Thank you so much. I guess we can't live down there all our lives, but we're not ready to leave the community any time soon."

"Keep in touch all the same," Gabriela said. "I know we only just met last night, but I feel so close to you already."

"Me too, Gabriela. I wish I'd known more girls like you when I was living up here. Maybe my life would have taken a different direction."

"It's not too late, Fox. In the meantime, just remember to come and visit us as often as you can, and don't forget that if ever the situation gets dangerous down there, you and Brand have a safe haven here with us."

"I won't forget," Fox reassured them. "Can I just ask one little favour before I go back to see how Brand is doing down there?"

"Of course, you can. What is it?"

"A hot shower."

"Be our guest," Ripley told her. "And don't worry, we surface walkers don't walk in on people in the bathroom."

They laughed together and hoped that it wouldn't be for the last time.

Once Fox had left, and they'd called in sick, Gabriela and Ripley went back to bed.

Ripley felt as though he were in paradise. His angel had never been quite as angelic as she was that morning. It was so easy to take a comfortable bed and the embrace of a loving woman for granted, and Ripley now realised that he usually did just that. He had only barely survived his underground adventure, and for several long minutes, he'd been sure he would never experience

99

another dawn or hold Gabriela in his arms again.

Likewise, Gabriela had begun to think her curiosity had lost her a loved one for a second time.

So, on that strange morning, with excitement and fear having subsided, they lay together peacefully and appreciated every second of it.

Ripley asked Gabriela to describe every step of her subterranean journey, from the moment she'd left the flat until the moment she'd climbed her way out of the tunnels.

As she explained her journey in as much detail as she could, it became clear that Ripley wouldn't have succeeded in finding her at all. He had been trudging west while Gabriela had been slowly making her way north. She had tried to push manholes open in order to escape but hadn't been able to dislodge them. It wasn't until she had reached a storm water pipe that led her out onto the Kedron Brook bikeway that she was free of her underground prison. Ripley could have walked around for weeks down there without ever finding her.

"You told Fox you didn't meet anybody down there. Is that true?"

She looked at him as though he were accusing her of dishonesty but didn't pull out of his embrace.

"What do you mean? Everything I said in front of Fox was the truth. Why would I want to lie to her?"

"No, that's not what I meant." Ripley wasn't even sure he knew why he had said that. "Of course, there's no reason you would have lied to her. After all, she did everything she could to help us."

"I didn't meet anybody down there at all. I dread to think what might have happened if Dart had stumbled across me instead of you."

"I couldn't stop thinking about that either," Ripley admitted. "From the moment I escaped him and resurfaced near Waterworks Road until I saw you lying asleep in bed next to Fox, I couldn't help but imagine that scenario."

He could tell that Gabriela was on the brink of crying, so he held her more tightly.

"It's all right, Gabs. It was a mistake to go down there, but all is well that ends well. We're both safe now. We won't go into the tunnels again, will we?"

She shook her head against his chest.

"But what if he comes after us? I mean, does he know where we live?"

Ripley thought about that for a moment. He tried not to shudder at the idea of Dart hunting them down. The tunnels had represented such menace and apprehension for him, and his flat such safety, that the terrifying possibility of danger coming after them up on the surface seemed so implausible. He asked himself whether Dart could possibly know where they lived.

"No, Gabs. The only tunnel dwellers who know where we live are Fox and Brand, and even though I've never met him, I certainly get the impression from her that they aren't the kind of people who would break our trust or put us in harm's way."

Gabriela sighed with relief, then quickly drew in a shallow breath as another idea formed in her mind.

"What?" Ripley asked, sensing her desire to ask him something.

"Well, what if he noticed me watching him from the window one day?"

"I doubt it," Ripley replied. "I don't even think it's possible to clearly see somebody through our bedroom window from the railway line. The light was always off when you watched from the window, wasn't it?"

"I think so, but I'm not sure. But Ripley, what if he followed you home last night?"

"That's not possible. I hit his shin so hard that I may very well have broken it. He couldn't have followed me in that state, no matter how athletic he is. As well as that, I didn't stop checking all around as I walked. Nobody followed me. Not even a possum could have escaped my attention."

"Good, that's that then," Gabriela said with a tone of finality.

"Let's get some more sleep. I'll take you down to Cold Rock for an ice cream later."

"Take me for an ice cream? You're not my father," Gabriela mocked him.

"No, maybe not, but you are my little girl. Do you want an ice cream or not?"

"Yeah, I don't feel like sleeping just yet. You can take me for one now, daddy."

17

Fox arrived in the Chambers just as Cooper was beginning the general meeting. He was standing next to the rich man's red letterbox, with the tunnel dwellers gathered in front of him and Brand standing by his side.

On seeing Fox, Brand raised his eyebrows.

She replied with a smile and a thumbs-up.

He whispered in Cooper's ear and the leader of the tunnel dwellers closed his eyes and bowed his head in relief.

"That's a relief,' Copper said.

He signalled for Fox to come over so that she could share the details with him, and once he had been full informed, he addressed the community.

"Fellow tunnel dwellers, please give me your undivided attention."

The echoing whispers died down.

"Some of you are aware of an incident that has taken place over the last twenty-four hours, but others are not. I have called this meeting today because it is essential in our egalitarian community that every one of you be given the same information as each other. We distinguish ourselves from the mass society of the surface walkers through our dedication to true and directly participatory democracy and our refusal of the pursuit of personal advantage and wealth at the expense of our comrades. One major prerequisite to such a social system is the accessibility of information and the opportunity for everybody to know what issues affect the community and, therefore, to partake in the resolution of any problems. This is both your right and your responsibility."

Cooper had their full attention.

"Two surface walkers entered deep into the tunnel system yesterday. They were neither drug addicts nor Brisbane City Council employees. They were just everyday citizens who had got curious."

A murmur spread across the assembly.

"Now, listen up. In order to protect our community from outside interference, we make it a rule to do whatever we can to dissuade surface walkers from coming down here; you know this as well as I do.

"On this occasion, Fox Terra met a surface walker who was down here looking for his girlfriend. Both of them were lost in the tunnels, and, as far as we know, neither of them discovered the Chambers. Fox has now assured us that they are both back home on the surface and that they have promised to stay up there and to mention our existence to no-one."

"How do we know we can believe them?" somebody called out.

"We don't know that, but Fox assures me they are trustworthy people. If they do come back down here, I want whoever finds them to bring them straight to me. However, I don't anticipate that they'll venture here again."

The gathering nodded its agreement.

"Where's Dart?" another voice asked.

"Dart has left the community."

"Why? Don't we need him?"

"We can do without him, despite his skills. He wanted to kill the surface walkers and I told him that murder was not part of our code of values. He armed himself and went into the tunnels."

"He wanted to hunt them down and kill them?" an incredulous voice asked.

"Yes, that was his intention. Thankfully, he didn't succeed. At any rate, it's perfectly clear that he can no longer remain a member of our community."

"What should we do if we find him?"

"I don't want you to look for him. He is no longer our concern. However, I think it would be a good idea if we paid a lot more attention to the protection of our person from now on. I don't know what his intentions are towards us."

Nobody spoke.

"I don't know how he'll survive in the tunnels by himself, but I suspect we will cross paths with him from time to time. This is why we need to take precautions."

Cooper surveyed the group. Dart had friends in the community, and he wanted to know where they stood.

"I have some questions for you all and I want you to answer honestly. Firstly, does anybody think Dart was right in wanting to kill the surface walkers?"

A resounding 'no' echoed through the chamber.

"Thank you. Secondly, does anybody want to leave the community and join Dart?"

Nobody answered.

"Good. Finally, does anybody think we should try to reintegrate Dart into the community?"

Cooper detected a 'yes' or two amid the voices that said 'no'.

"Very well then. If you want to talk to Dart and persuade him to come back to the community, then you may do so. However, he will need to convince the majority of us, and me as your elected leader, that we can trust him. Does that sound reasonable?"

Nobody objected.

"Do you have any questions?"

The tunnel dwellers looked at each other. Nobody seemed to have any specific questions. The news had come as a surprise, and they were too confused to really know what to make of it all. Everybody knew that Dart was jealous of Cooper and wanted to be their leader, but nobody could have guessed it would come down to this.

"Who will be the new tunnel runner?" one of them asked.

"That's a good question, and one that I can't answer just yet. If anybody is interested in taking Dart's place as the tunnel runner, please come and talk to me. If there are several candidates, we can put them to the test.

"I can't emphasise the point enough that we need to stand united more than ever. Please be careful out there. We don't know what he intends to do." He paused to let those last words sink in before adding, "That's all for now."

With that, Cooper stepped down from beside the letterbox, and the tunnel dwellers dispersed.

All they could do was try to get on with their routine. Some armed themselves, worried that Dart would turn on them, while others didn't bother, feeling certain that he would do them no harm.

18

"Darling, I've finished in the bathroom. You can take your shower," Suzanne Klipsch called from the bedroom of her three-storey home on Lansdowne Street.

Henry shouted something indiscernible that sounded as though it had been spoken through a mouthful of wine. He was still on the verandah, sitting in his favourite cane chair and looking down on all the quaint Queenslanders and cottages crowded across the lower reaches of the suburb. If he had known anything about history, he might have likened himself to a feudal lord overseeing his serfs.

Suzanne wasn't particularly worried about her husband's relaxed attitude because they still had plenty of time before they had to leave for the performing arts complex at Southbank. He rushed around enough as it was, working hard to help the construction giant he was also married to cut costs as much as possible. He deserved to take his time when he could, and, Suzanne had to admit, he could get dressed a hell of a lot faster than she could. He was always ready before her. So she let him enjoy his glass in peace.

Suzanne smiled to herself as she pulled the top drawer of her duchess open. She hadn't enjoyed a real night out since becoming a mother. But now that little Katie was old enough to be left alone with her grandma, Suzanne was free to spend an evening with her husband at last.

A slender, perfectly manicured hand reached into the drawer and removed a carved jewellery box from it. She placed the deceptively simple box on her bed and opened it by flicking a delicate brass latch with the tip of her index finger.

Curled and twisted on the red velvet lining was an array of pearl and diamond necklaces. They sparkled eagerly, as though each one was trying to impress her, begging to be selected for a night at the opera.

Her fingers caressed them.

She chose a pearl necklace that had been offered to her by her husband on the day of their fourth wedding anniversary. It was a glorious work of art. She held it up to her long neck and walked gracefully from the bed to the full-length mirror, passing the bedroom window, which faced south and provided her with a stunning view of the illuminated skyscrapers of the city centre.

Standing in front of the mirror in her black lace lingerie, she admired her slim body and didn't fail to remind herself that her husband was lucky to have such a gorgeous wife. He went to the gym now and then, when he had time, and he was in reasonable shape. But she figured he wasn't anywhere near as sexy as she was. There were other strong points about him though. She stroked the pearls that gently encircled her swanlike throat. Whereas he adored her slim body, she was mad about his fat wallet.

Suzanne pirouetted with the kind of elegance and poise that only a former student of ballet could have marshalled. She bent towards the bed and looked back towards the mirror in order to get a rear view of herself. Her buttocks were heavenly; smoother than silk and as seductively pale as the moon. Her skin peeked out through the obsidian lacework of her panties.

She had to give credit where credit was due, and all of the credit for a body that looked like it belonged to a twenty-something-year-old when she was in fact approaching the big four-oh had to go to her personal trainer, Kyle. He knew how to motivate her and he knew how she thought. He understood her so well it actually scared her a little.

Suzanne straightened up again and looked out the window. The next-door neighbours' house was considerably lower than theirs, so there was no way anybody could see into the bedroom. Only somebody living further down the hill and armed with a telescope or a pair of binoculars could possibly spy on her, and that anybody might actually do that never even occurred to Suzanne. She felt that she was in complete privacy up there on the third floor. Only flying foxes and owls could venture to pass by her bedroom window at night.

She looked across the city to where the highest light on the tallest skyscraper stood as an arrogant monument to the powerful construction company for which Henry worked. It stood erect over Brisbane, an enormous phallus that put the other towers to impotent shame.

She strutted away, displaying her delightful body to a non-existent audience, and opened her walk-in wardrobe. The choice of evening wear would have been mind-boggling for a down-to-earth woman, but for Suzanne, it was far more limited than she would have liked. She was sure that, at the opera, she would notice numerous women wearing gowns that would make her envious. Nevertheless, she had enough elegant clothing to cause her to think long and hard about what she would wear. There was her white silk gown that clung hungrily to her lean curves, but Henry would never let her wear that with black lingerie underneath. Even though she sometimes felt like provoking him, she had to admit it would make her look like a cheap slut. She would have to wear a little black number. She just needed to decide what type of fabric to wear – simple cotton, sassy satin…

The doorbell rang, interrupting her train of thought.

The front entrance was down on the ground floor, but the electronic buzzer could be heard on all three levels thanks to the smart home system that Henry had paid a small fortune to have installed. Everything electronic in the house was interconnected and centrally controlled, from the shutters and air conditioning, the locks and burglar alarms to the entertainment network and lighting. A security camera linked to the television, as well as a small screen built into the wall next to the door, allowed Henry and Suzanne to see who was there. But the door couldn't be opened remotely. So whenever somebody came, one of them would have to go all the way down to welcome the visitor.

Suzanne certainly wasn't going to answer the door in her underwear.

"Henry, can you get it?"

She waited for a reply through the silence that reigned within the enormous house. None came.

"Henry?" she called out again, a tinge of irritation in her voice. She didn't want to yell too loudly because Katie was sleeping soundly in her cot.

Henry still didn't answer.

The doorbell rang again. It sounded more insistent this time.

Suzanne rolled her eyes and huffed in annoyance. She knelt down and grabbed a T-shirt and pair of shorts from the neat piles of casual clothes stacked on a low shelf next to the long row of various types of shoes.

"Thanks, honey," she muttered sarcastically under her breath as she hurried out of the bedroom.

She could hear the shower running in the upstairs bathroom. At least, he had an excuse.

The doorbell rang again. It was longer this time, even more insistent.

Just as she reached the second floor, she heard Katie crying, her little voice demanding attention, ordering her mother to come back to the third floor. But Suzanne continued downstairs. Katie would have to wait a minute.

She didn't bother looking at the screen built into the wall. She simply reached out and opened the door.

19

Ripley and Gabriela were cooking dinner when his mobile rang for the first time that day. He rinsed his hands and grabbed it from the coffee table. It was Pete. With all the excitement he'd gone through, Ripley had completely forgotten about their workout that morning.

"It's Pete," he told Gabriela.

"Don't say anything!" she reminded him. They had made a promise to Fox, and Gabriela knew that they had to be very careful not to let their secret out.

"Don't worry, I won't," he assured her.

He accepted the call.

"Hi Pete."

"Rips, what happened this morning?"

"Sorry, mate. I slept in. I wasn't feeling too well." It wasn't really a lie after all.

"You lazy bugger! Don't miss too many workouts or you'll get out of shape and won't be able to keep up with the rest of us." Pete laughed.

Ripley felt like telling him not to worry about that, but he held his tongue.

"I'm feeling better now. I'll be back on Thursday."

"All right, Rips. Catch you then."

"See you, Pete."

He hung up.

"I completely forgot about Pete and the boys," he told Gabriela as he returned to the kitchen.

"It's understandable. It's all over now though. We need to put all of that out of our minds and get back to normal life."

Ripley nodded. It wouldn't be easy, but Gabriela was right. They would have to try to put everything that had happened behind them. Fox and Brand might come to visit them from time to time, but they would have to just act as though they were normal friends, as hard as that might be.

"Do you want to go to the cinema after dinner? A good movie will help distract us."

"Sure, why not? Do you know what's on?"

"Yeah," Ripley lied as he started peeling the carrots, a sneaky smile forming on his lips. "I wouldn't mind watching that new horror movie, "The Monster in the Sewers". What do you reckon?"

Gabriela laughed. "Very funny, you could have worked as a director in the fifties with a B-grade imagination like that."

"I'll finish the carrots and then check what's on," Ripley suggested. "I'm sure we can find a movie that has nothing to do with psychopaths or tunnels."

"I sure hope so."

———◦———

Ripley and Gabriela arrived at the cinema a good fifteen minutes before *Carol* was due to start. This meant that, allowing almost twenty minutes for advertisements, they were very early indeed. They were all alone, which was normal for a Monday night, especially considering the film they had chosen had already been showing for a couple of weeks. They sat in the middle seats of the fourth row from the back; their place of predilection.

"It feels strange in here all alone," Ripley said.

Gabriela held onto his arm. She knew exactly what he meant, even if he hadn't wanted to say it. Despite the scarlet curtains, comfortable seats, and relaxing music, they were in essence sitting abandoned in a dim concrete box. It was eerily reminiscent of being underground, even if nowhere near as dark. They knew that once the film started, the impression would vanish as the magic of the cinema took hold, but in the meantime, they couldn't help but think about the similarities between this world and the other.

"You want to know something, Gabs?"

She looked up at him with her irresistible chocolate eyes and made a purring sound that he knew meant she wanted him to continue. Ripley wasn't usually the most introspective man in the world, but from time to time, he would lose himself in thought. She loved it when he did that.

"I was just thinking about yesterday, or today rather, even though it seems like it was yesterday. In fact, it all seems like it was several days ago."

"Uh huh," she mocked him. "That's interesting."

"Forget it," he said, a little annoyed.

"I'm joking. I'm sorry. What are you thinking?"

He looked around the theatre. There was still nobody else. He might have suspected that time had decided to go on strike if it hadn't been for the music.

"Tell me, Rips," she prompted him. "I want to know."

"I was thinking about my encounter with Dart."

She squeezed his arm. "Don't torture yourself. It's over. We're on the surface. The ball is in our court. Dart can't hurt us now."

"I know." But he didn't sound so sure. "What I want to say is that while he was chasing me, which only lasted a few seconds, certainly no more than a minute or two, it seemed like time had slowed down, and I mean, become really slooooow."

"That's normal," she whispered reassuringly, sensing that he was more disturbed by the whole episode than she had realised.

"I know. Of course, it is. Time always seems longer when we're afraid or bored or sad, doesn't it?"

"Exactly. Down there, in the tunnels, it felt like days when it was really just a matter of hours."

"That's right. The thing is, well, what if time is really just a matter of perception?"

There was a long moment of silence.

"Is that what time is?" he continued.

"I don't know, Rips. I've never studied philosophy."

"Sure, neither have I. Maybe we should. I just think that it's a shame bad times always seem to last longer than good times. Today was great, spending time together, just the two of us. I mean, after what happened, I really appreciated it, and it seemed to last for ages."

"It was the same for me."

"It's a pity good times don't usually seem to last that long."

"You're right. But what can we do about it?"

"Well, maybe we can do something about it. If time is just perception, then we can control that perception and make the good times seem longer than the bad. By doing that, we could spend more time in our lives being happy than we do feeling sad or afraid."

Gabriela took a deep breath.

"I guess you're right, Rips. That sounds really profound. It's a little scary, but, at the same time, kind of exciting."

Ripley put his arms around her, and she kissed him tenderly. He slipped his hands up her blouse and caressed her breasts. He felt like having his way with her right there in the cinema and enjoying every long and thrilling second of it.

Her dreamy gaze told him she wanted that too.

His fingertips were brushing her nipples, and hers were undoing his fly, when voices emerged from within the sea of calm music.

A small group walked into the cinema. They laughed together as they noticed Ripley pull his hand out of Gabriela's blouse.

More people followed shortly after, and, before long, there were more than a dozen in the audience.

Ripley and Gabriela observed each person, and, although they were unaware of the fact, they were both wondering if somehow some of them were tunnel dwellers. As unlikely as it seemed, they supposed it possible that tunnel dwellers sometimes found the time and means to come to the movies. Perhaps there were even secret access points that led from the tunnel system straight up into the building, thus allowing them to get away with not paying.

The music and lighting faded, and the curtains were drawn back.

The screen came alive.

Ripley and Gabriela were plunged into the noisy world of cinema advertising, a far cry from the subterranean world of concrete and isolation they had been wandering through earlier that day.

20

The tunnel runner was watching the front of the Klipsch family's luxurious abode from the thicket of trees and bushes that grew along the thin median strip separating the upper southbound lane of Lansdowne Street from the lower northbound one. It would have been difficult for the average surface walker to stand there so motionlessly, but Dart had been sneaking through the streets at night for years. He knew not only how to run through narrow passages, jump over barbed wire fences, and crawl through pipes, but also how to stand perfectly still and hide in plain view.

Even as the hatchback's headlights swept across him and its driver got out just metres away from where he stood, Dart remained undetected.

His injured leg hurt when he walked and he knew that he would be unable to run at all for several days while it healed, but that was no reason to sit around in the tunnels and go hungry. As part of the community, it had been possible to take time off to rest whenever he'd been sick. There was always somebody ready to take up the responsibilities of any tunnel dweller who needed a break. But there was no turning back now.

Now that he was a lone wolf, Dart would have to fend entirely for himself. That meant he would have to keep launching raids on wealthy households, injured leg or not. He targeted those he considered leeches that sucked the blood out of their fellow surface walkers. From them, he procured the necessities of life, such as food and utensils, personal hygiene products, clothing, and other valuables that could be sold and that would, just as importantly, punish these people for their greed.

His invisibility from their point of view, as well as his ability to appear on the surface and then vanish without a trace, was a powerful weapon. The leeches could do little to protect themselves and their ostentatious palaces from his raids. However, now Dart had two worlds to feel disillusioned with; the superficial dog-eat-dog city above, and the weak, soon-to-be-exposed tunnel community below. He no longer belonged to either of them.

Dart hadn't burgled a Lansdowne Street address in quite some time, not for at least five months, so he'd decided it was time to strike again.

The Klipsch home was an extravagant monstrosity he'd noticed several times before. It was the kind of abode that was certain to be filled to the rim with the expensive trappings of surface walkers who received far too much and contributed far too little. It was a mansion Dart had always told himself he would reserve for a rainy day.

That day had come.

He shifted his weight slowly so that more pressure was applied to his uninjured leg. He needed to get some rest. He needed to treat his shin. He was pretty sure the bone wasn't broken, but his leg was hurt badly enough to make any physical effort painful.

He was intending to launch one of the most thorough raids he had ever undertaken. He knew exactly what he would look for, and he knew that he would be free to rest for at least a week if he found all of those items.

Success, however, depended on the inhabitants of the three-storey mansion. He had made a habit of checking all of the mail sent to Henry and Suzanne Klipsch. It was quite easy to do. He stole a stack of Woolworths catalogues from outside a deliverer's house and pretended to be distributing them. When he placed a catalogue in a letterbox, he had a look at whatever official mail was already in there. That's how he noticed the opera tickets that had been sent to Henry and Suzanne Klipsch a few days earlier. He had been able to read the tickets through the thin envelope in which they had been enclosed. He knew that they weren't going to be at home that night, but he hadn't counted on somebody else coming to housesit.

He carefully observed everything that happened as Suzanne Klipsch opened the door and greeted the older woman, who had driven the hatchback. He figured the visitor could only have been her mother. They looked remarkably similar, and both held themselves with the same poise, even if Suzanne's youth made her elegance more complete. They spoke together briefly, and although Dart could hear their voices, he was unable to make out much of what they were saying. Then, Suzanne ushered her mother inside and closed the door to the gathering dark.

There was nothing Dart could do but wait to find out what would happen. If Suzanne's mother stayed inside all night, he would have to forget about that particular house and find another place to raid.

He bent the knee of his unscathed leg and lowered himself to the ground until he was sitting. Then, he leaned against the trunk of the tree behind him and watched the front door of the house through the gaps between the leaves of the shrubs in front of him. He hoped that Suzanne's mother would leave. Maybe she had just dropped in to have a quick chat, unaware that her daughter and son-in-law had already made plans for the evening. Once they had told her they were going to the opera, she would hasten to assure them that she didn't want to hold them up and leave without any further ado. Dart would then be able to sneak into the house and take enough supplies to keep him comfortable while his leg healed.

That would be the ideal scenario, but he would have to bide his time. If living in the tunnels had taught him one valuable quality that was in short supply on the surface, it was patience. For a tunnel dweller, being patient could mean the difference between surviving underground and being forced to return to the kind of life on the surface that they had all sought so desperately to escape. So, gently massaging his sore leg, Dart sat back and waited.

———————— >o< ————————

Grandma took Katie from her cot and started pulling faces.

The infant immediately stopped crying.

Suzanne didn't have that special touch. She often got the impression her baby was capable of sensing that she wasn't really the sole object of her mother's thoughts. Even when she was cradling Katie and giving her daughter what she thought was her undivided attention, there were always other preoccupations weighing heavily on her mind.

Suzanne had put her career on hold in order to start a family, and she had done so begrudgingly. For her, although having a child was something that she'd always intended to do and that she didn't regret, it was a risk for her career and an inconvenience that reminded her that regardless of however hard she struggled to be equal to men in work and society, she was a prisoner of biology. She was the one who had to take time off work to look after Katie. Perhaps there were men who would consider staying home to raise a baby, but Henry wasn't one of them, and she had to admit she wouldn't want to be married to a man who would willingly stay at home to look after a baby while she played the role of breadwinner. She needed a husband like Henry, a hunter who provided his female and offspring with a bounty of fresh prey on a daily basis.

Unlike Suzanne, her mother had never felt conflicted about her role in life. She had been happy to dedicate her energies to motherhood, and, somehow, Katie knew this about her grandmother.

"You two will be all right?" Suzanne asked even though the question was unnecessary.

"I think so, dear," her mother replied, winking, as though she too could read Suzanne's mind. "I might take her for a little drive down to Kedron Brook Road later if that's fine by you, sweetie."

"Of course, it is. Do you still have the baby seat?"

"Yes, I keep it in the car all the time now."

"I have to keep getting ready or we'll be late. Make yourself at home, mum."

Suzanne dashed back into the bedroom and headed for the walk-in wardrobe. She took her T-shirt and shorts off and tried to remember which dress she had been on the brink of deciding to wear. She opted for a black silk number that Henry had bought for her when he was in China on a business trip. It was sure to make her the envy of every woman – and, for that matter, man – at the opera.

Suzanne lifted the dress over her head and straightened her arms, allowing it to slip over her body. It felt like a cool breeze.

Next, she selected a pair of high-heels without hesitating for a second.

After that, she returned to the duchess, from which she took a bottle of Hypnotic Poison. She sprayed the perfume on her neck before stepping past the window to check herself in the mirror. Smiling smugly, she caressed the pearls encircling her neck several times, and then she returned to her mum and Katie.

"You look gorgeous, dear. I hope Henry appreciates how lucky he is!"

Suzanne smiled. "I'm not sure that he does. Is he *still* in the shower?"

"I think so. He does take a long time for a man, doesn't he?"

They both glanced towards the door to the bathroom.

"He doesn't usually," Suzanne said.

"I hope he hasn't had a slip," her mother said, a hint of real concern in her voice. She always had been a worrier.

"Of course, he hasn't."

Suzanne went over and opened the door.

"Henry? We'll be late."

"I won't be a second."

"What are you doing in there? I hope you're having fun," she mocked him loudly.

"Let him be, sweetie. He's making himself nice and presentable for you."

Suzanne closed the door.

"Do you want a glass of Moët while we're waiting?"

"I wouldn't say no to a little champs."

Suzanne went down to the second storey, to where the kitchen and its two huge refrigerators held pride of place. She opened the one that was dedicated to drinks, appetisers, and desserts and took the cheapest bottle of champagne she could find among the ten or so kept in there.

By the time she got back upstairs, Henry had vacated the bathroom and was in the bedroom.

"It's good that you and Henry are taking the time to go to the opera together. It's important to spend time with your husband now and then. Your father was a slave to the wage. We didn't spend as much time together as we should have."

Suzanne sipped at her champagne. Her mother was such a sentimental soul. Even though she took after her physically, it seemed that her Auntie Margaret was right when she reminded her that, as far as personality was concerned, Suzanne was just like her father. The repeated observation wasn't intended as a compliment either. Everybody in the family had admired her father for many reasons, and she was grateful that he had brought her up to be a strong-minded and ambitious woman, but Suzanne had to admit that he certainly hadn't endowed her with the qualities of sentimentalism and tenderness. He had taught her to be a wolf, not a lamb.

"It's hard for Henry to get time off work. In theory, he can leave early, like he did tonight, but, in reality, he can't bear the thought of being seen as anything but completely dedicated to his work."

"I know that, Suze, but he also has an obligation towards you."

Suzanne was starting to get a little peeved. She hoped Henry wouldn't take as long getting dressed as he had in the shower. He was usually so much faster than her getting all set to go out. The sooner he was ready, the sooner they could be on their way, and Suzanne wouldn't have to listen to her mother rehashing the same old spiel any longer.

"I understand your point of view, mum. I wish dad could have spent more time with us too, but…" she thought about what she wanted to say. "Well, the point is, I need Henry to work. We need the money. Our income has fallen dramatically since I stopped working to have Katie."

"I know that, but you're not exactly broke."

Suzanne drained her glass of champagne.

"No, we're not broke, but we are doing it a little tough at the moment."

"What are you talking about? You have a magnificent home with a tennis court, a swimming pool, and a Jacuzzi, as well as a seaside apartment, and two luxury cars that most men could only lay a finger on at a motor show. You're doing all right. What do you have to go without? Is the problem that you have to drink Moët instead of Krug?"

"Yes, for example." Suzanne failed to recognise the sarcasm in her mother's voice until she had already replied. She felt silly for an instant. "What I mean is that we're used to a certain standard of living, so it's hardly reasonable to expect us to be able to accept anything less, is it?"

"Fine, Suze. Anyway, it's great you're spending a night together, just the two of you, no business partners or acquaintances. I hope you enjoy the show."

Suzanne lowered her guard and smiled as she refilled their glasses.

"We will, mum. Thanks for looking after Katie for us."

"Don't be silly. You know very well it's a pleasure for me to look after my little darling."

Henry opened the bedroom door. He was dressed to kill in a

silver lounge suit.

"Don't you look very suave, Henry!"

Suzanne nodded in agreement. *But not as handsome as I am beautiful*, she reminded herself.

Ripley and Gabriela had enjoyed the movie and were on their way home. They sat at the back of the bus and held each other tight. They were alone, apart from the driver. It seemed as though just about everybody else in the city drove everywhere. Nobody hailed the bus all the way home; it was like being chauffeur driven in a huge but rather grimy limousine.

They got off at the stop in front of Wilston Station, just metres from where the manhole that had enticed them to succumb to curiosity and head underground a little more than twenty-four hours earlier lay hidden in obscurity. A strange whim that had no basis in reason begged Ripley to jump the barbed wire fence once again and crawl through that inconspicuous manhole. He forced himself not to look in its direction.

Gabriela grabbed his hand and led him across the deserted road, as though she had sensed his thoughts with that most mysterious of feminine powers; intuition. They had promised not to go back into the tunnels, and, even more importantly, they now knew just how dangerous it could be for them.

"Let's get inside, Rips," she said, as though answering a question he hadn't even posed. "I'll rub some pawpaw ointment on your bruise."

He gripped her hand more tightly. His mind was playing tricks on him. There was nothing for either of them down there in the tunnels. He belonged with Gabriela, safe and sound in their bedroom, holding each other and making love like there was no tomorrow. That was how they would spend the rest of the night, and, in the morning, they would both get up and go to work as though they had just felt sick and needed a little time to rest. The morning would bring them back to a world of reassuring normality and easy routine.

Ripley was relieved to discover that the door to their flat was well and truly locked, just as it had been when they'd left for the cinema. At the same time, he found it unsettling that he had imagined it could have been otherwise. They'd decided that it wasn't possible for Dart to have any idea where they lived. There was no reason to think that he or anybody else had broken into their flat while they were at the cinema. Yet, Ripley couldn't shake the haunting notion out of his head.

He inserted the key into the slot and turned it. Then, he opened the door and slipped his hand inside, feeling for the light switch. He pressed it and a flood of comforting light hit like a warm sunbeam piercing winter clouds.

"What are you doing?" Gabriela asked, frowning at him.

"What do you mean?"

"Why did you open the door all funny like that?"

"What are you talking about? I just opened the door and flicked the light on."

"No, you didn't!" she almost shouted.

He obviously wasn't going to be able to pull the wool over her eyes.

"Shush, keep your voice down."

"Okay," she said more quietly. "Just tell me why."

He sighed as he pulled her inside, closing the door behind them. He didn't want to make a scene in front of the neighbours.

"Sometimes, just sometimes, I think you're a mind reader."

"I'm a woman. It's the same thing," she replied with a smirk.

"I guess I'm getting paranoid," Ripley tried to justify himself. "Is that such a surprise considering what we've been through, discovering an entire world beneath our feet and having it made perfectly clear that some of its inhabitants want to be our best friends while at least one other hates us enough to wish we were dead just because we live a couple of metres above the surface of this fucked-up planet instead of a couple of metres below it?"

Gabriela didn't know what to say. She wanted him to be the one to comfort her, to reassure her that there was no danger now that they were back in their world. She realised that it wasn't politically correct to expect that. The sexes were supposed to be equal in this day and age. A woman wasn't supposed to need a man to make her feel safe. But she did, and that was all there was to it. She wanted him to make her believe that the dark figure she'd seen jumping the barbed wire fence and vanishing underground was oblivious to the fact that the two surface walkers who had followed him, intruding upon his subterranean sanctuary where he felt removed from all that he hated about the competitive, bullshit-driven world of the city, lived just a few metres and one four-lane road away from the railway tracks that bordered the entrance to his dark home.

"Don't be paranoid, Rips. You got away from him once. You showed him that you're not the weak subject of society he thinks you are. He knows you're not a cowardly consumerist sheep. You showed him you can stand up for yourself, even down there on his turf. I need you to be strong for me up here too."

Ripley nodded confidently. She was right. He didn't need to be afraid of the tunnel runner. He had to stand his ground and believe in himself. He wasn't weak. The last twenty-four hours had strengthened him immensely, and he was only going to get stronger.

He led her towards the bedroom with the assurance she wanted from him and didn't let it waver as he pulled her clothes off and directed her into bed. Then, he pulled the curtains closed, without so much as offering one glance in the direction of the Ferny Grove railway line, before slipping into bed beside her.

21

Dart was starting to wonder how much longer he could put up with sitting there, leaning against the tree trunk while his arse grew numb, when a low grinding noise caught his attention. One of the automatic gates to the Klipsch household's double garage had started sliding open. Red lights glared at him like demon eyes as Henry's Lexus was backed down the short but steep driveway more quickly than good sense would have dictated. For an instant, Dart thought maybe the leech would spot his face glowing crimson in the rear-vision mirror and the game would be up, but in the next instant, he grew even more concerned as the rear of the car swung towards him. It seemed as though Henry was going to back into the median strip. What an embarrassing way to die that would be; crushed between a rich man's Lexus and a tree while waiting to break into the driver's house.

Dart could feel the heat and smell the fumes coming out of the car's two gaping integrated exhaust outlets, and he almost jumped up from where he sat.

But then, the Lexus stopped. Its tyres ground against the bitumen as Henry put it into drive, turned the wheel, and sped away.

Dart shook his head, admonishing himself for having come so close to losing his calm and giving himself away. The rich man was hardly going to back into the trees. There was no way he would risk scratching his precious automobile.

He shifted his weight, trying to make himself more comfortable, but only succeeding in making his sore leg hurt more under the strain.

"Come on, granny, get out of there!" he whispered to himself.

It was then that Dart realised the garage gate wasn't sliding shut as rapidly as they usually did in his experience. He didn't have time to think about whether he should make a dash for it or not. He had to react immediately.

He decided to take a chance. Without looking to see if there were any pedestrians in the street, taking their pampered pooches for an evening stroll, or observant neighbours watching from their verandahs, or even cars approaching from the left-hand side, Dart thrust himself forward and was able to roll under the gate just in time.

He ignored the pain that throbbed in his leg and lay flat on the concrete floor of the garage for a minute while he thought about whether he had reacted well and what he would do next. He had been wondering how he would get into the mansion without triggering whatever alarm system they had installed. That was no longer an issue. On the other hand, grandma was still in the house, and there was no way of knowing when she would leave, if at all. Dart had to decide what he was going to do.

He remained motionless and observed his surroundings.

There were shelves lining the walls of the garage, just above head height, and they were crammed full of all kinds of easily accessible sporting equipment and dusty, rarely used household appliances. The tennis racquets and golf clubs held pride of place close to where the boot would be when the Lexus was parked in the garage.

Dart noticed without surprise that there was no lawn mower, whipper snipper, hedge trimmer, or any other gardening tools in the garage. That was only natural; people like the Klipsch family could afford to pay for a gardening service to take care of such nuisances as keeping an oversized property in perfect order.

Dart was still noting his surroundings when the lights suddenly went out.

His heart jumped and he wondered who had turned them off.

He hadn't heard footsteps or any other evidence of movement nearby.

But his moment of panic soon passed as he realised they were probably automatic.

He remained lying on the concrete but lifted an arm above his head.

The lights flashed on again. He felt relieved, but he still had to make a decision. He couldn't wait in the garage all night until Henry and his wife returned.

He got to his feet and stepped slowly towards the door to the house. It was slightly ajar, but he couldn't hear any sound coming from within.

He raised a gloved hand to the door and thought seriously about pushing it open, but couldn't bring himself to do it. If he made his presence known, all his preparations and patience would have been for nothing. His hand remained pressed lightly against the door while he considered his options.

Even though life in the tunnels meant that Dart had to be strong, and at times brutal, he was also capable of being surprisingly gentle. The art of burglary required discretion and self-control at the very best of times. He had been caught in the act by surface walkers several times in his early days and had almost been apprehended by the police on a couple of occasions. The prospect of being dragged through the surface's impartial judicial system, which seemed to be designed to protect the powerful rather than to dispense true justice, had made him realise that he needed to be more careful. Being locked up in a confined area with all kinds of thugs would mean an intolerable existence for someone used to the freedom of the tunnels. More importantly than that, it would give him a criminal record, thus ushering in the end of a life of anonymity. Knowing that the house he was in was occupied at that moment, Dart had to be very cautious indeed.

His gloved hand pushed the door ever so slightly, making it move a centimetre. He was relieved to find that its hinges didn't squeak at all, so he pushed a little more, using minimal force.

Once the door was open wide enough, he squeezed his head through the gap. It was quiet inside the spacious abode. There was no vacant chatter from a television echoing along the corridors or seeping through the walls. He started wondering whether grandma had somehow left without him noticing. Perhaps, by some uncanny coincidence, she had gone out at the very moment he had rushed into the garage.

But he couldn't afford to make assumptions. He would have to play it safe. He waited a little longer, listening.

As the seconds crawled by, Dart started toying with the idea of taking that small but risky step that would place him inside the house, between the front door and the staircase leading up to the first floor.

He hesitated. His good sense warned him not to risk getting caught, especially when he couldn't run as well as usual. At the same time, experience and confidence told him that he could probably burgle the house even with the grandmother still in there if he put his mind to it.

While he was still considering how to proceed, a metallic jingling told Dart he wouldn't have to take a risk after all. It was the distinct sound of rattling keys.

Grandma was about to leave.

The jingling grew louder as she descended the stairs.

He pulled the door to the garage closed and took a few steps back. He remained perfectly still, hoping the lights would switch off, leaving him hidden in sweet obscurity.

They did, just as grandma, who was mumbling softly to Katie, reached the front door and left the house.

A few minutes later, the time it took grandma to secure Katie in the baby seat and sit down behind the wheel, Dart heard the car start up.

He stayed put until he heard her drive away, and then, as though some kind of switch had been flicked within his head, he changed from slow, patient mode to action mode.

He pushed the door open and crept upstairs as quickly as he could, letting his uninjured leg lead the other and pulling on the banister rail with a gloved hand.

As he emerged onto the first floor, his expectations were confirmed. The layout was just as he had imagined. To say that the luxury of the mansion was in stark contrast with the dingy tunnel world to which Dart belonged would have hardly begun to express how he felt whenever he committed burglary. The decadence of these people and their obsession with money sickened him.

As he slipped into the kitchen, he noted that every inch of the Klipsch abode stank of wealth and pretentiousness, from the shiny light fittings and elaborate coving to the top-brand white goods, marble bench tops, and professional quality oven. As far as Dart was concerned, despite its impeccable cleanliness and faint lavender scent, it smelled fouler than even the most congested sections of the sewer system.

He also noticed that almost all of the lights in the house seemed to have been left on. In his experience, this meant one of three things; that the occupant wasn't concerned about running up a big electricity bill, that the lights had been left on as a security measure, or that the occupant was planning on coming back within the hour. Dart hoped that it wasn't for the third reason, but he knew that he had to be prepared for that possibility. He had to move quickly.

He went straight to the American fridge and pulled its doors open. Food was his most immediate requirement, and even though breaking into homes was a risky way of acquiring supplies, it was not as risky as shoplifting when it came to gathering a large amount of food in a very short time. He took as much as he could and stuffed it into his sack before moving to the pantry and taking as many tins of vegetables, tuna, and sardines as he could find. Even the filthy rich kept staples in tins for the unlikely event of a rainy day. Perhaps it was due to some subconscious evolutionary need, or the guilty fear that the good life might be snatched away from them one day as a result of revolution or apocalypse.

His sack was just about full already, but it didn't matter, because Dart now turned his attention to smaller objects; the kind that could be easily transformed into the cold, hard cash that would allow him to provide for himself without having to commit burglaries for a while.

He left the kitchen and went up to the second floor, moving as though he knew the house intimately. He could somehow sense where the master bedroom was located.

The door was open but the light was off, unlike most of the others throughout the house, and even though he knew there was nobody inside, he couldn't help but feel a little uncomfortable. Its darkness was not like the gloomy, sheltering embrace of the tunnels, or even that of the garage. Dart was acutely aware that he was stepping into a person's most private place, and, despite his hate for surface walkers in general, he couldn't help but feel that what he was doing was not quite right. But he soon laid his qualms aside by reminding himself that his brief intrusion into their world justified by the very fact that it was necessary for his long-term survival.

He felt for the light switch and pressed it.

The pure opulence that appeared before him reinforced the conviction that he had no reason to reproach himself. The contents of the bedroom were worth more than most surface walkers' bank accounts, and he hadn't even looked in the chest of drawers or under the bed yet.

It was wrong for one household to be hoarding that kind of wealth. He needed some of it. It had to be redistributed. He would feel no pangs of guilt as he helped himself to it.

Dart's gloved hands pulled the top drawer of Suzanne Klipsch's duchess open and his gaze fell immediately upon the carved jewellery box. He smiled to himself. Imagination and wealth never seemed to come together. Or maybe it was just that Henry and Suzanne thought their alarm system was so reliable they didn't have to entertain the thought that somebody could break into their house and go through their belongings. That must have been it. Not even in her wildest dreams could Suzanne have imagined that a thief could enter her bedroom and violate her privacy.

Dart snarled at her self-assurance as he opened the jewellery box. He usually only removed items of particular value, but the tangle of glittering ornaments contained nothing that could be classified as a mere trinket. His snarl turned to a smile. When he looked at the intricately worked necklaces, rings, and earrings, he didn't see jewellery, he saw comfort. They were not beautiful to him. They were ugly symbols of greed and arrogance. But they were valuable in a very practical way. They would provide him with enough food and clothing to last him while he spent long days deciding what he was going to do now that he'd abandoned the tunnel community.

He put the jewellery box into his sack and moved around the ridiculously large bed, thinking how comfortable it looked. It must have been like a cloud to lie in. He imagined climbing onto it and falling asleep. He had never slept in a bed like that before and he probably never would. He certainly wasn't going to now either. He had heard of thieves falling asleep in a house they had been burgling. They had lost months of freedom for an hour or two of rest.

Dart knelt down and looked under the bed. Only old people kept money stashed under their mattresses, but he checked anyway, just in case.

There was nothing but perfectly vacuumed carpet.

Just as he was getting back up, he heard the front door open.

"It can't be!" he whispered to himself.

It had only been a matter of minutes since grandma had left the house, ten at most.

He had to act swiftly.

He hurried towards the bedroom door and stepped into the living area. A thud rang out as the front door closed. Grandma would be making her way up the stairs towards the second floor. It was too late for him to try descending them and waiting in one of the second floor rooms while she came upstairs.

He stepped back from the staircase and retreated into the bedroom. It was the only room he could feel quite sure she wouldn't enter. He would wait in there, listening carefully for the inevitable moment when she went to the toilet, and then he would make a hasty departure. There was no choice. That was how it would have to happen.

He switched the light off and stood silently behind the closed door.

Every few minutes, he shifted his weight from one leg to the other in a vain attempt to alleviate the pain of his constantly aggravated injury. Whenever he moved, even if it was ever so slightly, he made sure not to bump the wall or bedroom door. The floor was not a problem. An expensive and perfectly insulated home like the Klipsch's didn't have squeaking floorboards.

Grandma was watching TV. From what Dart could hear, the programme was a cooking competition between various contestants whose shared dream was to become a famous chef, like Jamie Oliver or Nigella Lawson, while, of course, winning a huge cash prize. Money was always at the root of everything surface dwellers did. Dart didn't find it entertaining at all, standing there in the dark and listening to the hosts giving instructions. All it did was make him hungry.

He hoped grandma would go to the bathroom soon.

The waiting continued, and he kept his breathing slow and steady so that it wouldn't interfere with his hearing. He knew that the bathroom was situated on the other side of the wall from where the duchess stood. If he heard any noise coming from that direction, whether it be the closing of a door, or the opening of a tap and the accompanying sound of water flowing through pipes, he would take a chance and get out of the house as quickly as possible.

As the minutes trudged by, Dart's mind started drifting away from his present predicament and directing itself towards the concern that had been nagging at it since he had clashed with Cooper. He had to decide what he was going to do in the long term. Being alone, sometimes for long stretches of time, was normal for him, and the other tunnel dwellers had always assumed that he was a natural loner. But it wasn't as simple as they thought. There was a difference between going off on your own on a regular basis and living in complete isolation from other human beings day in and day out. He felt empty inside when he thought about the prospect of living alone in the tunnels for the rest of his life. He couldn't do that. Nobody could.

His attention was brought back to the here and now, even though there was still no movement from grandma. There was a pleasant scent, and it was gradually growing stronger. It must have been seeping into the bedroom through the narrow gap between the door and the floor. He assumed it was coming from the living area. Grandma must have lit some kind of incense. He didn't know exactly what it was, but he recognised the smell and a sudden pang of nostalgia made him feel uneasy. Some of the tunnel girls lit incense sticks and candles that gave off the exact same fragrance in the Chambers. He hadn't realised until that moment just how very enchanting the scent was, and just how much he was going to miss it. He was going to miss a lot of things about life in the Chambers.

He shook his head, trying to chase any hint of regret away. If he didn't pay attention, he would never make it back underground at all.

A loud pop startled him, almost making him jump. It registered immediately. Grandma had opened a bottle of sparkling wine.

That seemingly insignificant sound got the cogs of Dart's mind cranking. He remembered he'd noticed a few bottles of sparkling in one of the refrigerators on the second floor, and he'd noticed an empty bottle somewhere, hadn't he? He

134

couldn't be sure. They were either memories or just imaginings. If he was right, and grandma had already had a glass or two of sparkling, then she would certainly go to the toilet soon. No bladder could hold a deluge of wine for long.

It would only be a matter of minutes.

22

The queue for the men's room was like a supermarket express lane compared with the endless parade of impatient princesses lined up outside the ladies'. Once Henry had relieved himself, he hurried over to the bar before it too was stormed by thirsty opera buffs. It was prohibited to take alcohol into the auditorium for some goddamned stupid reason, so Henry, like everybody else, would have to suck back a few drinks before the bell rang and the bar closed. It was always a competition to get orders in.

"Two glasses of sparkling, mate."

Henry walked over to the enormous plate glass windows that provided him with a panoramic view of Brisbane's central business district while allowing him to keep an eye on the ladies' room exit at the same time. Suzanne was still in that beehive of feminine activity. There was no telling how long it would take her to make her way out, but he would have to down her drink as well as his if she didn't hurry up.

He looked out over the nocturnal cityscape, only glancing briefly at the skyscraper being built by his company. It was one of three gargantuan towers of black and white that surrounded the central business district, dominating the anarchic mob of less imposing buildings. But he didn't want to think about work while he was at the opera. Instead, he surveyed the river and the Southbank Parklands, where a giant Ferris wheel was shining under soft violet lights. It looked like some kind of overgrown metallic flower with capsules for petals, but the capsules were empty as far as he could tell.

Henry felt a tender hand on his back and turned around to find his wife.

"Are both of those for you?" she asked, indicating the glasses with an elegant nod of her head.

He looked over her shoulder. There was still a traffic jam of high-heeled women lined up in front of the ladies' room door. They were looking at each other aggressively, ready to pounce on anyone who tried to jump queue.

He wondered what they were all doing in there that took so bloody long. They certainly weren't just urinating. Were they plotting some kind of conspiracy against men?

"I kept one for you just in case you ever emerged from wherever it is all the ladies – and I use that word in its loosest sense – are so eager to get."

"Well, thank you very much. This lady in the loosest sense will happily take it."

He surrendered the glass.

"You can stop staring at the other women now. You can stop imagining them naked in the ladies' room."

He smiled at her but quickly changed his expression as he noticed she wasn't amused.

Suzanne sipped at her sparkling.

She was a hypocrite. She'd been admiring the other men as well, only she was more subtle about it than her husband. Of course, it was only natural that her gaze should wander. There were so many gorgeous specimens of manhood dressed up in expensive suits that hugged their athletic figures. Some of them probably had the same personal trainer as her. People talk about six degrees of separation, but in a city like Brisbane, she guessed that it was more like two or three.

As Henry turned to look back across Southbank, his wife surveyed the crowded room around her like a queen inspecting her court, jealously ensuring that she was the most spectacular of the noblewomen.

She caught a couple of men in the act of staring at her arse. One of them was a man of at least sixty years of age. She didn't recognise him and quickly decided that he didn't seem to be anybody of great import. He was rather debonair with his grey hair and neatly trimmed moustache. He noticed that Suzanne had seen where he was looking and promptly lifted a glass of scotch to his mouth as he turned his attention back to his wife, who was blabbering on about something to another woman. The other man was younger and quite dashing with his dark complexion and fine yet somehow sturdy features. He was unashamed of the fact that he had been caught red-handed. He smiled at her, but she made a point of ignoring him, pretending that his interest wasn't appreciated.

Women were looking at each other too, while the men were sipping their drinks, chatting together, and checking their smartphones, or simply staring at the figures of each other's wives and daughters. They were oblivious to the bitter war of silent judgement that was going on around them. Interval wasn't just about going for a piss and downing a few drinks. It was far more important than that. It was the time when women had a chance to do what they had come to the opera to do in the first place. During those few minutes, out in the bright light of the foyer, they callously examined each other and tried to establish a sophisticated form of the hen house pecking order, and Suzanne Klipsch knew that she wasn't far from the top.

She noticed a woman staring enviously at her necklace and she could read the desire on her face. The woman was gorgeous, easily as ravishing as Suzanne, but the necklace she was wearing had nothing on Suzanne's. She wanted her necklace. She wanted Suzanne's exquisite pearls, but she couldn't have them. They didn't belong to her. She would just have to accept that fact.

Suzanne shivered with delight. She smiled at the woman triumphantly and took pleasure in watching her turn away in defeat.

She had just climbed a further rank in the pecking order.

The bell sounded the impending end of the interval. Everybody would have to make their way back to their seats.

Henry finished his glass and put his arm around Suzanne's waist. She raised a finger to her necklace and watched the reaction of two other women as she teased the pearls. She felt so pleased with herself. Henry was feeling pretty smug too as he gave her left buttock a quick squeeze.

Neither of them had any idea what was about to happen back home.

The important moment of quiet came just before an ad break, but it was not complete silence. Dart could hear a low rumbling noise. It was muffled by the walls, yet its impact upon his auditory sense was heightened by the utter darkness in which he was smothered. An advertisement for life insurance started up and drowned the sound out, so it wasn't until *after* he had heard it that Dart's mind registered the fact. He had to ask himself whether he hadn't simply imagined it.

The pause at the end of the ad break came. He had been waiting for it, an ear pressed against the bedroom wall. He heard the low rumbling sound again. There was no mistaking it. Grandma was snoring. Henry and Suzanne had left her to look after the baby and she had drunk herself to sleep.

"Nice work, granny," he whispered under his breath.

He picked his sack full of booty up and stepped towards the bedroom door. He opened it slowly and peered out into the living area. The lights were off and the kaleidoscope of colour from the television screen was playing on the grandmother's drunken face. She was snoring loudly, her head tilted back and her mouth wide open. An empty champagne bottle stood proudly on the coffee table, the weary victor of a devastating battle. A fine flute that had been drained empty and half a dozen candles encircled the bottle. Orange flames swayed slowly as though hypnotised.

All Dart had to do was leave the house and return underground with the spoils he so greatly deserved. He had squeezed the blood back out of the leeches.

He stepped out from the doorway and crept over to the staircase. The noise from the television provided him with cover, ensuring that his movements took place unnoticed.

He was about to start walking down the staircase when a breathy gasp took him by surprise. He didn't know what had drawn her out of her sleep. He was sure he hadn't made a mistake. Perhaps it was her inflated bladder that had made her wake up.

Whatever the cause, she was awake. There was no scream to expose her fear, or shout to indicate that she was angry. The gasp had been one of surprise, and Dart knew that he had to take advantage of that.

Without turning around, he hurried down the stairs. He moved quickly but carefully and opened the front door as though he were casually stepping out for a litre of milk from the local shop.

Then, he increased the pace. He slammed the door shut and dashed across the street and into the cover of the trees. He looked back and saw grandma come rushing out of the house. She looked around anxiously, and he was sure she was about to spot him.

She did.

Her mouth opened wide.

"Help! Thief! Help!" her hysterical voice cut through the night air like a knife. Dart knew he had to get himself underground as quickly as possible. He headed straight for the same manhole he had used to come to Lansdowne Street and escaped back into his own world.

23

After making love, holding each other in tight embrace, it hadn't taken Ripley and Gabriela long to fall asleep. Being safe in each other's arms meant so much more to them at that moment than it had before their separation.

But the blissful slumber wasn't to be without interruption. Ripley had been hoping to enjoy a sleep as deep as the ocean, but the waters in which he found himself were as troubled as they were fathomless. He shuddered several times and his hands thrashed out around him. His dormant mind had not come to terms with the fact that he was no longer in the tunnels and that there were no rats climbing up his legs and gnawing at him. He kept writhing in his comfortable bed, unintentionally kicking his sheet and blanket off.

Eventually, he woke up. He was shivering.

The initial shock subsided as he realised he was at home, in bed, next to Gabriela. His surroundings were hidden in the night. All was dark and silent. But unlike the darkness and the silence of the tunnels, he knew that he was safe. He was in his world. He could just make out the form of his bedroom's furniture and decorations which were softly lit by the filtered light coming through the curtains.

Ripley considered getting out of bed and stepping over to the window. Perhaps he would see Dart hanging around the railway line. But he resisted the temptation.

He pulled the bedspreads back up and was about to roll onto his side when he noticed a change in light.

The soft light penetrating the curtains had suddenly been replaced by flashing red. At the same time, he heard the roar of a powerful motor sending a solitary vehicle trundling along Newmarket Road. He briefly thought about pushing the sheets back and looking out the window, but before he'd even given temptation a chance to take hold, the red lights vanished.

Ripley buried his face in his pillow and attempted to go back to sleep. It wasn't going to be easy, but he had to try, even if it meant falling into a pit of nightmares once again.

———————————— ⇒◦⇐ ————————————

As the cast returned to the apron for the final curtain call, the auditorium thundered with the sound of several thousand hands clapping. The audience continued applauding energetically until the red curtain had descended and the lights were growing brighter.

Everybody was dragged back to reality, and the strangely powerful buzzing of countless voices filled the air as they started to comment on the opera and asked each other's opinions. They got to their feet and shuffled along the rows and into the aisles where ushers smiled as they exited.

"What did you think, honey?"

Suzanne tilted her head to one side as she thought of a clever critique – some words that were poignant and thought-provoking – so that the elderly couple behind her could overhear her and remark that the elegant woman whose shapely behind was wrapped in black silk and whose white swan neck carried immaculate pearls was not only stunning but also profoundly cultivated. Suzanne felt quite sure she recognised the pair, although she couldn't manage to put her finger on it.

Unfortunately, she was feeling tired and a little tipsy. She couldn't think of anything to say other than that she had found it delightful, so she didn't even bother to answer her husband's question at all. She just smiled prettily and shuffled along behind him. She was in a hurry to join the inevitable queue outside the ladies' room.

But there weren't anywhere near as many waiting as there had been at interval. Only five women stood there, knees frozen together. They were all very obviously impatient to evacuate the wine they had consumed. Suzanne figured that most of the other opera fans must have decided that they could hold it in until they got back home. She knew that she certainly could not.

Before long, she was inside the ladies' room and only seconds away from gaining access to a toilet cubicle. Her bladder sensed her anticipation and yearned to relax, so she placed her hands over her lower abdomen in an effort to ease the urge.

As soon as the cubicle door opened, Suzanne leaped towards it. The wafer-thin adolescent who came out was wearing tight pants, a vintage white blouse with black polka dots, and big red-framed glasses; no doubt a hipster from West End.

"Sheesh!" the girl gasped as Suzanne all but shoved her out of the way. In the privacy of the ladies' toilets, with nobody worth impressing, she allowed herself to abandon her customary finesse. And at any rate, she had no time for anybody she suspected might be a socialist.

Suzanne locked the cubicle door and wiggled her body as she hitched her dress up over her waist. She pulled her knickers down to her knees and squatted over the plastic seat, being careful not to let her buttocks touch where the hipster's had been.

While she was relieving herself, Suzanne heard one woman leave the cubicle next to hers. The rush of water and the drone of the hand-dryer that followed proved she paid attention to hygiene. It was amazing just how many women didn't. Come to think of it, she wasn't sure the hipster had washed her hands.

The momentary silence, disturbed only by the powerful whizzing sound that Suzanne was making as she felt the pressure flood out from inside her, was abruptly interrupted as at least two other women entered the ladies' room.

"Did you see Harriet Downer? I could have sworn that was her ex-husband with her, not her boyfriend!"

Suzanne had no idea who Harriet Downer was, but she wanted to eavesdrop on the conversation all the same.

"Oh, that's why you stuck your bony little elbow into my ribs? Why didn't you say something?"

"Because she was right in front of us, she would have heard."

"I didn't notice. I was too busy trying to hear what Mr Denison was saying."

Denison, Suzanne thought to herself. That was the name of the man standing behind her. She was right after all. He had friends in very high places. Every developer in town knew that he was the man to get through to in order to have a construction project accepted. He could get casinos built on heritage sites, apartments propped up on public land, and luxury residences constructed in national parks. He knew how to pull strings. He had earned his stripes way back when Sir Joh Bjelke-Petersen was running the state like a colonial branch of the Hitler Youth.

"And?"

"And nothing. I didn't catch a word."

Suzanne realised she had been holding it in while listening to the women. She let the remaining piss flow before reaching for the toilet roll.

But, as she reached for the flush button, she wasn't expecting what came next. She managed to stop her knuckle just in time.

"What about Suzanne Klipsch?"

"I hate that bitch!"

Suzanne let out a gasp, then closed her mouth. But she wondered whether it was too late. They may very well have heard her.

But they continued talking.

"You're just jealous of her."

Suzanne smiled as she pulled her knickers up, making sure they ran smoothly between her thighs.

"Jealous! Why would I be jealous of her? She thinks she's so much better than everybody else, but she's not."

144

"You hardly know her. I don't understand what you have against her."

Suzanne tried to recognise the voices but couldn't. The bitches must have been acquaintances of acquaintances.

"I've got something against everyone."

"You can say that again! But I suppose I can see where you're coming from. She loves her money, even more than we do."

They laughed.

"That's a worrying thought, isn't it? I thought *we* were the biggest gold diggers in town!"

"Her husband... What's his name?"

There was a brief silence.

"Anyway, he's not exactly George Clooney, is he? Compared to her, I mean. She's obviously with him for his money."

The other woman hummed in agreement.

"That's for sure. That monstrosity his lot is putting up must be bringing in some serious cash for them. No wonder he can afford to buy her pearl necklaces and silk dresses."

"Yeah, but I wonder if she knows he had to puff on Denison's big fat cigar to get it accepted."

That was the last straw. Suzanne peeled her dress back down and unlatched the cubicle door, but, by the time she had opened it, the women had already left the bathroom.

She quickly washed her hands and stormed outside. There were still quite a few people hanging around in the foyer, and she couldn't tell who the women she'd overheard were.

"Henry!"

"What's wrong?"

"Did you notice two women leave the ladies' room?"

He shrugged.

"Did you?" she repeated, looking around.

He frowned at her. "I don't make a habit of staring at the door to the women's toilets."

"Yeah, sure, but did you?"

"Yes, I saw two women come out just now. I think they've

already gone outside. Why? What happened in there? Did they try to touch you in your private place?" He smirked.

But Suzanne wasn't in the mood to laugh.

"You didn't recognise them?"

He shook his head.

"I have to know who they are,' she said, more to herself than him.

"Can you tell me what's going on?" he asked.

"I'll tell you in the car. Can we go home now? I'm tired. I need a hot bath and a strong drink. Mum must be getting impatient by now too."

Henry just shrugged his shoulders. There was no point insisting.

"Good," he said. "Let's go."

24

It took Henry a little under thirteen minutes to drive the eight kilometres that separated the performing arts complex from Lansdowne Street. Normally, it took at least seventeen or eighteen, but Henry had such confidence in his driving skills that he didn't hesitate to put his foot down and speed along Kelvin Grove Road at seventy-five kilometres an hour, running a red light twice at intersections where he knew there were no cameras.

It wasn't until the Lexus went rocketing up the steep slope of Montpelier Street, turning right when it reached the house with the tennis court on its left, that Henry and Suzanne realised something was very wrong.

Suzanne had been on the verge of falling asleep. She'd already told her husband about the bitching session in the ladies' room and had eventually decided to take his advice and forget about it. After that, used to his fast but somehow still smooth driving, she'd started to nod off.

But as they entered their street, she snapped awake.

"Is that smoke?"

Henry was already slowing down. In fact, he almost brought the car to a complete halt in the middle of the street.

She looked at him, hoping for reassurance, but saw a frown of grave concern distorting a face that was usually the epitome of self-confidence.

"I can smell smoke!" Suzanne complained. "Can't you smell it?"

Henry didn't answer her. His gaze was nailed to the street in front of him.

"Henry! Say something!" she yelled into his left ear. She needed to treat him as though her panic was his fault and that the blame for whatever had happened came down to him.

"Shut the hell up!" he roared at her. "You can see very well for yourself!"

But, as he turned to her, his frown expressing an unsettling mix of anger and apology, he understood that Suzanne couldn't see for herself. He realised that since they had entered their street, since the smell of smoke had reached their nostrils, she had been staring at him, using him to filter reality. She couldn't bring herself to look ahead through the windscreen.

"I'm sorry," he said more calmly. "Honey, I don't know any more than you do, but you can't just ignore this."

He parked the Lexus at the kerb and got out quickly but with a calmness Suzanne knew he was struggling to put on. He dashed around the front of the car and went to open the door for his wife, but she thrust it open, knocking him to the ground.

During that instant, as he'd left the car and moved across to the passenger door, she'd decided to look in front of her.

With one terrifying glimpse, the chaotic scene had hit her.

Henry pushed himself to his feet, but Suzanne was already running down the street towards the neighbours, who were standing with their backs to her.

They were watching her house burn.

It reminded Suzanne of the opera, the audience transfixed by the drama, only this was the real deal. Despite the shouting of firemen, the raised voices of shocked residents, and the horrible crackling of the blaze, they somehow heard Suzanne's heels hammering the bitumen behind them. They turned around.

"Suzanne!" It was Laura Pearce from number seventy. "Suzanne, your mother's safe!"

Laura had read her mind. Suzanne had never felt very close to her neighbour, but at that moment, she was her best friend in the entire world.

Henry arrived and pushed his way past his neighbours,

148

ignoring their attempts to console him. He stopped in his tracks just a metre from a policeman who thought Henry was going to try to get into the house and was getting ready to block him off. Henry just stared at his house as hungry red flames licked it into oblivion and black smoke billowed up into the night sky. Firemen were fighting the blaze and it seemed as though they were winning the battle, but it was obviously too late. The damage had been done.

Then, all of a sudden, he turned to the policeman.

"My baby!"

"She's fine, Mr Klipsch. Your mother-in-law is safe too. She tried to call you but your phones must have been switched off for the opera."

Henry was stunned. This man, whom he had never met before in his life, knew all about him.

"They're safe?"

"Yes, they're fine. Look!" The policeman pointed back in the direction from which Henry had come. Suzanne had found her mother and their daughter. All three were holding each other in their arms.

Henry forgot about his house and ran over to them. He felt left out. He too wanted to be held.

The neighbours gave them some space and just stared alternately at them and the remains of their once opulent home. With every passing moment, the flames died down a little. The firemen had the situation under control.

"I'm so sorry… I'm so, so sorry…"

"Stop it, mum. It wasn't your fault."

The distraught woman's face was buried in her daughter's shoulder. Her sobbing apology was muffled.

Suzanne was holding Katie in her left arm and stroking the back of her mother's head with her right hand, which was shaking with the shock of what had happened.

"I couldn't stop it!"

"I know you couldn't, mum. It wasn't your fault. I'm just

thankful you're both safe."

Suzanne looked at Henry angrily until he understood what she wanted from him.

"Mum," Henry always called her that when he was trying to be sensitive. "It wasn't your fault."

Suzanne scowled at him over her mother's head. She looked as if she wanted to spit in his face. Henry knew why. It wasn't because he hadn't said what she'd wanted him to say. It was because it hadn't sounded sincere.

"It was just an accident," he said calmly.

It still didn't sound like he meant it, and he understood why; because he didn't. It clearly was her fault. She had continued drinking until she'd fallen asleep and left the stove or the iron or something like that on. Henry wanted to ask her what had happened but thought better of it. He bottled up his anger, or frustration, or despair, or whatever the hell it was that he was feeling, and turned away from his wife.

A few of the neighbours, who had witnessed the tense interaction between Henry and Suzanne, stepped forward to comfort him. But he didn't want their sympathy. He was too proud for that, and anyway, what was the use of pity when his home and contents insurance meant he would be able to buy an even more luxurious house. His insurance broker was a close friend who had never let him down. Henry knew that he was still in a state of shock. He hadn't expected to come home from the opera to find his house lighting up his usually dark and quiet street like a campfire, but it wasn't going to make him have a nervous breakdown.

He strode over to the policeman separating the bystanders from the firemen.

"Officer, can you tell me what happened?"

The policeman looked over to Suzanne's mother as though wondering why she hadn't told her son-in-law, but it was obvious that she was too rattled to recount the series of events.

"Of course, Mr Klipsch. For the moment, all I know is what

your mother-in-law told me. None of the neighbours witnessed the disturbance."

"Disturbance?"

"There was an intruder, I'm afraid."

"You mean to say that this fire was deliberately lit? Are you looking for the son of a bitch?"

"Yes, Mr Klipsch, we are looking for him. However, at this stage, we don't believe the fire was deliberately started. Your mother-in-law said she'd been reading when she noticed him in the house. He didn't threaten her or react violently. He just left as quickly as he could. Once she'd recovered from the fright, she tried to follow him, but he disappeared down a manhole."

"He went down a manhole? Are there officers chasing him?"

"Yes, there are."

"Down in the sewers?"

"Yes, it won't be easy locating the individual, but we're trying."

"Good." Henry nodded, obviously impressed with the seriousness with which the police were treating the case.

"Did he take anything?"

The officer looked over to Suzanne and her mother.

"She's not sure but thinks he was carrying a bag. The fire prevented her from getting back inside."

"So, how did the bloody fire start?" Henry was trying not to yell. It wasn't out of respect for the policeman, a mere public servant who earned far less than he did, but out of fear that Suzanne would overhear and think he was trying to put the blame on her mother.

"There were some candles and aromatic oils in the living room and she thinks they were knocked over during the commotion."

Henry shook his head but resisted the temptation to utter a single word. He pushed his tongue against his hard palate.

"Essential oils are highly combustible."

"Yes, indeed they are," Henry hissed, no longer able to hold back. "Did you say she was reading?"

"That's what she informed me."

"She reeks of champagne. Did you notice that, officer?"

"I did, but there's no law against a grown woman drinking on private property. If I can just make a suggestion, Mr Klipsch; these accidents do happen, and the intruder is to blame for this terrible situation, not your mother-in-law."

"Yes, thank you, officer. I don't need you to give me advice regarding my personal affairs."

"Very well," he capitulated. "I understand. Will you need assistance finding temporary accommodation?"

"No, I can manage that myself, thank you. If that's all, I think we'll get away from here for a while."

"Just one thing before you go. Do you have any idea who would do this?"

"No. I don't know anybody who makes a habit of breaking into houses and then disappearing down manholes."

"You don't have any enemies?"

"Hold on a second. I thought you said it was an accident."

"Yes, I did, but there could be another motive at play. The intruder may have been looking for something in particular."

Henry shrugged.

"Just a possible line of enquiry."

"I doubt it very much. I have plenty of enemies, but they have far more sophisticated ways of getting on my nerves."

He turned away from the policeman and decided he had better talk to his neighbours for a while, more for their benefit than for his. They told him that it was outrageous and that they hoped the police would catch the burglar. They reminded him to be grateful that nobody had been hurt. But none of them offered to let the Klipsch family stay with them while alternative accommodation was organised. No matter. Henry didn't mind. He wouldn't have opened his door to them if their houses had burned down either. At any rate, he would have refused any such offer.

He went over to Suzanne and took Katie off her so she could

give her mother all her attention. He was eager to leave Lansdowne Street as quickly as possible. He couldn't stand being there any longer. He was quickly growing sick of the other residents looking at them with sympathy, and he couldn't even be certain that their sympathy was sincere.

"I'm so sorry, Henry. I'm so clumsy. You must come and stay with me while you try to work out where you'll go. You can stay as long as you like."

"No, we really couldn't," Henry said.

"Yes, we will, mum," Suzanne accepted. "That's very kind of you."

The bitch!

"Yes, thanks," Henry found himself saying. "We won't bother you too long. I'll organise a nice flat to rent in the city centre tomorrow and we'll be out of your hair by Saturday."

He kissed his daughter on the forehead. She wasn't even crying, the brave little girl. At least grandma had been able to save her; that was all that really mattered.

"Let's get out of here," he said, and led the women back to his Lexus, walking with dignity and self-control.

The neighbours watched silently as he did a graceful three-point turn and left Lansdowne Street.

———◦———

Dart had no idea the house he had just burgled had gone up in flames or that his escape through a manhole had been observed. If he'd known, he would have been worried and forced himself to weave his way through the sewers until he'd reached one of the most hidden of the disused overflow chambers to be found on the north side. But he was tired and sore, and, above all, hungry. He wanted to get back to where he had left his belongings and bedding.

He moved slowly through the tunnels, using his torch not so

much to guide him as to confirm the turns and branches that he expected to come across. The frequency of the thumping of tyres on manhole covers overhead verified which road was above, because he knew how much traffic each road or street carried at any given time of the day.

Nothing was out of the ordinary. Dart was sure of that. He would have noticed anything odd. The only movements he observed were those of rats scurrying away from the light and cane toads hopping through the filth of the tunnel floor.

He didn't find his way unexpectedly blocked by police constables in gas masks and Wellington boots or highly-trained sniffer dogs trying to catch a whiff of any odour other than rank air and raw sewage. After all, there were no officers down in the sewers. Henry Klipsch had been told a lie to placate him.

Police cars were patrolling the streets of Newmarket and Wilston, as well as other surrounding suburbs, in a more than optimistic attempt to spot somebody climbing out of a manhole or walking down a back street. They were on the lookout for a man covered in grime and carrying a bag full of stolen goods. The police assumed the thief had just gone down the manhole in order to make a quick escape before resurfacing once he thought the coast was clear. The notion that anybody could stay down there for more than a few minutes hadn't even occurred to them.

Once Dart had arrived at his hangout, he made himself comfortable on the high maintenance platform he was using as a bed and opened his sack. He removed the jewellery box and carefully placed it on his bedding before digging deeper into the sack and taking a tin of tuna and a tin of baked beans. It wasn't much of a meal, but he just wanted to get some food into his stomach before going to sleep.

25

It felt strange going back to work on Tuesday morning. Ripley's colleagues didn't fail to notice that he seemed out of sorts, but they misunderstood the reason why, and he was by no means eager to illuminate them. They assumed he was still getting over his illness, but in fact, Ripley's quiet and unenthusiastic behaviour was the result of an overriding sense of boredom. Back in the familiar environment of the office, he realised more clearly than he had since finding Gabriela safe at home that the adventure was over, and the monotonous and comfortable routine of life was set to resume.

He knew he should have felt somewhat relieved, if not completely happy. But he didn't. There was something about the tunnels that fascinated him. He felt drawn to them and was aware that if he let his guard down, if he looked at a manhole cover for a second too long, or allowed himself to gaze out his bedroom window towards the railway tracks while he was getting ready for bed, then maybe, just maybe, he would succumb to the urge for one more taste of subterranean adventure.

Ripley looked around his office. His colleagues were working, their attention devoted to organising files and checking emails. There was nothing wrong with his job, his conditions were decent and the atmosphere was pleasant, but after what had happened that weekend, it all seemed somehow absurd. It seemed mundane and unimportant.

Ripley went to make himself a coffee. The tunnel dwellers had decided to abandon a life of comfort for one of simplicity, even if it meant they faced challenges on a daily basis. He could understand why they wanted to live together in their own community, disconnected from a world whose values didn't suit them, but he couldn't imagine how they could have come to make that decision in the first place. He had never known instability in his family and had never been abused or rejected. Perhaps some things were impossible to understand without experiencing them. What seemed like an unfathomable decision to one person must surely have been a very natural reaction for another. Brand and Fox appeared to be content with life in the tunnels, at least for the time being. But what if they decided to have children one day? And more immediately, what if Dart turned on them all?

Ripley drank his coffee slowly and told himself to forget about all that. If Brand and Fox felt like developing a friendship with a pair of surface walkers, then he would receive news from the underground through them. But on a day-to-day basis, he had to put the drama behind him and count his lucky stars that both he and Gabriela had escaped unharmed. They could so very easily have ended up as skeletons waiting to be discovered by maintenance workers several years down the track.

———◦———

That evening, Ripley and Gabriela had a light dinner. They didn't feel hungry, just confused. They sat in front of the television as the evening news came on, sipping pumpkin soup with croutons and fresh cream. Winter was going to be a cold one; the air had begun to bite a little and the sun was losing its strength.

"How was it, going back to work?" Gabriela asked him, even though her instincts told her what his answer would be.

Ripley thought for a moment and scooped a spoonful of soup out of his bowl.

"Rather strange," he replied.

156

"Same here. I can almost understand why they want to live down there."

"Really?"

"Can't you? The camaraderie, the control and responsibility over what happens in your community, the shared values?"

"Yes, I can understand that, but I don't think I could ever understand wanting to live down there. I'd miss the creature comforts of the surface."

Gabriela nodded. "I do admire them though."

Ripley looked at her as though her remark had been one of the most profound he had ever heard.

"I haven't really thought about it like that but I suppose I agree. Most of them escaped difficult situations on the surface and created what was, until we ruined it, a solid community based on respect and equality. That *is* admirable, isn't it?"

But Gabriela was frowning now. "We did ruin it, didn't we? If we hadn't gone down there, Dart would still be with them. Do you think he'll hurt them? Is he that-"

"What's wrong?"

Gabriela, mouth wide open, pointed at the television screen.

Ripley followed her finger.

The charred shell of a splendid hill-top house stood behind the svelte silhouette of an attractive but excessively made-up reporter.

"Is that in Wilston?" he asked.

Gabriela's reply was to turn the volume up so they could hear what the reporter was saying.

Her voice was husky, quite sexy really, despite the seriousness of the information being conveyed.

"The fire broke out when candles and oils were knocked over while she was pursuing the alleged burglar. Fortunately, Mrs Hammersley was able to rescue her baby granddaughter, and both of them escaped unharmed, but the home is beyond repair and will have to be demolished. Although she was unable to provide police with a detailed description of the intruder, Mrs

157

Hammersley claims he ran with a limp and says she witnessed him make his escape down a manhole.

"Police inspected the manhole and immediately began scouring the streets of Newmarket and Wilston but were unable to trace the suspect. Police urge anybody with information to contact Crime Stoppers."

Ripley turned to look at Gabriela. He wanted to know whether she knew what he was thinking.

She just looked back at him, slowly nodding in silent agreement.

"It's Dart!" Ripley whispered, not daring to say that dreaded name too loudly.

"It sounds like it. He was limping away *and* he disappeared down a manhole," Gabriela repeated the facts.

"And this happened right here in our area, where we know he comes almost every night."

"And we know he is in a desperate state of mind right now and probably low on resources."

"He could have killed that woman and the baby!"

Ripley took the remote and flicked through the channels, trying to find more details on the incident.

"That's why there was a fire engine racing along Newmarket Road last night."

"I didn't hear it," Gabriela said.

"No, that's because they don't put their sirens on at night unless absolutely necessary. I just noticed the flashing lights."

"Why weren't you asleep?"

Ripley sighed. "I was having nightmares. I woke up in a cold sweat."

"About Dart?"

Gabriela moved closer to him. She hadn't realised just how much the encounter had distressed him.

"About the tunnels in general; the dark, the smell, the rats, the disorientation."

Gabriela held him in her arms.

158

"You poor thing, you woke up from a nightmare only to find that what had caused it was still haunting you in the real world."

Ripley didn't particularly appreciate being called a poor thing, but her embrace was comforting, so he just hummed his agreement.

"I was hoping we would never hear another word about Dart ever again," he admitted. "I wanted to believe that we'd left him underground and that he wouldn't bother us up here."

"It's no longer us he's after. He just wants to get provisions from the wealthy. That's obviously why he targeted a mansion."

"Sure, that's all very well. I don't have a problem with the tunnel dwellers stealing food, clothes, or whatever provisions they need from supermarkets or even the homes of the rich, but I do have a problem with people's lives being put at risk. If this maniac decides to wage a one-man war between the underground and the surface with no regard for others, it becomes our problem. We have a duty to the public."

"I agree with you. But what can we do?"

"I know we said that we wouldn't, but, maybe it's unavoidable."

"Rips, we made a promise to Fox and Brand."

"I know. That's why it's so hard. We have to choose the better of two evils."

"So, which one will we choose? Can you make that decision?"

"We have to, Gabs. Not making a decision is a decision in itself."

She took another mouthful of pumpkin soup. It was starting to get cold.

"What would we tell Crime Stoppers? *Hello, yes, we know the burglar who escaped down a manhole. He was part of an underground community, but after trying to kill my boyfriend and getting into an argument with the other tunnel dwellers, he broke away from them and is now living on his own in the sewers – sorry, how do we know this? Well, it's a funny story – at least, funny in a black humour kind of way – we just went into the sewers because we were curious and – oh, where is he now? We don't know exactly, somewhere under Brisbane...*" She turned to Ripley and frowned. "Oh, that's strange, they hung up on me!"

"Okay, I suppose you have a point. So, we should just ignore what happened, is that what you're saying?"

"I just think we ought to wait until Fox and Brand come to visit us. They helped us down there. They quite possibly saved our lives. We can't stab them in the backs."

Gabriela's choice of words made him think about his shoulder. It didn't hurt much now, but he could still clearly remember the blow. It was almost as though Dart was right there behind him with his blunt axe ready to come crashing down.

"We owe it to them, Rips. We should talk about it with them."

"Fair enough," Ripley gave in. He had to admit that they did indeed owe it to the others to act carefully and to protect the secret of their existence. "I hope they come soon."

"You miss them, don't you?"

"I suppose I do."

"So do I," Gabriela admitted. "I wonder if they miss us too."

26

Gabriela's question was answered the very next day. It was quite late, around ten o'clock, and Ripley was doing what he had told himself not to do as he put his pyjamas on. He was standing in his bedroom with the light switched off, watching the railway tracks for any sign of movement. It was the third time he had found himself being drawn towards the window that night. The first had been while he was cooking dinner, and the second after ironing his shirt for the morning. This time, however, it wasn't in vain.

Once the 10:14 train had rolled along towards Newmarket Station, its carriages mostly empty, two shadows appeared on the far side of the tracks. It was as if they had materialised from nowhere, but Ripley knew the trick all too well now. He felt the hairs on the back of his neck prick up and his mind made him think that the spot on his shoulder where he had been struck suddenly hurt again. But, as the figures sprinted towards the platform and jumped up onto it, he recognised them. Fox and Brand were coming to visit already.

Ripley smiled to himself and drew the curtains closed.

Fox and Brand had moved faster than he could have thought humanly possible. He was leaving the bedroom when Gabriela almost ran into him. Panic was written all over her face.

"There's someone at the door!" she hissed at him.

"Don't worry. It's just Fox and Brand."

"It might be Dart!"

"Don't be silly," Ripley laughed at her. "Dart doesn't know where we live."

"We don't know what he knows!"

Ripley put his hands on her shoulders and tried to calm her down. "It's Fox and Brand. I saw them crossing the railway tracks."

"You were at the window? I thought you said that we had to stop that."

"I know I did," he confessed. "But, well, I just can't help it."

He pushed past her and strode over to the door.

The visitors smiled at him with a warmth and familiarity that belied the infancy of their relationship. The two couples felt close after just a few hours together, but the truth was that they still knew next to nothing about each other.

Behind the smiles, there was a shadow of doubt and concern. Ripley noticed it immediately.

"Come in," he said.

"We're sorry to come so late," Fox apologised.

"Not at all," Gabriela said. "You're welcome any time. I'll make you some tea."

"Thanks."

Ripley made some room for them all around the coffee table.

"Have a seat. We were hoping to have a visit from you. I think there's been some news regarding Dart."

"We know," Brand replied. "That's why we came."

"You know about the house that burned down on Lansdowne Street on Monday night?"

"Of course," Brand affirmed. "We live underground, not on the moon. We follow the news closely and pay particular attention to weather reports so we know which storm water drains and low-lying tunnels to avoid when a heavy downpour is going to hit."

Ripley felt a little silly.

"I take it you agree that it sounds like Dart?" he asked.

They nodded. "It sounds exactly like Dart," Brand said.

"And yet," Fox added, "it's not his usual way of doing things."

Gabriela came over with the teacups. "What do you mean by that, Fox?"

162

"Dart is the tunnel runner. That's one of the most highly regarded positions in the community. We're in the process of selecting his replacement and Cooper has been trying to convince everybody that we can manage without him, but the fact remains that Dart played a major role in our ability to survive underground. His thefts provided us with funds that were used to purchase essential items that can't be stolen directly. We will go on without him. We have no choice. But it's going to be difficult. The big problem is if he turns on us. We can't watch our backs all the time."

Ripley felt the urge to look over his shoulder right then but resisted it for the sake of his dignity.

"Dart has been a thief most of his life; certainly ever since we've known him. As far as we are aware, he is one of the best burglars in the city. He has never been caught and has never left any clues behind. He has no criminal record, and, as far as we can tell, his victims don't even realise they've been burgled until weeks or even months later most of the time."

"But that's not what happened this time," Gabriela pointed out as she poured the tea.

"No, it's not. That's what I mean. I think he's becoming unstable. I'm worried about him. Brand and I, in fact, all of the tunnel dwellers, have been busy thinking about how his absence is going to affect us, but we haven't thought much about him. He's all alone in the tunnels and, even though he knows how to look after himself, he must be lonely. Even Dart can't live without human interaction for very long. He's bound to end up going crazy."

"I think he's already there," Ripley said.

"He could get a lot worse, Ripley. Believe me, he could. If he loses control of himself, he will become very dangerous, either for himself or for the public. I think what happened on Monday night makes that clear. The Dart I know despises the rich, but the Dart I fear he is becoming could hate them with such a passion that he starts doing more than just stealing from them. I

163

think he's capable of killing."

"I'm *sure* he is," Ripley said. "I almost proved that when he caught me down there."

"Did you come to warn us to be careful?" Gabriela asked.

"No," Brand replied. "We know that you are already being careful. We came because we want your advice."

"Why do you want *our* advice?"

"We just need a different perspective."

"What is the general consensus in the community?" Gabriela asked.

Fox and Brand looked at each other. It was Fox who answered. "We'd rather know what you think first if it's all the same to you. What do you think we should do?"

It was Gabriela and Ripley's turn to look at each other. They hadn't expected Fox and Brand to come to them for advice. They had no experience making decisions about dealing with such situations. Surface walkers had state authorities that managed, to varying degrees of effectiveness, matters of social disruption and deviance. They weren't used to having a direct say the way tunnel dwellers were.

"We considered going to the police," Ripley admitted, "but decided it wouldn't be fair on you and the others. We promised we wouldn't tell anybody about your community."

"Thank you," Fox said.

"I don't know what other options we have," Gabriela pointed out. "The only other course of action is to just ignore him and hope he calms down."

"I don't think he will though, not all alone. He's bitter and resentful. He hates surface walkers and now he hates other tunnel dwellers too. He thinks that nobody understands him and considers us weak in our convictions. I'm afraid his bitterness will brew and grow stronger."

"So, our choice is between telling the police what we know about him and ignoring him, and we have to choose the latter," Ripley concluded.

"That's what the community decided too."

"And do you both agree with that?"

"Like you said, Ripley, we don't really have a choice."

"There is a third possibility," Fox suggested. "But it's unlikely to work."

"Go on," Gabriela encouraged her.

"We could try to convince him to come back."

Brand shook his head at her. "We can't do that, Fox. For one, he won't listen to us, and, more importantly, he has rejected our code. He refuses to accept Cooper as our elected leader. Now that he has shown his true colours, thanks to Ripley and Gabriela, we wouldn't be able to trust him even if he came back."

"That's settled then," Fox said. "We have to try to forget about him."

Ripley filled their teacups.

"I'll never forget him. I've never been so scared before in my life. We can try to ignore him, but we won't forget him."

"I just hope he doesn't make the news again," Gabriela said.

"I couldn't agree more," Ripley added.

"Are you hungry? We've got some pumpkin soup that I can heat up if you like."

"No, we're fine. Thanks all the same, Gabriela. Actually, we should probably head off. We've all got work to get back to tomorrow."

Fox and Gabriela gave each other a hug. Gabriela noticed how firm the tunnel dweller's body was.

Ripley opened the door for them and had a quick look outside.

"You're getting tunnel instincts, mate," Brand remarked quietly as they stepped outside.

"I certainly am. Come back soon."

"Thanks. We'll try to."

They jogged out to Newmarket Road and faded into the night.

27

Ripley had forgotten to set his alarm for a six o'clock start before going to sleep. But it didn't matter. His biological clock woke him up before dawn. His sleep had been far more restful than the previous night's, and as he crept out of bed and put his tracksuit on, he figured that the visit from Fox and Brand was to thank for that. They were like guardian angels, except that they came from below rather than above.

He quietly slipped out of bed, trying not to disturb Gabriela. It was going to be a cold morning, and, even though Ripley desperately wanted a cup of coffee and some toast, he forced himself to resist the temptation. He needed to go for a jog and do a workout with his mates. He had to get back into the routine that had seemed so adequate and fulfilling just a few days ago, before he'd tasted adventure and primal fear. Exercise was not only good for his health but could also mean the difference between being a victim and being a victor. Every assumption he had held about the safe and orderly nature of life in Brisbane had been torn down like a flimsy curtain to reveal the truth; that there was no knowing when he might have to fight tooth and nail for survival.

Unbeknownst to them, Pete, Ben, and Oscar were going to play an important role in helping Ripley keep out of the tunnels. They were his best mates and an important link to the surface world. It was a shame he couldn't tell them that. Ripley's secret could never be revealed. He could never be truly honest with them again, and he knew that was going to be difficult.

Before stepping outside, he drank half a glass of water and checked that he had his key to the flat and four dollars for a cappuccino after the workout.

The sky was cloudy but didn't threaten rain. The slight breeze that swept along the side of the block of flats made him pull his sleeves down over his hands, but he knew he wouldn't be cold for long.

He was pleased to notice that none of the other residents were around. They didn't usually leave their flats until half past seven or eight. It wasn't that he had anything against them, just that he liked to be alone when he woke up.

There were a few cars and trucks rushing along Newmarket Road, but apart from that, the morning was calm.

Ripley walked briskly along the road to warm his legs. He passed the fabric shop with its awning that covered the footpath and continued between the phone booth and red letterbox. When he reached the Youth Advocacy Centre at the corner with Vardon Street, he turned right and increased his pace until he felt warmed up enough to break into a slow jog.

The park was already a hive of activity. Locals were walking their dogs, jogging, and cycling. A well-sculpted personal trainer was making a group of women do sit-ups and punch his hands. As Ripley jogged across the grass to where Pete was doing a few chin-ups on the bar next to the bicycle path, he wondered whether those women would ever need to use such techniques to defend themselves the way he had and whether it would be enough.

Pete dropped to his feet.

"Hi, Rips. Are you feeling better?"

"A lot better, thanks. I'm going to work out hard this morning."

"Good on you. Hopefully, Ben and Oscar won't be late today. I'm just going to do a couple more sets to warm up."

"I'll do some push-ups," Ripley said. "I want to focus on my shoulders, triceps, and pecs."

As he pushed up with all his might, feeling the energy coursing through his body and the tension of the previous few days being expelled with each breath, Ripley wished he could share what he had been through with Pete. Their friendship went way back to high school, and Ripley thought he could trust Pete with any secret, but he resisted the temptation and just concentrated on keeping his back and legs straight so that he got the maximum benefit out of the push-ups.

After three sets of twenty, he decided to take a little break. He didn't want to wear himself out before the others arrived.

Pete shook his arms for a minute, then started doing squats.

"Here they are, the lazy buggers!" Pete called out.

Ben and Oscar had come together in Ben's car and parked in the small gravel car park under the tall eucalypts that grew next to the hockey field. Parking was easy at that time of the morning. It wasn't until seven that the steady flow of office workers looking for a parking space would come swooping in like crows to an open rubbish bin.

"Hello fellas. Warmed up?"

"We certainly are. What took you so long?" Pete asked.

Ben pointed his thumb at Oscar. "You-know-who had trouble waking up."

They were complete opposites, both physically and in terms of personality. Ben was tall and skinny and had a huge mop of curly reddish hair. Oscar was comparatively short and had a stocky build like a rugby player. His dark hair was short but his auburn beard was increasingly long. After years of growing slowly but surely fatter, he was now becoming rather muscular thanks to the regular workout sessions. Ripley thought that if they could merge to become one person, he would have a perfect physique.

"What's the plan for today?"

"I haven't planned anything," Pete admitted. "How about you, Rips? It must be your turn to choose."

"I wouldn't mind an obstacle course run. We could do some hurdles, crawls, and balancing, and then do five sets of dips, squats, push-ups, and chin-ups to finish."

168

"All that? You really meant it when you said that you wanted to work out hard this morning."

"Are you up for it?"

"Hell yeah!" Ben and Oscar chorused.

"Take us through the course slowly, Rips."

He looked up and down the length of the park that stretched along the northern bank of Enoggera Creek. There were plenty of obstacles provided by the city council.

"All right, let's go!"

He started jogging towards the narrow footbridge that crossed a drainage canal leading into the creek.

They checked behind them to make sure there were no cyclists speeding along the path before they crossed the bridge. On more than one occasion, Oscar's short temper had found him so annoyed at reckless cyclists that he almost knocked them to the ground. So far, though, he had resisted the urge and just hurled abuse at them.

On the other side of the canal, Ripley turned sharply to the left and jumped the set of low hurdles.

The others followed closely, clearing the hurdles with ease.

Then, he jogged over to a length of concrete piping that was just big enough for an adult to crawl through on hands and knees.

They all managed to make it through.

He led them back across the narrow bridge and over to the wooden barriers separating the road from the bicycle path to do some balancing practice.

The workout lasted for twenty minutes and all four were thoroughly exhausted by the time they had completed Ripley's set.

Once they had cooled down, Ben drove them over to Alcove. If there was one thing better than some intense exercise in the morning, it was sitting back and drinking a coffee with mates, even if they could only spare fifteen minutes before they had to leave for work.

The tattooed woman who ran the café didn't need to ask what they wanted. She knew their order by heart; two cappuccinos with full-cream milk and no sugar, one with light milk and one sugar, and one soy latte.

They sat down at a low table that had been cut into the shape of an ironing board and Oscar started talking about his plans for the weekend.

Ripley only pretended to pay attention to the conversation. A couple of young women sitting at a table near the entrance to the café were chatting about a topic that was far more interesting to him. He was sure he'd heard them mention the house on Lansdowne Street.

He kept looking at his friends and nodding as they spoke.

"It's so scary. I don't think I've heard of a burglary happening anywhere near Lansdowne Street before," one of them said. Her voice was irritatingly high-pitched, but Ripley was concentrating on the words, not the delivery.

"Really?" the other encouraged her.

"No, I don't think so."

"Maybe there have been other burglaries but they just haven't made the news."

"I guess that's possible. It might have been the fire that made the story newsworthy. In any case, I hope the police catch him. I live with two other girls and they're often away for the night screwing some guy. I don't know what I'd do if I was confronted by an intruder."

The other woman laughed. "You'd probably invite him into your bedroom."

"You bitch!" she retorted in mock outrage. "But seriously, it's disturbing."

"Do you know who lived in the house?"

"Of course, everybody who is anybody in Wilston knows Henry Klipsch. He works in construction, for Meriton, I think. You know that huge skyscraper that's being built. He's involved in that."

"He's homeless now though."

"I wouldn't worry about that. You can be sure he's not taking the family to the Salvation Army for dinner."

"He must be furious."

"I suppose he is, but what can you do?"

"They said the burglar used a manhole to escape. That's crazy, isn't it? On my way home last night, I kept looking at manholes, half expecting one to suddenly pop open and a maniac covered in shit to leap out at me like a bogeyman."

Ripley knew exactly how she felt.

"Do you think he actually lives down there?"

"No way! Nobody could live in the sewers, but he must know how to use them to get from one place to another."

"What a freak! I can imagine this happening in Inala or Woodridge, but not here in Wilston or even Newmarket, whichever Lansdowne Street is in. It's so wrong."

"Technically, it's in Newmarket, isn't it? Anyway, do you think it was just random? Maybe it was personal."

"I don't know. They said on the news that the fire was an accident, and my mum's neighbour knows Henry Klipsch. He doesn't think it was personal."

"So, it could happen to any of us."

"I guess it could."

"Hey, it's already a quarter past seven. I have to go."

"Okay, catch you later."

"Bye."

Ripley suddenly realised that his coffee was sitting on the table in front of him and that he hadn't been following his friends' conversation at all, but it seemed they hadn't noticed. He picked his mug up and, after some preliminary sucking at the foam, drained half of it in one thirsty gulp.

"I've got to go," Pete announced. "I'll try to come along on Saturday. No guarantees though."

"Me too," Ripley added.

"Oh, you're back from la-la land?" Oscar asked mockingly.

"Yeah, sorry, I've had a lot on my mind with work," he lied. "See you later."

He drained his mug and put four dollars on the table before heading off.

18

That evening, once Ripley had entered his flat and switched the light on, he discovered that the adventure was far from over.

It wasn't the fact that his privacy had been violated that rattled him the most, or that something might have been stolen. What really filled Ripley with a sense of dread was that there was no doubt Dart knew where he lived.

"How?" he asked himself aloud as he stepped into his flat.

Without moving from the doorway, he looked around. He could feel his senses suddenly kick into action as he tried to take in every detail. But apart from the obvious, there was no way of telling that anybody had been in his flat at all.

His first concern was to know whether Dart was still there. After that, he would read the message on a small sheet of writing paper fixed to the wall directly opposite the door. A thin-bladed filleting knife stuck out of the sheet at a vicious angle. He recognised it immediately, even though he rarely used it, because he always bought his fish already filleted. The sharp blade was usually kept hidden away in the cooking utensils drawer under the kitchen bench.

Ripley's heart skipped a beat as he heard a muffled sound behind him, like the dull thud of a soft-soled shoe.

He was sure that Dart's axe would crack his skull open before he had enough time to spin around.

He jumped forward into his flat and, at exactly the same time, dropped to his knees, just as he had done before crawling through the concrete pipe during the exercise routine that very morning.

He wasn't far from the note and was ready to pull the knife out of the wall. He knew that he was capable of sticking it deep into Dart's body. He knew for certain that he wouldn't hesitate for even a split second.

But, without getting up, he spun around to check where Dart was.

Nothing.

He was nowhere to be seen.

There was just the grey cat that Ripley had often noticed inspecting the rubbish bins standing at the doorway. It was looking at him with curiosity, trying to figure out what strange game the human was playing, and whether it could join in.

Ripley felt stupid. He had panicked for nothing.

Or had he?

He still had no idea whether Dart was in there or not.

He looked towards the bedroom. The door was closed. That was normal. Ripley and Gabriela always closed it when they left home. But did that mean anything? Fox had told them about Dart's ability as a burglar, surely he was used to making it look as though nothing had been disturbed. He hadn't damaged the door when he'd broken in, assuming he had entered via the door at all.

Ripley couldn't see the bathroom door from where he was. Perhaps Dart was in there.

He would have to arm himself before inspecting those two rooms.

But then, despite his fear and anger, a logical thought managed to creep into Ripley's mind and reined him back into a world of relative sanity. If Dart had left a note, he didn't intend to kill the recipient before he'd had a chance to read it. It only stood to reason, and, although Dart had given Ripley the impression he was a maniac, the fact that he had been able to survive in the sewers for so long proved that he wasn't irrational. There was definitely some kind of method to his madness. That was what worried Ripley the most about him.

He stood up, trying to stop his knees from shaking, and

stepped over to the open door.

The cat leaped away as he pushed the door closed.

Drawing a deep breath, he looked across to the note. Then, he exhaled.

After four more deep breaths, he could feel his knees regaining their strength. He walked over to it, trying to ignore the terrifying blade stabbed through the paper and into the wall.

Surface Walker Ripley,

I would like to congratulate you on your commendable escape from my realm. Despite what you must think, I am not the kind of man who engages in physical violence on a regular basis, but I have occasionally been forced to fight for survival before. On the other hand, I suspect that you are entirely unfamiliar with the need to resort to force. Therefore, forgetting the pain that you caused me when you struck my leg with your hammer, I feel obliged to tip my metaphorical hat – I rarely have the need to wear one – to you. I believe that you could have dealt me my deathblow, but instead, you were merciful and let me live. Nevertheless, I cannot forgive you for having breached my privacy just as I am sure you will not forgive me for having breached yours. However, I want you to know that there is a reason for my actions and that I wish to make my intentions perfectly clear so that any further action I undertake will be completely justifiable.

I am willing to forget about your intrusion into the tunnels if you can keep your mouth closed about what you discovered down there. My survival, and that of your new friends, depends on it. If you go to the police or tell anybody else about the existence of the tunnel dwellers, I swear that I will punish you and your girlfriend.

Thank you kindly for your understanding and be sure to destroy this note immediately.

Best regards,
The Tunnel Runner

Ripley yanked the filleting knife out of the wall and plucked the note off it. He took the blade back to where it belonged in the kitchen and struggled not to imagine what Dart could have done to him with it. He was so angry that he could hardly control his own movements, and as he jerked the drawer open, his fingers lost their hold on the knife. It fell, and Ripley only just got his right foot out of the way before it stabbed into the floor like a dart. This made him even angrier.

"How dare he!" he shouted to himself. He felt the urge to rip the message to shreds. But he resisted. He still had the presence of mind to know that once he had calmed down a little, he would want to read it again.

He picked the knife up carefully and placed it in the drawer from which it had been taken before going back to the door and opening it.

He looked at the keyhole, only to find that it was in perfect condition. There was no sign of forced entry at all.

Looking along the side of the building, he saw the grey cat stalking along the fence, just below where a few birds were fluttering around. He wondered if the feline had witnessed Dart's bold, daytime break-in.

He went back into his flat and locked the door. He would never leave it unlocked ever again, even when he was inside. Never ever again.

"How did you find out where I live? And how did you get in here?" he asked aloud.

The second question particularly bothered him. It was terrifying enough to know that Dart had entered his home and left a death threat pinned to the wall, but not even being able to comprehend just how he had got in was intolerable. It meant that Ripley and Gabriela never had been and never would be safe. It proved that the walls and windows and door that were

176

supposed to protect them were nothing more than a bad joke to Dart.

The windows? That must have been how he did it.

Ripley went to the bedroom and opened the door quickly.

He breathed a sigh of relief. It was empty. Everything was exactly how it had been that morning, for whatever that was worth.

He checked the window. It was locked from the inside. Dart couldn't have come in that way.

The kitchen windows?

He checked them too. The windows and security grill were locked and hadn't been hampered with. Dart had certainly not gained access through the kitchen.

The bathroom window?

Ripley went into the bathroom, but even the briefest of glances confirmed what he suspected; no grown adult could fit through it. The opening was too high and, more importantly, too small.

"How did you do it?" he asked uselessly, his confusion increasing his anger. "How did you get in?" he hissed. "I'll kill you. If you come near me or my girl, I *will fucking* kill you!"

Ripley forced himself to take a deep breath. His rage surprised him. It frightened him. He felt as though he was discovering a primaeval drive that had been hidden deep inside his every fibre all his life, some kind of animalistic potential that had remained suppressed and unnecessary in his quiet, modern life.

For the first time since he had escaped from the tunnels, he truly believed that he was capable of killing Dart. He knew that if it came to the crunch, he could do it. There was no moral reason why he shouldn't. There was no obligation to restrain himself from doing whatever he had to in order to survive.

That realisation was immensely liberating.

Ripley held the note up and read it again.

It was written by somebody who had a perfect command of the English language, and Ripley admonished himself for having assumed that a misfit who lived underground must have been poorly educated, if not completely illiterate.

"How did you find out where I live?"

He scanned the text and stopped when he came to the tell-tale sentence: *My survival, and that of your new friends, depends on it.*

That was the answer. Ripley had no way of knowing whether the tunnel runner had dropped the hint intentionally or accidentally, but it was definitely the answer. He had followed Fox and Brand. He had shadowed them all the way to his flat.

Ripley was beginning to understand just how formidable an enemy the tunnel runner was. He could follow anybody anywhere and enter secured private property with the greatest of ease. It was terrifying.

He decided then and there that he had to keep what had happened from Gabriela. She had already been put through enough and didn't need to know about this.

He took the note to the bedroom and hid it in a tattered copy of Reginald Hill's *Fell of Dark*. He wasn't prepared to destroy the letter, because he couldn't shake off the notion that he might need to refer to it later.

Then, Ripley suddenly remembered the damaged wall. He went back to the kitchen and opened the door to the cabinet beneath the sink. Hidden behind a bottle of dishwashing detergent and a pack of scourers was a pile of miscellaneous tools and bric-a-brac that included a small pot of putty.

He flipped the lid open and found that there was some still left inside. It wasn't exactly the same colour as the paint on the wall but it was close enough to white to go unnoticed by Gabriela, and probably even the real estate agency if they ever decided to leave the flat – an option that was becoming more attractive by the minute.

Once he had filled the hole and smoothed the putty out, he sat down on the couch and tried to calm his nerves and think about what he was going to do. One thing was for certain, he would have to deal with the situation by himself. It was between him and Dart.

It was already dark outside and Ripley was expecting Gabriela to arrive within a few minutes. He had to pretend it was just a normal evening. That meant putting the news on and getting dinner ready. That was the easy part. What would be more difficult was acting as though he wasn't angry and unsettled.

At the same time, Ripley decided that he couldn't go to sleep without making an attempt at properly securing the access points to the flat. He had no idea how Dart had entered his home but he guessed the door was the most likely weak point. Perhaps the tunnel runner had simply picked the lock.

There was a sliding bolt lock that he could use to secure the door from the inside. There was no way anybody could open the door with that put in place. However, Ripley would have to slide it locked once Gabriela was already in bed and remember to unlatch it again as soon as he woke up in the morning in order to avoid arousing suspicion. And he would have to repeat the routine every day because of Dart's threat.

Ripley pushed himself up from the couch and walked across to the television. The news report flashed on and chased the uncomfortable silence that reigned in the flat away. It instantly made Ripley feel a little more at ease.

He took his shoes and socks off, putting his shoes on the rack next to the door and his socks in the dirty laundry basket in the bathroom. He was so rattled by what had happened that he had to think carefully about how he usually acted in the evening. It wasn't coming naturally. He reminded himself to go to the fridge and grab a bottle of Cooper's Celebration Ale.

As he sipped his beer, Ripley thought about weapons. He was going to have to make sure he was armed at all times. He would need to have a means of defending himself hidden somewhere easily accessible. He had stored his hammer, along with his torch, under the bed. That was perfect. He went into the bedroom to check that it was still there. It was. Then, he lay down on the bed and reached underneath it without lifting his head from the pillow, but he couldn't get a hold of the hammer or torch. He got out and repositioned them closer, then tried again. This time he could reach them without moving his head far off the pillow. He could arm himself quickly if attacked in the dead of the night.

Back in the living area, he sat on the couch and drank his beer in front of the television. He still didn't feel safe, but he was slightly more confident that he was ready for Dart if he should come. But, Ripley reminded himself, Dart would have no reason to come after him, because he had no intention of breaking his promise and telling anybody about the tunnel dwellers.

He sat back and watched the news, hoping that there would be no more reports about burglaries or house fires.

19

Henry wondered whether the lift would ever stop as it quietly hurtled upwards. It felt like he was being blasted into space. He wasn't sure that Suzanne would approve of having to catch a lift up to the seventy-second floor every day for however long they would have to stay in Soleil Tower, though he knew she had a soft spot for a good view. That was one of the things she had most appreciated about Lansdowne Street. Like him, she got a kick out of looking down over the city and those who lived beneath her. But he wasn't sure that the apartment would be enough to win her over. They had never lived in the city before; it wasn't exactly the Australian dream. Any respectable family either lived on a country estate or in a fashionable inner-city suburb, but never actually in the centre of town.

The lift slowed down. It hadn't taken that long after all, but still, using a lift to come and go from home, even temporarily, would not be to Suzanne's liking. She was used to just walking up a short flight of stairs.

A sensual female voice announced the seventy-second floor as the lift came to a smooth stop. The doors glided open to expose an immaculate corridor. "Going down," she announced once Henry had stepped out.

He checked the numbers in polished brass and followed the corridor to the right.

As he reached out to swipe the key card, he held his breath. He hoped it would be as impressive as his director had promised. He didn't want to live under his mother-in-law's roof for any longer than necessary.

He pushed the door open and stepped inside.

The lights flicked on automatically.

He smiled. All the latest in domestic technology. That was something Suzanne would appreciate.

The apartment was new, just as he had been told. Nobody had occupied it. Considering the fact that construction and finishing had only just ended, it was no surprise that he would be the first to use the company's apartment.

Henry walked through the kitchen and living area. It was fully furnished and far more modern than the equivalent rooms in his house had been. Suzanne would approve of that too.

He walked over to the wide balcony and opened the sliding doors. The night view was spectacular. He could see the Story Bridge directly in front of him and, to his right, all along the south bank of the river past the Kangaroo Point cliffs. He could imagine Suzanne sitting there in the evening, admiring the night lights of the city.

It seemed like the kind of place where they would be very comfortable for a few months while they started looking for a new house.

Henry took his mobile phone from his jacket pocket and called his wife.

"Honey, it's beautiful! It really is! Do you have time to give it a look tonight? I need to get back to them tomorrow. Somebody else is interested."

He listened to her reply and smiled.

"All right, I'll meet you in the lobby. Call me when you get here."

He hung up and dialled another number.

"Hello. Listen, mate. Do you have any news about this son of a bitch?"

Henry frowned as he listened.

"Can't you put the screws on them? This isn't good enough. What did they say they were doing?"

"What do you mean *nothing*?"

"But I was the victim of a serious crime and my mother-in-law witnessed it. She told them the bastard went down a manhole. That means he might still be hiding out in the sewers like the fucking rat he is! Tell them I'm paying big bucks in taxes and that I expect some bloody service to justify that. They have an obligation to do their utmost to catch this criminal."

"Mate, you're pretty close to the commissioner. Can't you use your clout with him to get a reaction out of these bludgers?"

He listened.

"I want them to send a few boys in blue into the sewers to catch this bastard. I know the premier wants to watch the budget, but I don't think neglecting to provide the people who support him with a little law and order is the way to go about it. Maybe you should remind him of the assistance our company has rendered as well."

He grinned.

"Good, thanks for that, mate. Keep me informed."

Henry put his phone away and strolled into the kitchen, hoping to find a beer or two in the fridge.

No such luck.

He wandered back to the balcony and took in the view again. He had taken losing the house relatively well, as had Suzanne. They had lost a few personal possessions in the fire, but all of their family photos had been backed up on the net. They would be happy living in the city for a while and then they would buy a house they liked even more than the old one. All the same, he wanted the thug who had almost cost his mother-in-law and his daughter their lives to be caught.

He leaned against the balustrade and looked down onto the lane. The height was staggering and made him feel a little dizzy. It occurred to him that he was about as far away from the sewers as anybody in Brisbane could get. That would be another positive aspect to point out to Suzanne.

His telephone rang.

He pulled it out and checked who was calling.

It was Suzanne, ready to come up and pass judgement.

30

The following evening, while Henry and Suzanne were enjoying an expensive cocktail at Esquire, his phone rang.

"How's it going, mate?"

Henry listened for a few seconds.

"Good on you. That's more like it!"

He stuck his chin up in the air triumphantly.

Suzanne guessed what the call was about and what her husband had just been told. She put a hand on his shoulder in silent congratulations. They were an unstoppable pair, destined to win. Their house had been burgled and burned down just a few days ago but instead of getting down in the dumps and losing perspective, they had handled the blow like champions. Now, they were one more sleep from moving into a gorgeous apartment and getting on with finding a new house. But there was no rush for that. Suzanne had a feeling she was actually going to enjoy living in the city for a while.

"Thanks again, mate. I knew I could rely on you to get the wheels in motion. You know how it is. I work hard for my money, like you. We should expect everybody else to do the same, shouldn't we?"

He laughed.

"What are you up to tonight?"

Suzanne waved a finger at him.

"No problem. We're having a quiet one too. We move into the apartment in the morning, so we'll get to bed fairly early – not that we have a lot to shift."

Henry laughed.

"Yeah, I suppose I *am* taking it pretty well; new beginnings, new adventures, all that, right? We might do some shopping tomorrow."

He smiled.

"She loved it. It's only natural. It's a great place. We'll throw a fireworks party if we're still living there when Riverfire comes around. We have a view all along the river from the Story Bridge to the Captain Cook Bridge."

"I'd appreciate it, mate. Thanks for that."

Henry put his phone away and sipped his cocktail.

"Do you know who that was?" he asked Suzanne smugly.

"Of course, I do. That's great news. Do you think the police will catch him?"

"Probably not, he could be anywhere by now. The point is that he might try to burgle another house in the future. I don't really give a damn if he gets caught or not. Strange that, isn't it? What annoys me more is that the police don't seem bothered enough to even try."

"They will now though."

"They'd better. I'll be following it up."

"I still can't believe it. I mean, you hear about this kind of thing on the news but you don't expect it to happen to decent people like us in a quiet suburb like Wilston."

"No, it makes you wonder why, doesn't it?"

"Probably because we have the most beautiful house in the area," Suzanne pointed out.

"We *had* the most beautiful house," Henry corrected her. "Some people just don't understand how the world works. They see successful people, those who have a good job and plenty of money, and think they too have some kind of right to those things. It's jealousy, that's all it is – jealousy and laziness. They wish they had an expensive car and a big, comfortable home, but they don't want to work for it. They aren't smart or motivated enough to do what's required to obtain the fruits of a successful life, so they just go and take what they don't deserve."

185

"And destroy what they can't have."

Henry had the urge to say that if anybody had destroyed the house, it was her mother, but he didn't want to ruin what was turning out to be a rather pleasant evening.

"We should take it as a compliment that the scumbag targeted us," Henry said, thoroughly amused at his way of putting a positive spin on the incident. "It's quite flattering really."

Suzanne laughed.

"That's going a bit too far, dear. Really!"

"Why can't people just keep their hands off other people's property? Everything we have, we've worked for."

"Not exactly *everything*," Suzanne reminded him. She was thinking about his considerable inheritance.

"Well, almost everything. My point is, you get what you work for, and if you don't work enough, then you deserve to live in the streets, or the sewers, like an animal."

"It's in the hands of the police now," Suzanne said, then drained her glass dry.

"So it is, but I'll give them a little shove along all the same, just in case they don't pull their weight. Your mother has taken it well too."

She placed her glass delicately on the table before staring sternly at him.

"What? She has," he said.

"No, Henry, she hasn't. You just don't pick up on it. You may be clever and pragmatic but you have a big problem understanding what's going on in other people's minds. She was absolutely petrified. She told me about it. For a moment, she thought that she and Kate were going to die."

"When she noticed the house burning?"

Suzanne shook her head in disappointment. "No. She meant when she woke up to find the intruder standing at the top of the stairs."

"Wait a minute! She was asleep, drunk on champagne?"

"Henry, how dare you!"

186

"She told me she'd been reading!"

"She must have been reading before she fell asleep."

"That's not what she told the police though."

"Listen, Henry. Just drop it. The fire wasn't her fault and that's all I'm going to say about it!"

Henry glanced around. People were starting to give them funny looks. They were on the verge of making a scene in one of Brisbane's most prestigious restaurants. Suzanne was right. It wasn't her mother's fault. But for some reason, Henry kept forgetting that. The fact that both his wife and mother-in-law had lied about the precise circumstances of how the episode had unfolded only made it more difficult for him to accept that the fire hadn't been her doing.

He finished his drink.

"Do you want to eat here, darling?"

Suzanne remained silent for a moment, and Henry hoped she was just thinking about how she was going to answer his question and not fuming about what he had said about her mother.

"I wouldn't mind going to Augustine's tonight. I think we deserve a treat, don't we?"

"We do indeed, after everything we've been through."

31

A solitary jogger made her way along Lansdowne Street, eager to do what was required to prevent her from gaining even a gram of fat. The chill air and the stubborn darkness that were waiting for the sun to chase them away didn't discourage her. The sky was clear, and on the horizon, just beyond Eildon Hill, a pink glow signalled the impending dawn.

It was just after six o'clock in the morning and the street's residents were mostly still in bed.

Apart from the eerie, charred hulk of what had been the Klipsch residence, nothing was out of place.

But that was about to change.

The girl jogged off the bitumen and onto the verge as two vehicles turned into Lansdowne Street from Abuklea Street and drove slowly up the narrow strip of bitumen. There was nowhere for the police van and city council truck to park, so they stopped in the middle of the street.

Four police officers, suited up in boots and rubber trousers, got out of the van, and one council worker wearing a similar outfit descended from the truck.

"All right. That's the house up there." The sergeant pointed across the median strip towards the ruins of the house that had occupied the highest point of Lansdowne Street. "So, this must be the manhole just here."

The council worker went over to the manhole cover and inspected it. There was no bitumen overflow blocking the cover and the lifting holes were clear of dirt and debris.

"Could he have lifted it by hand?" the policeman asked.

"It's not impossible, if he was strong enough. But it's not just a

188

matter of strength either. These buggers are hard to get a grip on. We use a heavy-duty magnet to take them off. Nobody lifts them manually these days. He was alone?"

"As far as we know. The witness didn't see anybody else. She didn't say anything about seeing him remove it, so I suppose he must have opened it beforehand, in preparation for his getaway."

The council worker shook his head and put his fingers through the holes. He pulled on the cover and lifted it fractionally but wasn't able to remove it.

He shook his fingers.

He couldn't use gloves because the holes weren't big enough.

"I'll try using hooks."

He grabbed two sturdy lifting hooks from the van and put them through the holes. Then, bending his knees, he pulled up.

The cover lifted off.

He dragged it well away from the hole.

"Not easy?" the sergeant asked.

"No, this fella's no weakling."

"Could he have pushed it up from below?"

"He could have. Bloody dangerous though. If he had lost his footing on the rungs in the pipe, he would have fallen one heck of a long way."

"Maybe he had some kind of harness."

"Who knows, maybe he did. We've had gear stolen from our warehouse before."

"Really? Did you report it?"

"We certainly did, but your lot didn't find them. No wonder if they're squatting in the sewers."

He looked down the manhole. The sewers had presented him with a number of hazards over the years, such as the presence of toxic gases, but the risks usually associated with them were well-known and taken into consideration. On the odd occasion, he had found graffiti and candle stubs, presumably from kids in search of a cheap thrill or two, but he'd never considered the idea that thieves used the sewers as a hideout.

"Do you really think you'll catch this nut? He may very well know the sewers better than I do."

"I thought nobody knew the sewers better than you."

"That's what I thought too, but I'm suddenly not so sure."

"I don't know if we'll catch him. I can think of better ways of spending a Monday morning. I'm just following instructions from the powers that be."

He glanced around at the houses, making sure that nobody was watching them, and lowered his voice. "This Henry Klipsch appears to be an important bloke. He must have friends in high places. I get the impression he's put pressure on us to get a result."

"Bloody rich bastards!"

"Let's just get this over with before my boys fall asleep."

"Sure, just give me a second to cordon the cover off."

He grabbed a roadwork sign and red plastic barrier from the truck.

"Jack, go and park her somewhere out of the way."

The driver started the truck up and moved it slowly along the street.

"Same for us," the sergeant instructed the driver.

He followed the council truck.

"We're starting to get some onlookers," the council worker said.

Curtains were moving behind a window to the right of the front door of the nearest house. A child was watching them, nose pressed against the pane.

A little further along the street, a jogger was leaving his house. He pretended to do some stretches but was actually just observing the scene. He showed no sign of being confused about what was happening. It was more than a little obvious, and everybody in the street knew about the manhole.

"They won't have much to look at in a minute, once we're in the sewers."

As soon as the two drivers were back to supervise the manhole opening, the others got ready for the descent.

"All right, I'll go down first," the council worker explained. "I have to check the air quality down there, but even if it's safe, we'll still need to wear our masks. Sewers are notorious for toxic gases and also bacteria from human and animal waste."

"Animal?" one of the constables asked.

"Of course, mostly rats, sometimes toads too. Okay, put your masks on."

The officers fastened their masks. They looked like elite soldiers getting ready for chemical warfare rather than cops chasing a street criminal.

The council worker put his on and carefully climbed into the manhole. He lifted one gloved hand up towards them and made a fist. They understood the meaning; don't lose your grip, whatever you do, because it's a bloody long way down! Then, he climbed down the pipe.

At the bottom, he switched a device on to check the air quality, and then, once he was satisfied that it was safe, turned his headlamp on and radioed his colleague up top.

"Send them down."

The policemen descended one at a time.

"All right, put your headlamps on. I've got the map here. Sergeant, come up front with me. Your boys can follow us, but they need to stay close. I don't want any strays."

"Got that?" he asked his men.

They nodded. Even though the masks muffled their voices, they could still hear each other.

"I don't know what looks normal or what looks strange down here," the sergeant explained. "If you see something out of place, just put your hand up, like this." He showed the council worker what he meant.

"Understood. Ready? Let's go."

They moved off along the sewer, and within a few seconds, the policemen felt completely lost. They were relying on the council worker to lead them through that gloomy underworld. He had prepared a map highlighting the places he wanted to check in advance. There were a number of spots which were wide and high enough to provide a person with adequate living space. If the suspect was still in the vicinity, he would certainly be in one of those places. All the policemen had to do was follow him, watch their step, and, of course, be ready to make an arrest.

As the men advanced, the beams of light coming from their headlamps played on the grimy tunnel walls like giant fireflies. They were well aware they were making noise, but there was little they could do to prevent that. When they walked on dry tunnel floor, which is what they tried to do, their boots made a scraping sound. When they walked through the putrid water that was unavoidable in some stretches, their movements made an unpleasant sloshing sound.

The sergeant kept expecting to see a human silhouette suddenly illuminated by the light from their headlamps, but after every twist and turn, there was nothing but more concrete tunnel. It was a strange man-made landscape that somehow seemed as though no man had ever set foot in it before.

After about ten minutes, the council worker came to a halt at what appeared to be a door. It was made of solid metal, and instead of a doorknob, it had a huge latch securing it.

He signalled for the constables to step past him so that when he opened the door, they could go in first. He was happy just being the guide. It was their job to do any manhandling.

He pulled back on the clip. At first it resisted, but then it gave way with a loud cracking sound.

The door, however, wasn't so obliging, and he had to kick it in.

He stepped back to let the police enter first.

"Clear!" one of them called back, disappointment obvious in his voice. They all just wanted to find the freak and get out of the sewers.

The sergeant stepped in next and looked around the tiny room.

It was no bigger than a closet and he had to wonder why such a big door protected such an insignificant storage area. There were half a dozen rusted shelves attached to the far wall and one of them had a coil of wire cable on it. The others were empty apart from a thick layer of dust. The sergeant looked down at the floor and towards the corners.

Nothing.

"All right, next stop."

They moved back out and the council worker closed the door again. That was one of the first rules of the sewers. Always keep a door closed unless you want to be the one who is sent down to clean the crap out of a vault after the next flood.

They continued along the tunnel, passing under a manhole cover that shuddered every time a vehicle drove over it. They headed downhill, and, little by little, the sewer floor became wetter. Even though their boots protected them from the thick liquid and their masks minimised the foul odour, they still felt sickened.

The next stop was a large chamber. The light from the council worker's headlamp was consumed by the deep darkness.

He stepped further forward, out of the tunnel and into the chamber, moving his head from side to side so that he could study its features, and his eyes widened as he spotted a maintenance platform with bedding lying on top of it.

Before he'd even had enough time to fully register the significance of the find, a filth-covered man dashed out from under the bedding. Within a fraction of a second, he'd jumped off the platform and out of the light.

"There he is!"

The sergeant marched forward and the constables followed him. The added light from their headlamps helped to brighten the chamber.

"Stop! Police!" the sergeant shouted. But he was shouting into thin air.

"Where is he?"

"He's gone!"

"Where the fuck has he gone? He was right there in front of us."

They looked all around the chamber, shining their lights into the shadowy corners.

The only other way out was where the tunnel continued in front of them, but if he had gone that way, he had to have slipped right under their noses.

"Follow me!" The sergeant took the lead, running along the tunnel faster than good sense would have dictated.

The constables ran at his heels, so close behind him that they would end up slamming into him if he were to stop suddenly.

Now that the game was afoot, the council worker found himself designated to the rearguard, and that didn't bother him in the slightest.

As they ran, the tunnel seemed to straighten out, allowing them to catch sight of the suspect. He was a long way ahead of them, and the sergeant immediately understood that this was a young man for whom this forbidding maze of darkness and déjà vu was home.

He came in and out of view several times as their lights bobbed up and down, and although the sergeant couldn't see him very clearly, he could tell that the man's dark clothes were covered in a film of dust and grime. More importantly, he could see a chain wrapped around his body and what looked like a hatchet in his right hand.

"The suspect is armed!" he called back to his men without turning his head for fear of losing balance and momentum.

His voice carried through the tunnel.

Without a doubt, the suspect had heard him and understood the significance of those words.

The policemen knew they had little hope of catching up with him, and, as the tunnel opened up into another chamber, they saw their target climb a wall with ease and squeeze himself into a pipe they could have sworn wasn't wide enough for him.

194

"What the hell! He's a bloody rat!"

The sergeant ran over to the hole and looked down into it.

He saw a face look back at him from the other side, just a few metres away. It wasn't the face of a monster, just the hardened face of a young man who had grown up in a tough world. He had already seen hundreds like it.

"Give it up, son. You can't stay down here for ever," the sergeant told him calmly before trying to catch his breath.

Then, the face disappeared.

Pulling his mask off, even though it was against the guidelines he'd been given, the sergeant put his hands on his hips.

The constables did the same.

All of them drew in deep breaths of rank air as they waited for the council worker to catch up.

"There's a room in there," the sergeant said.

"Yes, I know."

"Well, how do we get in?"

He sighed and pointed to the map. The sergeant watched as his finger traced a route through several passages.

"Otherwise, we crawl through that pipe. If we fit, that is."

"Forget it! Let's go back to where he was sleeping. Maybe we can get some clues to his identity from whatever he's got stashed there. If he even has an identity, that is."

The sergeant turned away from the hole. He had come so very close to catching his man.

"Sir, he's bound to go back to his bed later," one of the constables said. "We could wait for him."

"No, he won't. He's too cunning for that. He'll just steal some blankets from somewhere else."

"You mean off people's clotheslines?"

"Off clotheslines," he repeated. "Yes, that's probable. I think we've got more of a chance of getting our hands on him up top than down here. We'll go back to his den and have a look around, and then we'll get back up to patrol the streets."

The council worker took the lead again and the policemen

followed him back to the first chamber. They were disappointed to have missed an opportunity to make an arrest but relieved to be on their way out of the sewers.

"I can't believe how fast he was running!" one of the constables said to the others.

"We should add sewer pursuit to the training programme," another joked.

"Fuck that!"

"If we see him again, we should just shoot the bugger. We could say it was self-defence. There are no cameras down here to prove otherwise."

"Constable! For the record, I didn't hear that, but don't let me hear it again. Understood?"

"Yes, sir."

They arrived in the chamber where Dart had been forced to abandon his nest. The sergeant still couldn't understand how the suspect had slipped past him unnoticed.

He climbed onto the maintenance platform to get a closer look at the bedding and used his telescopic baton to sort through the sheets and blankets, just in case there were any nasty surprises in there.

But there was nothing at all.

He turned his attention to the two bags that Dart hadn't had time to take with him. They were sitting ominously against the chamber wall.

He held the first one at arm's length as an instinctive precaution, and then leaned in closer so that his headlamp shone into it. He tipped the bag upside down and its contents vomited out. There were tins of meats and vegetables, nothing else.

"We've found his food reserves," the sergeant said, not very triumphantly. "But you can be sure he didn't break into a house like Henry Klipsch's with the intention of nicking just a tin of baked beans."

He pulled the other bag closer and opened it up.

"This might be more interesting. What have we got here? A lot of clothes; T-shirts, shorts, socks, and undies. They're all nice and clean, believe it or not."

He tipped the contents out.

"A few books, a torch, some batteries. Hey, it just clicked, he was running through the sewers without a torch!"

He turned to the others. "How the heck did he do that?"

"He's a fucking sewer rat, that's how!" one of the men explained.

"Is there anything that might be from the burglary, sir?"

"It doesn't look like it. Maybe he didn't get a chance. Or maybe he has some stolen cash or jewellery on him. Let's get back up top. I've got a feeling he'll try to steal some more food and clothes. We'll take all this stuff with us so he has to come up and play on our field."

The sergeant passed Dart's belongings down to his men before giving the council worker the go-ahead to lead them back to the manhole.

The police patrolled Newmarket and Wilston all day, watching for anybody who looked even remotely like the suspect they had come so close to catching. They spoke to bemused locals and told them to beware of anybody stealing clothes from their backyards. But, as the sun sank behind the mountains in the west and flying foxes replaced crows in the sky over Brisbane, they had to admit defeat.

Dart hadn't surfaced that day. Waking up to a patrol in the sewers had given him a fright it would take a while to get over. He had never come so close to be being caught before, and he had never encountered policemen in the sewers.

He had bided his time underground with nothing to eat and no books to read. It had been a long and boring day, but he'd kept himself busy thinking about how Ripley could have been so stupid as to ignore his warning.

The more he thought about it, the more his anger brewed. He'd told the others not to trust a surface walker and he'd been proven right. Their future was in jeopardy because they hadn't been strong enough to kill the intruder. Now, it was too late. The authorities knew he was down there, and he would never feel safe again. That couldn't be undone. It was out of his hands now. But he could still keep his promise. He could and he would. Unlike Ripley, he was a man of his word. As soon as darkness had spread its black cape over the city, he would resurface.

32

Ripley was standing at the window, peeping through the slightly parted curtains.

All was quiet on Newmarket Road. There was no traffic at all that night. The weather was getting colder and the residents of Wilston were staying at home in the evening, snuggled up in front of the television with a cup of hot chocolate, instead of going to yoga class or the local gym.

But Ripley wasn't thinking about his neighbours. He had the tunnels on his mind. Gabriela's curiosity had drawn the both of them towards the underground in the first place, but Ripley was the one who was struggling to put it behind him.

He turned around and let the curtains fall back into place.

Gabriela was sound asleep, not a care in the world.

He wished he could do that.

He crawled into bed, cuddled up to her, and waited for Morpheus to claim him.

It felt like a second later, but nearly twenty minutes had passed when Ripley's drowsy mind was dragged from the intangible zone between the worlds of sleep and wakefulness. A dull shuffling had disturbed him, as though something heavy but soft was being pulled along a rough surface.

He lifted his head from his pillow and listened. It wasn't his imagination. It wasn't a nightmare. He really could hear it.

The bedroom was smothered in darkness, only a faint rim of light indicated the outline of the curtains.

Ripley relied on his hearing to tell him what was going on. He had to make sense of the strange noise.

He tried to work out where it was coming from. It sounded like it was above him, on the other side of a ceiling that was undoubtedly little more than a sheet of fibro, but that made no sense. It couldn't be coming from up there.

He thought he was probably overreacting, but he got out of bed slowly, making sure not to disturb Gabriela, and knelt down on the floor. He reached under the bed and pulled the torch and hammer out.

The shuffling sound was becoming more distant now. It faded until he could hardly hear it any longer.

He let his muscles relax a little.

The relief was brief. A distinct sliding sound and a loud thud broke the silence. It was followed by a horrible sloshing, like liquid being shaken in a plastic vessel.

There was no doubt any longer, somebody was in the flat, and that somebody could only be Dart. The mystery of how he had broken in had been solved.

The disturbing sound grew louder. Dart was splashing some kind of liquid all over the place.

Ripley's eyes widened as he sniffed the air. There was no mistaking it; he could smell the sharp odour of petrol.

He felt like shouting, asking the tunnel runner why he had come to burn them alive even though they had kept their promise. But it was too late for that. Dart hadn't come for conversation.

Ripley flicked his torch on and gripped his hammer tightly.

He flung the bedroom door open just in time to see Dart step onto the back of the couch and leap up to the ceiling manhole. He pulled himself up through it and put his head back down.

Ripley shone his light at Dart's face.

"I warned you, surface walker!"

"I didn't tell anybody! Why are you doing this?"

But Ripley's reply was ignored.

Dart lit a match and his smug smile glowed for an instant, then, he let the flame fall.

It went out before it hit the floor, but he lit a second and a third simultaneously and both drops of golden light glided down through the darkness and exploded as they kissed the petrol-drenched carpet.

Ripley didn't see Dart's face disappear or hear him shuffling back along the ceiling. All his attention was on the furious blaze.

His fire alarm went off, adding to the terrible din.

Within seconds, Gabriela was out of bed and at his side.

"Fire! Rips, what have you done?" she screamed.

The accusation infuriated him, but he ignored it. He took her hand, without dropping his hammer, and pulled her towards the door. He struggled to unbolt it and turned the doorknob.

It didn't open.

"Open the door!" she shrieked.

He tried again.

"It's blocked! Quick! The bedroom window!"

The fire was already crawling towards the bedroom. The smoke and heat it was generating was intense. The nightmarish smell of petrol, melting plastic, scorched carpet, and acrid smoke was so powerful they were beginning to lose their grip on reality. They could hardly breathe.

They squeezed into the bedroom, between the door jam and the licking flames, and ran over to the window.

Ripley tried to open it, but it wouldn't budge.

"Son of a bitch!" he roared as he lifted his hammer and brought it crashing down against the pane of glass.

It shattered into a thousand shards.

Ripley dragged the head of the hammer along the frame in order to clear away the jagged edges of the pane before helping Gabriela up onto the sill.

"Jump!"

She hesitated.

"It's not far. Just bend your knees when you hit the ground!"

She screamed for courage and jumped.

Ripley waited for her to get out of the way before making the leap himself.

He bent his knees as his feet came into contact with the ground and rolled onto his side.

They wasted no time in getting to their feet and spent several seconds sucking the fresh night air in before either attempted to speak.

It was Ripley who broke the heavy silence first.

"We're all right, Gabs! We're all right!"

"What happened? Was it Dart?"

Ripley nodded, his body shaking.

"Where is he?" she asked, the whites of her eyes visible as she looked around.

Ripley looked around too. He looked up towards the roof and out towards Newmarket Road. He could almost feel the cold steel of Dart's hatchet against the back of his neck, getting lined up for the beheading.

33

"We need to get the others out!" Gabriela shouted at Ripley.

The fire was already lapping at the window frame. What had been their bedroom until moments ago was now just a flimsy box struggling to contain an inferno.

Smoke was also billowing out of the kitchen window and it was only a matter of seconds before the blaze had spread to the neighbouring flats.

Ripley felt a pang of guilt. Those people had nothing to do with any of this. Dart may have lit the fire, but Ripley couldn't pretend that his hands were clean.

He didn't know what he would say to them. He didn't know how he was going to explain the fire. The petrol that had been doused all over his living area would be detected. Nine times out of ten, the fire brigade's arson investigators could pick a deliberately lit fire before they even set foot inside the ruins of a building.

"Listen to me, Ripley!" Gabriela was shaking him, and for a second he thought she'd lost control of her senses. But she hadn't. He was the one who wasn't reacting well. He had been so busy worrying about what he would tell his neighbours that he'd failed to recognise the fact that if he didn't act quickly, he wouldn't have a chance to explain at all.

He ran around the side of the building.

The fire was strangely quieter there. He could still hear it devouring his flat like a famished beast from another world, but he could also hear other noises, ones that should have been equally unsettling, but yet were reassuring. He could hear the high-pitched beeping of fire alarms and the shouts of the building's other inhabitants.

The door of the flat next to his was tugged open and his neighbours came rushing out. They were half-naked and still not quite awake, but they were well and truly alive.

He helped them down the stairs and Gabriela led them out front.

Ripley hurried along to the other flats and banged on their doors so hard that he put a dent in one of them. But what did it matter, the whole place would be a blackened and twisted waste by the time the fire brigade arrived.

The occupants come rushing out like bees from a smoked hive. Even though their eyes were wide open and their movements rapid, they still seemed to be asleep.

"The fire brigade! Does anybody have a phone?" Ripley shouted.

"They're on their way," somebody said. Ripley didn't recognise the man. "Is everybody out?"

"I think so."

"What about number five?"

"There was no answer. They might be away."

"We can't take that chance." He frowned as he looked at Ripley's hand. "Can I borrow your hammer?"

In the panic, Ripley had forgotten he was still carrying his weapon.

He handed it over and watched as the man strode up to the door of number five and pounded at it. He watched him as he disappeared inside, admiring the stranger's ability to keep a cool head in a crisis but also worrying whether he would ever come out again.

He did, carrying a little boy over his shoulder. The child's mother followed; stunned, not yet fully grasping that she was awake.

The man handed the hammer back and Ripley thought to himself that this was the kind of person he might need to help him with the tunnel runner. But he couldn't just ask him for help, and to do what, be an accomplice to murder?

Ripley stumbled back towards the front of the house.

Just a few minutes earlier, he had been in bed with Gabriela. Now he was standing outside a burning building with eight people, and the numbers were growing. Neighbours from nearby houses were running over to help. But there was nothing else to be done. Everybody was safe now and the building was beyond help. All they could do was wait for the fire engines to roll up.

Ripley put his arms around Gabriela.

"You need to talk to me," she whispered in his ear. But he could tell that she would have screamed at him if they had been alone. "Then, we need to get our story straight."

Ripley nodded.

"I'm guessing we've only got about a minute to do that," he said.

He had no choice. He told her the whole story, and then they created a convenient version of their own. They wouldn't tell the police about Dart, they wouldn't break their promise to Brand and Fox. They had no idea why the firebug – whoever he was – had decided to target them.

Gabriela told him that she thought they should try to find Brand and Fox again. As much as she hated the idea, she thought it was even worth going back down into the tunnels one more time if that was the only way of getting in touch with them. They needed to discuss what course of action to pursue.

Ripley told her he agreed, but in fact he didn't. He had already decided what to do about Dart. There was only one way of putting a permanent end to the reign of terror.

34

Ripley and Gabriela moved in with her parents. It was going to be strange living in her childhood home as adults. They had never even spent the night together under her parents' roof before, but Ripley had a good relationship with them and they made him feel welcome and comfortable.

"Hello, Ripley," Jan welcomed him warmly. "How was work?"

"All right. Actually, really good. I don't think about the fire while I'm working."

"You poor boy! What do you want for dinner tonight?"

"Don't make a fuss, Jan."

"No, no, no, I don't want to hear any of that. You need a good meal to help you feel better. Just tell me what you want."

All the attention made Ripley feel uncomfortable, even though he knew Jan enjoyed looking after him.

"I'll let you think about it. Oh, and you have a letter."

She walked over to the coffee table.

"It was hand delivered. See? No stamp."

Ripley read the few words that were scratched in pencil on the envelope. *For Ripley and Gabriela* – that was all.

He knew who had sent it instantly, but he didn't understand how they had found where they were living.

"Thanks, Jan. What do you think Graham would like tonight?"

"It's your turn. Don't worry about what he wants."

"Well, how about a roast?"

"Perfect, lamb with pumpkin, sweet potato, and Brussels sprouts?"

"That sounds perfect. Let me know if I can help," he offered.

"Don't be silly. Just go and relax. Have a shower if you like."

Ripley decided to take her advice, but not before he'd read what Brand and Fox had to say.

He ripped the envelope open and removed the letter.

Ripley and Gabriela,

Thank goodness you are both alive! When we heard about the fire that destroyed your home the day before yesterday, we thought you were dead, even though all the news reports said that nobody had been killed. It wasn't until we saw you leaving this house yesterday morning that we felt sure you were both fine.

We really don't understand why this happened. Anyway, we don't want to write too much in this letter, just in case it falls into the wrong hands. Meet us outside at midnight if you can. We'll be waiting for you. We have to talk about the situation.

Best regards,
Fox and Brand

Ripley folded the letter and put it back in the envelope, then he hid it in the wardrobe in the spare room, which was where Gabriela had grown up through her teenage years. He would show it to her once she got home, but he didn't want her mother to stumble across it in the meantime. Jan was a bit of a sticky beak, and, even though she would never open their mail, he knew that she was capable of reading a letter from an already opened envelope.

He went to the bathroom to take a shower.

As the warm water ran over his body, soothing him, making him feel just a little safer, he asked himself the question that bothered him once again. He wanted to know how Brand and Fox had found them, and more importantly, he desperately needed to know whether Dart had followed them again.

Ripley read until midnight. Gabriela had been planning on doing the same but fell asleep and ended up using her novel as a pillow.

He pushed her gently until she woke up.

"Is it time?" she whispered.

"Yes."

They got out of bed slowly and tried to walk as quietly as possible across the wooden floor. The house was an old Queenslander, and, although Gabriela's father had kept it in good condition, he hadn't gone to the trouble of making sure that none of the floorboards creaked.

The bedroom window was already open, despite the chill weather. Ripley had left it open intentionally so they could climb out easily and noiselessly.

As he crawled through and lowered himself to the ground, he couldn't help but have a flashback of his previous exit via a window, just two days earlier.

The smell of the smoke and the heat of the flames still haunted him.

He held his arms out to help Gabriela.

"We mustn't make a habit of this," she said.

"My thoughts exactly."

He turned his attention to the street.

"Look, there they are," he said, pointing.

Beyond the paling fence and native shrubs that delimited the property were the familiar forms of Brand and Fox, standing on the far side of the road, next to the gnarled trunk of a leafless frangipani.

They crept over to the gate, opening it ever so gently, and crossed the street.

Brand and Fox hugged them, and Gabriela thought she felt a

tear on her cheek as her face pressed up against Fox's.

"We're all right, Fox," she reassured her.

"I know, but for a while there, I was a bit concerned."

"How did you find us?" Ripley asked.

"Easy," Fox replied. "Gabriela told me her family name once and I remembered it. I used the telephone directory to suss a few likely addresses out, and then, earlier this morning, I saw your mother come back from the shops. You're her spitting image."

"That's my Fox," Brand congratulated her. "We might have to change your name to Hound."

She gave him a wink. "Thanks, but no, Fox suits me just fine."

"Well done," Ripley said. "Watch out for Dart though. I think he's been following you."

Brand looked up and down the street.

"So it seems," he said. "I promise we won't lead him to you twice."

"Let's not talk here," Fox said. "There's a park a few streets away."

"All right, let's go there," Gabriela agreed.

Fox led the way. It only took them a minute.

"We can sit under that gazebo for a while," Fox suggested.

They all walked across the park to where the round wooden structure stood and sat down in the complete darkness it provided. Its roof shaded them from the moonlight that gave the rest of the park a luminous edge.

"Dart threatened me," Ripley began. "He broke into our flat and left a note stabbed into the living room wall with a filleting knife. He said that if I told anybody about the tunnel dwellers, he would kill me."

Brand and Fox sighed. "Did you?"

"Of course not, we promised you that we wouldn't."

"I think that Fox was right about Dart. His isolation is driving him mad."

"Madder," Fox corrected him.

"What are we to do?" Brand asked. "If he wants you dead, he'll keep coming after you. He must have heard the news by now. He must know that the fire didn't kill you."

"Maybe he'll think we've been punished enough for whatever we did to make him loathe us," Gabriela suggested.

"Maybe." Brand didn't sound convinced. "We can't come to your parents' house again, Gabriela. We've been paying special attention to covering our tracks since the fire but we can't guarantee he won't succeed in following us eventually. We need to meet somewhere else if we want to keep in touch."

"How about somewhere further away from this area, a public place that you can get to easily by using the tunnels, but a place on the surface all the same."

"Somewhere halfway between the underground and the surface," Fox said. "I know, how about the Powerhouse?"

"That's a great idea," Ripley said.

The Powerhouse was a huge concrete building on the riverbank in New Farm. It had long since ceased to be used to generate electricity and now housed art displays and hosted theatre performances and rock gigs.

"We go there quite a bit, especially to the free gigs on Friday evenings," Fox said. "Is this Friday good for you two?"

"I think so. Do you have any plans, Rips?"

"No, Friday's fine."

"So, that's settled," Fox said. "We'll meet you there then, and we won't talk about you-know-who. Agreed?"

"Agreed," they chorused.

"But don't forget about him. Watch your step," Brand reminded them.

"The same goes for the two of you."

Fox and Brand left the gazebo and disappeared into the night.

"They're right. We still have to be careful, Rips. He's still out there."

He tapped the bulge under his track pants where his hammer was strapped to his waist with a short length of rope. She hadn't noticed that he'd taken up the habit of carrying it with him absolutely everywhere he went.

"I know," he said. "Come on. Let's get back to bed."

"Actually, I wouldn't mind staying here for a minute first," Gabriela whispered huskily. "It's far more romantic sitting under a gazebo on a moonlit night than being stuck in one's childhood bedroom, if you catch my drift."

Ripley smiled. "I think I do."

35

Flying foxes beat the air with their leathery wings as they moved from tree to tree. Their dark forms rose high above the parkland and the bleak industrial bulk of the Powerhouse. The building's brick and concrete mass contrasted starkly with the lawns and trees of New Farm Park.

Ripley jumped as a cyclist overtook them from behind, neglecting to sound his bell.

Gabriela was also startled.

They had both noticed each other's reaction, but she hadn't seen his right hand slip inside his jacket, reaching for the hammer.

"Bloody cyclist!" Ripley complained. But he was more annoyed that he'd been taken by surprise than by the cyclist's behaviour. He needed to stay calm but aware.

They had met after work and caught a bus from the city to New Farm. The idea that Dart could have followed them ought to have been too ludicrous to give any serious thought, but they both knew that if he was capable of shadowing Brand and Fox, they had to assume he was capable of tracking them with his eyes closed.

Ripley turned them both around so they were looking along the dark path behind them. Apart from flying foxes in the air and a couple of possums on the ground, there were no other signs of movement.

"Come on, Rips. He can't have followed us here. He doesn't know where we work."

"Doesn't he?" Ripley whispered sceptically. "What if he heard us talking to Brand and Fox one night?"

Gabriela shivered. The thought of Dart eavesdropping on them in the privacy of their own home was a dreadful one.

"Even if, somehow, he does know where we work, we didn't see him in the bus on the way here."

Ripley nodded. He imagined Dart noting the bus they had caught, guessing where they were going, and then sprinting through the tunnels to arrive at their stop before the bus. Surely that was impossible.

They continued towards the Powerhouse. The path curved down towards the river.

Up on Riverbend Terrace, patio heaters were blazing and people were chatting loudly as they sipped their Friday evening drinks.

Ripley and Gabriela walked up the stairs and through the modern glass doors that pierced the thick red brick walls of the building. They went to the bar, where a tall young man with blond hair and a short girl with dark hair were busy serving schooners of beer and glasses of wine.

"What do you want to drink?" Ripley asked.

"Some white wine, I think. Is there a wine list?"

Ripley was reaching out to take one from between a couple of women who were waiting for their drinks when a hand tapped his shoulder.

Every muscle in his body tensed and he had to force himself to turn around.

Brand noted the look on his face.

"Sorry, I didn't mean to scare you, mate."

Fox looked at Ripley sympathetically.

"Fox!" Gabriela gave her a hug.

"How are you two going?" she asked, even though she knew the answer. "Are you holding up all right?"

"We're doing our best."

"Remember," Brand interrupted. "Tonight we're going to relax."

"Can I get you a drink?" Ripley asked them.

"No, I've already got some drinks for all of us," Brand informed him. "A bottle of white wine and a few boutique beers. Is that all right?"

"Sure," Ripley said. "I'll get the next round then."

"Don't worry about it, Rips. I've got it sorted out in here."

"You mean that you can get into the cellar?"

Brand coughed and tapped his nose. "No questions, please."

Ripley didn't like the idea of drinking stolen beer. The Powerhouse was the kind of place he wanted to support, not rip off, but he didn't want to offend Brand after everything he'd done for them.

"Cheers, mate. Should we go and check out the resident band?"

"Infinite Void? Yeah, they're not bad," Fox said. "They've got a kind of underground sound."

"Right up your alley," Gabriela pointed out.

Brand led them into Turbine Hall, a vast space where the vestiges of the former powerhouse matched the music perfectly. Concrete pylons, brick walls, and steel girders provided an impressive background for the angst-ridden voice, throbbing bass, powerful drums, and frenetic guitar.

There were no seats available, so they stood at one of the tables.

"Keep the table for us. We'll be back in a second," Brand told them.

He and Fox walked off and descended a flight of stairs.

"As much as I like them and accept their way of life, I don't think they should steal like that," Gabriela said quietly.

"I know. Let's let it go for tonight. I'll tell Brand next time that I'd rather buy my drinks."

"It's amazing though, isn't it? They can go almost anywhere they want in Brisbane."

When Brand and Fox came back with the drinks, they all listened to the band without speaking for several minutes. Ripley held Gabriela from behind and they swayed to the music. He rested his chin on her shoulder and breathed slowly into the curtain of her hair.

214

36

The two couples decided to make a habit of going to the Powerhouse on Fridays, and Ripley and Gabriela grew a little less nervous with each passing week. Ripley even stopped carrying his hammer with him after a while.

"You know what's kicking off soon?" Brand asked the others as they leaned against the balustrade of Riverbend Terrace one evening, watching the lights of the Powerhouse dance on the muddy water of the river.

They shrugged.

"The Ekka!"

Ripley, Gabriela, and Fox glanced at each other.

"What did I say?" Brand asked.

Fox put a hand on Brand's shoulder, signalling for him to hold his tongue.

"I didn't tell him," she explained to Gabriela.

"It's all right," Gabriela said. "Brand, when I was little, I used to go to the Ekka. One year, something terrible happened."

She stared at the river.

"Don't worry. I'll tell him about it later," Fox said.

Gabriela didn't say anything for a long moment.

The others respected her silence.

Ripley took a sip of beer and put an arm around her.

Brand looked at Fox questioningly, but she just signalled for him to wait.

Eventually, Gabriela turned to them and spoke. What she said was the last thing they'd been expecting.

"That was the last time I went to the Ekka. It was so long ago. I think I'd like to go back, just one more time."

Ripley was stunned.

"Are you sure you could cope with it?" he asked.

"That's just it. After all I've coped with over the last few weeks, I think I could."

Fox shook her head in admiration.

"I know we told you we wanted to pay for our drinks," Gabriela whispered to Brand, who was still confused. "But I don't suppose you could get us into the Ekka for free? From what I've heard, it's ridiculously expensive nowadays."

Brand winked at her.

"You'll have to go back underground," he warned her.

She hesitated, and for a while the others thought she would refuse.

"No problem. For old times' sake."

Ripley couldn't help but smile to himself.

On Saturday the eleventh of August at four-thirty in the afternoon, they met in the grounds of the Old Museum. The huge nineteenth century building of red brick stood in a pocket of calm just next to the screams, sirens, and carnie music of Side Show Alley. A concrete wall separated it from the Ekka grounds.

On the other side, thrill seekers were being tossed and turned, dipped and swung, and spun and shaken on the monstrous mechanical arms of the Ranger and the Hangover. Lights were flashing like a multi-coloured electrical storm high on crystal meth.

Even the air that drifted across from the other side of the wall was different. It was laden with the fatty odour of dagwood dogs and the equally nauseating saccharine scent of fairy floss.

The contrast between the frenetic activity of Side Show Alley and the stubborn calmness of the Old Museum grounds couldn't have been starker. The wall was a frontier dividing two completely different worlds, but such a wall was no obstacle for a tunnel dweller.

Gabriela didn't know what to make of it all. It was an obnoxious symbol of society's obsession with incessant consumerism and shallow distractions. The noise and excitement and tacky throw-away gadgets and toys, the greasy food being gobbled up voraciously by obese bogans; none of it appealed to her.

And of course, there was that other reason she had always avoided the Ekka, that personal one.

Fox read her thoughts and placed a comforting hand on her shoulder. "If you think it's a weird place to you, think about us. We're used to quiet and darkness. It's like another world for us."

"Is that why you come here?"

"I suppose it is. It's a change from the routine. Listen, you know it's not too late to call it off if you want."

"No, I won't do that. I'm all right."

Fox searched her face.

"Really," Gabriela assured her. "I want to have a look. I want to challenge myself. I still can't believe that there is a secret tunnel allowing access to the show grounds."

Brand overheard her comment.

"There's almost no public or private site bigger than a house that can't be entered via the underground network. I wouldn't say that nobody knows about them, but rather that so few members of the public do to make them any problem for the authorities. There are council maps illustrating the sewage and storm water systems, as well as disused storage rooms, but these maps are probably only used on rare occasions by a handful of council employees or subcontractors when planning maintenance work on a specific section of the system."

"So, the tunnel we're going to use will take us under that wall and into Side Show Alley?" Ripley asked. He wanted to be able to imagine just where they would arrive.

"Not exactly," Brand replied. "I want you to listen carefully."

Ripley and Gabriela nodded their agreement.

"The tunnel is *very* narrow."

Gabriela groaned to herself. She'd had enough of tight squeezes to last her a month of Sundays. But she wasn't going to be put off. She was determined to go ahead with it.

"We'll crawl through and emerge in an alcove at the back of the Show Bag Pavilion. I'll check that the coast is clear and then we'll walk casually out of the pavilion. All you need to do is move when I move and stop when I stop."

"Understood," Ripley agreed. He was enjoying every minute of it already.

Brand looked around. They were alone.

"All right, let's go," he said, heading off towards the rear of the Old Museum. He led them to a manhole whose cover he had loosened a few days earlier.

"Give me a hand, Rips."

They dragged the cover off and Brand crawled inside first.

"Don't worry about trying to put it back now. We'll leave the grounds like everybody else at closing time, and I'll come back and pull the cover over the entrance later. Ready?"

Brand climbed down the ladder and into the darkness.

Fox followed him, then Gabriela, and Ripley took the rearguard.

As they walked through the darkness, their heads bowed like monks on a pilgrimage, Gabriela told herself that this would be her last adventure beneath the streets of Brisbane. She couldn't bear to keep doing it. The very sight of a manhole cover or storm water drain was beginning to make her skin crawl.

It soon became clear that Brand hadn't been exaggerating. The invisible walls closed in on the group until they could feel them pressing against their arms, smothering them the way a gang of schoolyard bullies would intimidate a likely target for lunch money. It didn't bother Brand and Fox in the slightest, but

Gabriela was finding it more emotionally challenging than she'd expected. Ripley, despite trying to tell himself otherwise, had to admit he was actually enjoying it.

The tunnel seemed to continue closing in as they advanced. With every dragged step, they could have sworn the passage became narrower. Both Gabriela and Ripley shared the same impression, but they didn't communicate their thoughts with each other. They made their progress in silence. The only contact they had was every minute or so when Ripley reached forward and took her by the hand to encourage her to maintain the effort he knew she was making.

In reality, their impression about the walls was entirely false. The sides of the passage remained at the same distance, and, although they were forced to keep their heads bowed and their arms by their sides, the squeeze wasn't as bad as they had imagined it to be after all.

Their shoes scuffed against the rough ground as the tunnel curved to the right, and as the darkness grew less formidable, the music and screaming of Side Show Alley intensified and drowned out the rhythmic sound of their footsteps.

Little by little, the level of light penetrating into the tunnel increased, until it was strong enough for Ripley to make out the entangled silhouettes of his three companions in front of him. Light and darkness danced awkwardly together as Brand, Fox, and Gabriela shuffled along.

Then, the silhouettes vanished abruptly.

Ripley reached out for Gabriela's hand but failed to catch it.

She was no longer there.

In front of him was a circular grill that allowed light and chill air in. Through it, he could see the maniacal machines of Side Show Alley scaring the wits out of their human prey. He'd never understood the fascination with rides and always thought of them as being rather silly, but from the darkness and isolation of the tunnel, the whole phenomenon struck him as being nothing short of absolutely absurd.

He heard Gabriela groan somewhere to his right. She too had thought the journey was already over, but Brand was leading them down another passage. This one was so narrow they had to turn sideways and slip along like stick figures trapped on a sheet of paper. He could hear Gabriela breathing heavily, fighting back panic. He followed the sound and succeeded in taking her by the hand.

After several more turns, the tunnel widened again, and Ripley heard the reassuring sound of feet on metal rungs.

They were on their way up.

He squeezed Gabriela's hand.

They climbed slowly, being careful not to miss a rung, and Brand and Fox helped them out into a space that was equally as dark as the tunnel. They still had no idea where they were except for a vague feeling that they were on street level.

"Wait here," Brand whispered.

What happened next went smoothly and quickly, as though it had been rehearsed a dozen times before.

A door opened, ever so slightly, then a little more, and Brand slipped through with serpentine ease.

A moment later, it opened again.

Fox pulled Gabriela through.

Ripley hastened to follow, and before he knew it, they were weaving a passage through a crowd of bewildered mums and dads who were being dragged around by commanding children on the hunt for chocolates, whoopee cushions, and monster masks.

The cover was perfect. Their entrance hadn't been noticed, and within seconds, Brand had led them out of the Show Bag Pavilion.

Ripley shook his head in disbelief as he noticed that Brand and Fox had managed to pick a few things up along the way. Just like the enslaved parents all around them, they were carrying a stack of show bags.

"How did you do that?" Gabriela asked.

Fox just shrugged her shoulders. There was nothing to it for them. Stealing was as simple as tying shoe laces.

"Guys, we didn't strictly procure these according to the usual procedure."

Ripley laughed.

"I need a chocolate fix. I'll make an exception, just this once."

Brand handed him a Bertie Beetle bag.

Fox looked at Gabriela and winked.

"What the hell!" she surrendered. After braving that particular stretch of tunnel, she figured that a treat was in order.

"There are bigger thieves than us in the world," Fox told her apologetically.

"I'm sure of that," Gabriela agreed.

Brand looked around.

"Where shall we start the fun and games?"

He was as excited to be there as the horde of children swarming all around the Ekka grounds.

"I want to see the fluffy little animals," Fox answered.

Gabriela and Ripley exchanged a glance and read each other's thoughts. Fox always spoke and acted so seriously. The tough life she had made it through before joining the tunnel dwellers, as well as the difficulties of living underground and the constant need to watch her back every day when she went to the surface to steal provisions, meant that she had been forced to act with a high degree of maturity. The challenges she faced were greater than the mundane responsibilities and stresses of Gabriela and the young women she knew in her circle of friends. Every time they met, Gabriela's appreciation of the difference between them grew. But rather than create a gap, it somehow made them even closer.

Brand wasn't surprised by her suggestion at all.

"What do you think?"

"I love animals too," Gabriela volunteered.

"All right," Brand concluded, looking around to get his bearings. "I think it's this way."

He pointed vaguely towards the north and set off through the crowd, biting the head off a Freddo Frog as he walked.

Ripley followed him closely, and the girls trailed not too far behind, trying to keep the pace while they chatted together.

"Fox, could you tell me about Brand?"

She smiled at Gabriela, obviously amused.

"What is it?"

"Nothing. I just love the way you always ask about people's lives."

"Sorry. I know I'm nosy."

"No, I mean it. You're interested in people, and I like that about you. It's a novelty for me. Everybody underground already knows all about everybody else."

Gabriela almost blushed.

"What do you want to know? I've told you about how we met, haven't I? When he was asleep in the park and I pinched some of his stuff."

"Yes, you told me about that, but not about before that, before you met him."

Fox thought about it, looking in front of her to where Brand was, as though watching him would help her get the facts straight.

Then, she began.

37

"Brand's story isn't a pleasant one," Fox warned her quietly. "Like mine, I suppose. That's the case for most of us. Only a handful of the tunnel dwellers decided to live underground for reasons entirely unrelated to the fact that they had disastrous home lives, and even fewer are still in regular contact with their families. You've probably observed how Brand is calm and in control, but I can tell you he gets angry sometimes, especially when something, any little word or image or situation, reminds him of his former life as Barry Craig." Fox made sure to whisper that forbidden name. "For example, any mention of lawnmowers," she went on, her voice no more than a nervous breath.

"Lawnmowers?" Gabriela repeated the word as a hushed question.

The expression on Fox's face told Gabriela that she knew it sounded ridiculous.

"You must never mention any of this to anybody, not even Ripley. I'd rather it stayed between us. I shouldn't even be talking to you about it."

Gabriela put her hand over Fox's.

"You have my word."

"I trust you," Fox said. "You know I do. Well, as I was saying, he doesn't get angry very often, and he tells me that he doesn't believe in hate or holding grudges, but he can't help feeling upset when he thinks about his dad and what he used to do. Whenever that happens, he tries to deal with it by listening to Nine Inch Nails, KMFDM, or Rammstein and doing countless repetitions of push-ups and chin-ups until he works it out of his system."

Fox pulled Gabriela along so they didn't lose track of Brand and Ripley in the crowded passage leading to the animal sheds.

"Like I said, he's not often angry. I think his self-control is one of the reasons I was attracted to him in the first place."

"That makes sense," Gabriela agreed. "After all, he quickly forgave you for stealing his belongings."

"Yes, that's true. Anyway, to get back to the story, and just remember, you asked me to tell you this, so don't blame me if you don't like what you hear."

"I won't," Gabriela assured her.

"Brand!" Fox called out loudly.

He stopped in his tracks, worried about why her voice sounded so urgent.

"Gabs and I need to go to the ladies'. Can you two wait for us near the lamb enclosure?"

"Sure thing."

Fox pulled Gabriela off into the crowd so the boys couldn't see them.

"Actually, I really do need to go to the toilet," Gabriela admitted.

"Do you know the way?"

"I've got no idea, but we're bound to stumble across them if we walk around for a while."

"Let's try over there," Fox suggested, pointing beyond a row of bushy Moreton Bay fig trees that had been pruned to resemble giant umbrellas. There appeared to be an inordinate number of women hovering around a small brick building next to a hotdog stand.

"As I was saying, Brand's family was rotten, and I mean rotten *to the core*. Of course, I never met them, but I was tempted to pay them a visit one Halloween. It was shortly after we'd got together and he'd told me all about himself. I can't remember exactly why, but we'd got talking about Halloween and something that came up in the conversation reminded him of an episode involving his dad.

"I remember being so outraged that I wanted to play a trick on him that would be far more memorable than the usual trick-or-treat fare. Sure enough, Brand, in his cool-headed manner, was able to talk me out of it. He also reminded me that taking revenge on surface walkers from our past was against the code."

"What he told you must have been terrible to make you so furious."

"Well, here it is, since you want to know so badly. Just remember, you asked for it."

Fox took a deep breath and stopped Gabriela under one of the fig trees. They were at the end of the toilet queue, behind a group of teenage girls who were chatting loudly and stuffing hotdogs into their mouths. They all needed to pee so badly their thighs were pressed together under short skirts.

"Brand's parents were really screwed up, even worse than mine. He told me that life started to get out of control when his mother got sick of his dad and ran away with his brother, I mean Brand's uncle, of course. He knew what Brand's dad was like and had tried to warn her when they'd first started going out. She hadn't listened to him because she thought he was just jealous of his brother. She soon fell pregnant with Brand... sorry, am I going too fast for you?"

"No, not at all," Gabriela encouraged her. "Keep going."

"Where was I? Okay, later, when she eventually ran off with Brand's uncle, he wanted to go with them, he wanted to live with his mum and uncle, but they didn't want him. His own mother didn't want to take him with her!"

"Why?" Gabriela asked. "What kind of mother wouldn't want to take her own child with her?"

Fox lifted her palms to the sky in a sign of absolute bewilderment. It was a question she had asked herself many times before.

"Brand stayed with his father. I think he was about seven or eight years old at that time.

"As he got older, he started to look more and more like his mother. His dad used to tell him that he had *her fucking nose* and *the same annoying frown as the whore*!"

Gabriela was speechless.

"So, his dad used to do whatever he could to take his anger out on Brand. He would make him do all the housework and flog him around the back with a horsewhip if he found one drop of water on the dishes after Brand had dried them or a single speck of dust on the floor after he had swept it. He never let Brand have friends over and he never let him go to a friend's house."

"He treated him like a slave," Gabriela said absently.

"I guess that's one way of putting it. Another would be to say that he treated him like a witch or heretic. He did to Brand what he wished he could do to his mother."

Gabriela gasped loudly.

"Hold on! No, that's not what I'm saying, Gabs," Fox clarified. "I don't mean anything like *that*, but, yeah, he tortured him. There's no other way of putting it."

Gabriela whispered her next question, as though ashamed to even be asking it. "Is that where the lawnmower phobia comes in?"

Fox lowered her eyelids for a moment and then flicked them up again.

"I'm afraid so. It was because he looked so much like his mum. His dad hated him for it, as though it was Brand's fault that he had received more of his mum's genes than his dad's, as though he had actually chosen to take after her."

"That's nuts!"

"Yeah, and that's exactly how Brand describes his old man – *nuts*. At least, that's one of the nicer adjectives I've heard him use."

"And the lawnmower?" Gabriela dreaded the question, but she just had to know.

"It took place a couple of times. You know those moments in your life that only last a few seconds but are repeated so often in your mind that it seems as though they used to happen all the time?"

Gabriela nodded even though she couldn't really think of any such moments, not off the top of her head at any rate.

"The first time, his dad was mowing the lawn while Brand was weeding the garden. I've never mown a lawn myself, but you know how you don't really have to concentrate very much on what you're doing? I mean, how people have time to think while they're doing simple tasks like that, whether it's mowing, doing the dishes, or sweeping the floor?"

"Yeah, I know exactly what you mean," Gabriela said. "It gives you a chance to sort things out in your mind."

"That's how it is for most people. But for Brand's dad, it gave him time to dwell on dark thoughts that would have been best left alone."

"I think I know where this is going," Gabriela said, and Fox could tell by her expression that she did indeed.

"I can't imagine what it must have felt like to have my dad, and as you know, mine was no angel, push my face close to spinning lawnmower blades. What I do know is that Brand never got over it, and probably never really will. The good news is that he got away from his dad before it was too late."

Fox and Gabriela had entered the toilet block and rushed into the earliest available cubicles, thus happily ending a conversation that neither of them wanted to pursue any further.

Once they had relieved themselves, the girls navigated their way through the jostling crowd and into the animal sheds.

They found Ripley and Brand staring vacantly at the children eagerly lined up to touch lambs, llamas, and kids.

Fox noticed one mother, who was wearing jeans that looked as though they were about to split at the seams, glance suspiciously, and none too discreetly, at the pair. She then checked to see where her daughter was.

Fox smiled to herself. Even though she wasn't a mother, she could understand the woman's concern, and the boys were

227

staring so intently at the children. She crept up on Brand and whispered into his ear.

"A penny for your thoughts, young man."

He turned to her.

"I was just wondering whether we would ever bring children here to see the animals."

"Oh, that's so cute. Were you really?"

"Really."

She kissed him on the cheek.

"I was asking myself the same question," Ripley added.

"We're not so different after all," Fox mused. "Two couples stumbling through life, trying to find their way. We just live on different sides of the street."

"Different sides of the street," Brand repeated. "Yeah, that about sums it up."

Gabriela tried to hide the pity she had for him behind a relaxed smile. She didn't want him to sense that Fox had shared his story with her.

"Are you going to line up with the children?" Brand asked, patting Fox's taut bottom.

"Yes, I am."

Gabriela joined her, ignoring the fact that they looked silly, being the only motherless women in the queue. She had to admit that it was kind of fun anyhow. The Ekka wasn't so bad after all.

Ripley watched Gabriela as she stepped into the enclosure behind a pair of girls who were approaching the smallest lamb with unwarranted caution. He watched her tickle the ears of one of the lambs and laugh with Fox as the animal licked at her. She giggled and smiled, and Ripley felt a sudden wave of pride and admiration for her. After everything they had been through, that they'd put themselves through by getting involved in a world that was none of their business, she was still smiling. She wasn't going to let it get her down.

38

"Where should we go next?" Fox asked once she and Gabriela had had enough of stroking animals.

"How about we go for a stroll through Side Show Alley? I've never understood why people are attracted to paying good money to have themselves shaken like cocktails," Ripley offered.

"Me neither," Brand agreed. "Let's go and try to work it out."

It wasn't easy staying together in the crowd. People were walking all over the place and paying little attention to each other. It was as though nobody else mattered at all. Obese family after obese family barged their way through the throng, sometimes intentionally pushing people aside with their bulk in a rush to get to the fast food stalls. The stench of body odour, boiling fat, and, worst of all, fresh vomit was sickening.

Ripley looked up as a pod full of screaming teenagers twirled overhead. He had to wonder what enjoyment they could possibly be getting out of it.

To his left, he saw a shooting gallery where boys were trying to win a fluffy toy for their girlfriends. He could understand the point of that at least.

From a little further along the alley came the ghastly howls and wicked laughter of the Haunted House, and for some reason, Ripley found himself drawn to it. Perhaps he was no different from the thrill seekers whizzing through the air after all. He too could be sucked into the inane pleasures of the overbearing whirlpool of noise, light, and movement that was begging for him to empty both his mind and his wallet.

Before he could take evasive action, he was trapped between

an enormous young woman with two overfed boys hanging from her arms like monkeys on a sugar high and a middle-aged man who was holding a hamburger and giant cup of Coca-Cola against his man boobs and seemed oblivious to the fact that both items were dripping their contents onto a T-shirt that was unable to cover the flabby mass of his belly.

Ripley had to turn sideways to slip between them and avoid being smothered.

He managed to do that, but when he looked around, he found that he had lost track of the others. They'd been in front of him a few moments ago, but now they were nowhere to be seen.

He made his way ever closer to the Haunted House, where a werewolf with flashing red eyes was ripping its shirt open with hairy, mechanical arms, and a ghost was hovering over the doorway, ready to spook any who dared enter.

Ripley knew that Gabriela wouldn't want to go into the Haunted House. That would be impossible for her to manage. But there was no reason he couldn't have a quick walk through. The skeletal hands and lurching mummies would be a light-hearted laugh compared to the real dangers he had faced in the darkness below the city. It would only take a minute, and then he would call Gabriela and catch up with the gang.

"Come on, young man. You're never too old for a thrill in the Haunted House!" the friendly carnie in the ticket booth reassured him.

Ripley paid the eight dollar fee and took his ticket.

"This is the way, step inside," the carnie hissed, no trace of joviality left in his voice, and in the second it took Ripley to realise that it was merely a well-practised act, he let a stab of panic prick his already susceptible mind.

He walked up the steps and felt a cool breeze from a fan hidden inside the ghost blow down on him as he passed beneath it.

Before stepping inside, he decided to turn around and look at the crowd milling around the rides and stalls. He could see

Brand, Fox, and Gabriela down near where an elaborate merry-go-round had come to a halt to let a mob of parents place their children on ponies, swans, and lions. He wanted to call out to them, but the incredible racket of sirens, howls, screams, and crappy dance music meant it would have been futile.

He looked at the ticket booth by the bottom of the stairs and noticed among the crowd that one person was standing perfectly still, staring at the Haunted House as though mesmerised by its otherworldly powers.

Ripley's skin broke out in goose bumps as the face turned towards him and a chilling grimace that was a mix of complete surprise and pure hate met his gaze. They weren't the kind of goose bumps a mechanical phantom or rubber zombie could ever give him.

They were born of real terror.

Dart shoved a family out of the way, ignoring their junk food smothered cries of protest, and jumped the gate in front of the ticket booth.

Ripley saw that he had a chain wrapped around his body and was clutching his hatchet in his hand. He had come to the Ekka armed, and nobody had even batted an eyelid. Ripley could hardly believe it. Perhaps everybody had simply assumed he was part of a woodchopping team.

The carnie shouted at him to stop, but his words were ignored.

As Dart came bounding up the stairs, Ripley disappeared through the entrance.

There was nowhere else to go but straight into the Haunted House.

The darkness inside was interrupted only by a disconcerting assault of bright white strobe lights and dimly glowing red and blue lamps. Despite the conditions, Ripley had to run, and he couldn't afford to slip up. Dart was right behind him and was more of a menace than any tacky sideshow monster could ever be.

He barged through a clutch of teenage girls who were staring expectantly at a possessed maiden lying in a soiled bed while an exorcist's right arm made jerky mechanical movements back and forth, thrusting a radiant silver cross at her.

The girls didn't complain. They just laughed at Ripley, mistaking the cause of his fear. Then, an instant later, they let out an ear-piercing volley of squeals. Ripley didn't know whether it was because the possessed girl had suddenly twisted herself into a hideous knot, or they had caught sight of Dart's hatchet. He didn't dare look back to find out.

He stumbled through the maze of rooms, using his hands to guide him along the walls. He had to escape back to the relative safety of the real world.

He lurched forward through what felt like cobwebs, but they failed to stick to his body the way real gossamer would. Rubber spiders were hanging from the ceiling too, but they had no effect on him at all as they bounced off his face and swung like pendulums.

As he rushed into the next room, Ripley almost tripped, but he managed to stay upright by pushing himself off a wall.

A crazy butcher was hacking a hapless victim to pieces on a rustic cutting table. The thud the cleaver made as it struck sent a shiver through Ripley's body. He couldn't help himself from imagining Dart's hatchet sinking into his skull, cracking it open with the most ghastly of sounds.

It would all be over. He would never hold Gabriela in his arms again.

Dart had no right to do that, to take his life, to take anybody's.

Ripley knew that he should have been furious, but his fear overrode his rage. That was part of the instinct to survive. The primaeval part of his mind that had taken control of his actions, that was guiding him, had chosen the emotion that was most likely to get him out of the predicament alive. Fear was making him flee as quickly as his legs were capable of carrying him. Rage would have slowed him down or pushed him to confront Dart, and that would have been a fatal error.

Don't look back! He's right behind you! You've got to keep running!

He was dashing through the torture chamber now. Skeletons chained to a fake stone wall were rattling like wind chimes, and a half-naked damsel in distress was being whipped by a horny demon with a hungry grin.

He shoved past a couple of young lovers who were making out. The young man had purple hair and his left hand was groping under his girlfriend's similarly coloured tartan skirt.

"You won't get away this time!" the voice behind him boomed, and Ripley's shoulder throbbed as he remembered the hatchet blow it had been dealt down in the tunnels, when for the first time in his life, he had known what it meant to be the object of murderous intent.

Daylight was growing stronger. Ripley could see a rectangle of white light in front of him.

He'd almost made it.

His right shoulder rammed the door and sent it crashing open.

He squinted as he used the railing to propel himself down to the ground, but no matter how fast he ran, he knew the tunnel runner would catch up with him sooner or later.

Looking back for a split second, he saw that Dart was as close behind him as he'd imagined, and he was angrier than ever.

"Stop!" the carnie yelled at them. "I've radioed the police!"

"Fuck your police!" Dart shouted back.

Some people were screaming hysterically, and others were laughing nervously, ignoring their gut feeling and forcing themselves to believe that it was some kind of bizarre act. One man dropped his hotdog as the pair pushed past him and seemed more distressed by the loss of his junk food than by the deadly pursuit he was witnessing.

Nobody tried to help Ripley. Of the hundreds of people they weaved through or bowled over as Dart chased him through Side Show Alley, not one single human being dared get involved.

233

People were shouting out for the police, but Ripley didn't notice any officers as he fled. He didn't know where he was going either. He didn't have time to think.

He soon found himself at the railway station.

He jumped the ticket gate and forced himself to keep running even as it dawned on him that he was heading straight for a dead end.

He glanced over his shoulder, almost losing his equilibrium as he did so, and saw Dart so close behind him that he could probably have swung his chain around Ripley's neck and brought him down like a lassoed calf.

Ripley was almost at the end of the platform now, and he knew he had no choice but to jump onto the tracks and keep running. He had to ignore the pain in his legs and keep his breathing under control. There was nothing else he could do. Run, run, run until he either lost Dart or found a weapon with which to defend himself. He refused to admit that neither of those outcomes seemed very likely.

"What are you doing, mate? You're fucking crazy!" a man in a broad-brimmed Akubra yelled at Ripley as he jumped onto the tracks and landed so heavily that, for a terrible moment, he thought he must have hurt himself too badly to keep going.

Ripley wanted to shout at the man to help him, not mouth off. But he couldn't spare the precious breath. His muscles were depending on him to suck every bit of air he could get deep into his lungs.

"There's a train coming any second now! Get off the bloody tracks and stop horsing around!" the man roared.

Horsing around? What was happening was so inconceivable that bystanders were telling themselves it was all a game. To admit they were witnessing a predator hunting his quarry was just too primitive a concept to comprehend.

As Ripley pushed himself to his feet, relieved that he hadn't been injured, he heard Dart land on the coarse gravel behind him.

234

A moment later, he felt the chain strike his right ankle.

He yelled, more out of fear than pain.

The people on the platform screamed out for them to stop, and Ripley could hear a child crying.

But the chain hadn't wrapped around Ripley's ankle, he could still move, and gritting his teeth, he staggered forward.

They kept running for several hundred metres more, but the pace soon slowed to the point that either one of them might have collapsed from exhaustion at any moment.

"Fuck it!" Dart shouted in defeat.

Ripley turned around, realising that his voice had come from quite a distance away.

Dart was lying on the tracks, breathing heavily.

Ripley found it difficult to believe.

He looked beyond the tunnel runner and saw the man in the Akubra rushing towards them from the station.

Another man soon followed his lead.

They were both agitated and waving their hands. Now that Dart no longer presented a threat, they had mustered enough courage to back Ripley up.

But there was something else in the way they were gesturing, and it didn't take Ripley long to work out what it was. He could feel the tracks starting to tremble under his feet, making his already shaking legs even less stable.

"Get up, Dart!"

"I can't!"

Ripley ran over to him.

It didn't make any sense, but he just couldn't bear the thought of letting the train crush Dart.

"You have to get up, right now!"

As he closed in, he understood why Dart couldn't move. He'd got his foot caught on a section of rail and was trying in vain to pull it out. His chain had also got tangled around his leg. Ripley had never seen him so vulnerable. He was as pathetic as a sacrificial lamb.

An image of the butcher from the Haunted House flashed back into Ripley's mind. He remembered how mechanically he had hacked at the bodies of his victims; how easy and void of emotion the machine had been.

He blinked the image away. The tracks were vibrating more violently with every second.

"Hold still!" Ripley urged him, as he unlaced his shoe and tugged his foot out. After that, he quickly unravelled the chain.

Dart breathed a sigh of relief, but it was drowned out by the deafening blast of the horn as the train came roaring into view.

The driver applied the emergency brakes, but it was obvious that the yellow and silver juggernaut wouldn't come to a halt in time.

Ripley grabbed Dart's shirt and pulled him up and off the tracks, ripping it in the process. The two rolled down into the gutter beside the railway line as the train went grinding past.

"Why?" Dart wheezed.

"I don't know," Ripley replied. "I may kill you yet, but we need to get away from here before the police catch us."

He struggled to his feet and held his hands out to help Dart up. Looking down on him, he noticed a strange triangular mark on the tunnel runner's chest. It had been exposed when his shirt got torn, and Ripley wondered whether he had got it during some kind of rite of passage.

But now was no time to ask.

"There's an entrance to the tunnels just over there."

Dart pointed a little further along the gutter.

Ripley looked over to the train. It now blocked the line of sight between them and the group of witnesses.

"Let's move!" Ripley ordered him, wrapping the chain around Dart's neck.

"What are you doing?" he started to protest, but Ripley wasn't going to have any of it.

"Shut your trap and move!"

Dart obeyed, leading them towards the entrance.

Once they were underground, Ripley pushed his prisoner to the concrete floor and held the chain firmly with both hands.

"I don't know why I decided to save your life just now, or why you still want to kill me, but, one way or another, it all ends here."

"You broke your promise; that's why. You gave me no choice."

"I didn't break my promise. I didn't tell the police about the tunnel dwellers."

"They came down into the tunnels. It's no coincidence, is it? I'm not stupid."

"No, you're not. But you are misinformed," Ripley stated calmly.

"What do you mean?"

"You burgled that house in Wilston?"

"How did you know that?" Dart asked with genuine surprise.

"It was on the news. The house burned to the ground."

"What? I didn't set it on fire!"

"Maybe not on purpose, but it happened, and the woman inside saw you go underground."

"Shit!"

"Exactly."

"So, it wasn't you after all?"

"No, it wasn't," Ripley said, and he felt a great sense of relief at being able to tell Dart that.

"I nearly roasted you for nothing."

"That's right," Ripley said. But he was no longer angry. There was only room for relief, and he knew that he was on the verge of breaking down in tears.

"And you decided to save my life after all that? You do know something about honour."

"Yes, I do. You shouldn't judge people simply by whether they live above or below the surface. That's pretty narrow-minded, isn't it?"

Dart just shook his head, making the chain rattle.

237

"If I take the chain off, will you behave?"

"Of course, I give you my word. I owe you my life."

Ripley decided he could trust him. Dart may have been a violent sociopath, but he had already demonstrated to chilling effect that he was a man of his word.

He removed the chain.

"What happens now?" Dart asked.

"I don't know. That's up to you. If you want to live underground and come up to steal from the rich, then keep doing that. I don't like people who have more than their fair share either, but try not to burn any more houses down, all right?"

"That sounds reasonable. I'm going to be all alone though. I don't know if I can survive like that, mentally, I mean. You must think I was either born mad or bad, or double shots of both, but it's not like that. I've just been struggling to look after myself and those who have chosen to live underground. I don't want to be a victim."

"I don't think you were born a bad person, Dart," Ripley said. "You are a victim of circumstance, but you need to take control of yourself before you end up doing something that can't be undone. You're a man of values, not a monster. You don't really want to hurt others, but you will if you let this hatred continue. You should make your peace with the tunnel community, and you should do it soon, because you're going to need them as much as they're going to need you."

"You're right, but they'll never forgive me."

"I can talk to them."

"No, please don't. I'd be too ashamed."

"What are you going to do then?"

"I need some time to think about what has happened. Do you want me to do something to thank you for saving my life?"

"No, I don't," Ripley assured him. He wanted Dart out of his life for good; nothing more, nothing less.

"Thank you. Thank you so much," he said, hanging his head.

"Does that mean I can go now?"

"Yeah, you can go."

Dart got up and vanished, leaving Ripley staring into the darkness.

All he could do was hope the tunnel runner really would change.

39

Ripley didn't know where to go from there. In all likelihood, a crowd would be milling around the railway line, trying to work out how both a maniac and the young man he had been hell-bent on killing could have simply disappeared into thin air. At the same time, he didn't have a torch and wasn't keen on wandering through the tunnels in the dark, even if the problem of Dart had been resolved.

But he didn't really have much of a choice.

He stumbled further along the tunnel, the same way Dart had gone, using his hands to feel along the grimy sides.

After a few long minutes, the distant glow of twilight lured Ripley down a narrow tunnel to his right, and he found himself emerging into the makeshift car park that served the exhibition grounds.

A family was squeezing into a four-wheel drive that was barely big enough to accommodate all of the show bags and stuffed toys they had collected. They had spent a small fortune on cheap products that would end up in the rubbish bin within a couple of weeks.

Ripley stayed where he was while he scanned the car park to make sure nobody was on the hunt for a dishevelled man carrying a chain.

The chain! He let it slip out of his grasp. It would no longer be necessary.

His mobile phone started beeping repeatedly as it picked up the network again. He had messages, several of them, and he could imagine the frantic questions that Gabriela's voice would be throwing at him.

Where are you?
Where should we meet?
Why won't you answer me?
I'm freaking out, Rips! What's going on?

He closed his eyes and smiled broadly. It was all over. Then, drawing a deep breath and exhaling, he dialled his message bank and lifted the phone to his ear. He would be able to put her mind at rest, tell her that thanks to a turn of events neither of them could have ever anticipated, Dart had renounced his burning desire to destroy them.

He listened to the messages, each one asking where he was, but each more pressing and fearful than the last, and then he called her.

"Ripley!" she shouted down the line, her voice heavy with both relief and anger. "Where did you run off to?"

"Where did I run off to?" he echoed her. "You don't know the half of it, but I can't tell you over the phone. I'm outside the Ekka grounds now, and, to be perfectly honest, I don't feel like going to the trouble of sneaking back in."

"That's fine by me. I don't think I can stand this place any longer. Some surface walkers are such hideous bogans!"

Ripley laughed.

"You sound like a tunnel dweller. Listen, I need to talk to the three of you right now. Can you meet me at York's Hollow?"

"Where's that?"

"Maybe you know it as Barrambin? It's that pond between the golf course and... actually, even better, make it the golf course. It'll be empty by now. All the golfers will have gone to the bar. Let's meet on the green, just across from the car park, all right?"

Gabriela conferred with the others.

"Okay, we're on our way!"

Ripley dashed across the car park and onto the golf course without being noticed by any passers-by as far as he could tell. There were no golfers on the green, just as he had expected, and, for the first time since he had run for dear life into the Haunted House, he was able to let all tension flow out of his body.

He sat on the ground, leaning against the rim of a sand bunker.

It really was over. He would no longer have to look over his shoulder every time he walked the streets. The idea wasn't easy to believe. Dart had been a shadow lurking behind every corner and ready to spring out of every manhole for so long. His hatred had been so intense, but he had accepted Ripley's act of human kindness with true gratitude. He wasn't an evil monster, just a misguided person who had been mistaken about Ripley and Gabriela, who had made an assumption about them based on his bitter resentment of everybody who lived on the surface.

Ripley felt confident he'd made the right decision in sparing Dart's life. This was a young man who just needed the help of his peers to get him back on the rails. If only he would accept it.

The others didn't take long to arrive. Fox spotted Ripley first and pointed him out to Gabriela and Brand. Even from a distance of several hundred metres, Gabriela immediately recognised in Ripley's posture some subtle sign that confirmed her suspicions.

She ran across the green and threw her arms around him. Before she had even begun to speak, he felt her tears on his cheek.

"Dart?" she whispered fearfully.

"It's all right now. He won't bother us any longer."

Gabriela pulled her head away and stared at him wide-eyed. "Did you…?"

"No, just the opposite. I saved his life."

"You did?" Brand asked. "From what?"

"From a train."

"Shit!" was all Brand could think of to say. "All right, how about you start at the beginning? We lost sight of you near the Haunted House."

Ripley pulled Gabriela onto his lap and wrapped his arms around her like he would never let go.

Brand and Fox sat on the grass beside them and listened intently as Ripley gave them a blow by blow account of the encounter.

Nobody interrupted, not until Ripley gave one particular detail that he hadn't realised was of any significance at all.

"What did you just say?" Gabriela twisted so that she was staring straight at his lips.

Ripley repeated, "He has a triangular mark on his chest, like a burn. I just wondered if perhaps it was from some kind of tunnel runner rite of passage."

"Well, no, it isn't," Fox said. "We don't do anything like that. What's wrong, Gabriela?"

"It's just that, well, it might be nothing."

"Spit it out, Gabs!" Ripley urged her.

"What does the mark look like?"

"Like I said, it's triangular. Well, it's a burn. The point at the top is clearly defined but the lower edge a bit blurry, as though there had been less pressure there."

"How big?" she asked.

"It's hard to say exactly."

"How big?" Gabriela insisted. "Could it have been made by an iron?"

"An iron?" Ripley repeated thoughtfully. "Yes, that's it, without a doubt. It was as though somebody had pressed an iron against his chest."

Gabriela was trembling. Her jaw was moving, but no words escaped her mouth.

"You're scaring me," Ripley said, grabbing her by the shoulders. "What is it?"

"Tell us, Gabs!" Brand said.

Fox jumped to her feet as understanding struck. She knelt beside Gabriela and took her hand, holding it tightly in an attempt to reassure her.

"I think I understand," Fox said softly. "There is only one reason Gabriela could have such a strong reaction to such a seemingly insignificant detail," she added for the benefit of the men, unintentionally making them feel insensitive and dull.

"I don't get it," Brand admitted.

Fox stared into Gabriela's eyes and the two women communicated silently in a way that no male could ever comprehend.

"It has to do with her brother," Fox said simply, her voice understating the meaning that simple sentence carried.

"Gabriela?" Ripley asked. "Your brother was burned by an iron?"

She moved her gaze from Fox to him and nodded. "Yes, my mother told me about an accident that happened when he was little. She never forgave herself for it. He was an active child..."

"Like Dart," Fox added.

"...and one day, while she was doing the ironing, the phone rang. She answered it, but before she could tell the caller that she had to turn the iron off, my brother had pulled on the cord."

"It struck him on the chest?" Brand asked.

"Yes, and left a burn."

"That can't be a coincidence," Ripley said. "Can it?" he asked the others.

"And he went missing at the Haunted House," Fox reminded them. "That's where Dart saw Ripley. For all we know, Dart has some vague memory of the event and goes back there every year."

"That can't be a coincidence," Brand agreed. "This is incredible! I can't imagine how you must feel, Gabriela."

"To tell you the truth, I don't know how I feel either," she said. "What I do know is that I need to talk to my parents."

"You're going to tell them?" Fox asked. It was clear from her tone that she wasn't sure it was a good idea.

"Do you think I should wait?"

"I just think you ought to talk to Dart before you broach the topic with them. It's a delicate situation, to say the least, and you don't want to make any rash decisions. It would be helpful to know how much he remembers about his childhood."

"What happened after you pulled him off the tracks, Rips?" Gabriela asked. "Did you talk together?"

He finished the story, explaining that he had forced Dart underground and that they had spoken about the misunderstanding. He told them Dart had decided to remain in isolation.

"I'm sure we could convince everybody to let him back into the community," Fox said to Brand.

He shrugged.

"It wouldn't be easy, but it could be done. The community would demand a formal apology."

"Do you think you can find him?" Ripley asked.

"I'll look after it," Brand assured him. "It might take a while though."

"I can help," Ripley offered.

"No," Brand told him. "I think you and Gabriela need some quiet time together."

"Thanks," Gabriela said. "You're right about that. I need to let this sink in. The more I think about it, the more certain I am that it can't be a coincidence, but all the same, it's no easy feat to suddenly change the way I consider Dart. One minute, he's a violent madman, and the next, he's just a confused little boy who needs to be shown some love."

"Could you face him, Gabs?" Ripley asked.

"I have to try," she whispered. "I have to know."

40

It didn't take long for Brand and Fox to track Dart down.

The following night, Gabriela's sleep was disturbed by a nightmare whose meaning was all too clear.

She was at the Ekka, not with Ripley and her tunnel dweller friends, but with her parents. They were standing outside the Haunted House, part of a crowd of obese mothers and fathers gobbling away at hotdogs and slurping soft drink through fat lips. There were no other children in the crowd, only adults.

The children had been lined up at the entrance to the Haunted House and were being prodded inside, one by one, by a fork-wielding man in a devil suit. His perverse face with its twisted grin was far more terrifying than the tacky costume he wore.

One little boy, a shorter version of Dart, let out a solitary scream as the devil forced him inside.

All the while, maniacal carnival music was playing, and hidden speakers spouted the cackle of a witch and the howl of a werewolf.

Gabriela turned to her parents to find expressionless faces.

The other mums and dads around seemed equally unconcerned.

A man in a Harley Davidson T-shirt told his wife, who was licking the insides out of a meat pie, that he was bored and wanted to go watch the precision driving show.

Gabriela woke from her nightmare to find the bedroom completely dark, except for the rectangular window through which moonlight shone.

The sound came again, and she knew what had roused her.

Tap, tap, tap at the window.

She could see the silhouette of a slender index finger, and, even though she knew it was Fox, her pulse quickened.

"Ripley," she whispered.

He was fast asleep. He had suffered his fair share of nightmares recently, so she was pleased his slumber was no longer troubled. Knowing that Dart had stopped hunting them was part of the reason he could sleep well. His exhaustion was another.

"Ripley," she said more loudly, shaking him gently.

He groaned and rolled away from her.

Tap, tap, tap.

Gabriela got out of bed and drew the curtains open to find Fox's keen eyes trying to see through the glass. She opened the window quietly and felt the bite of a chill breeze.

Fox looked past Gabriela and started to blush. "I hope I'm not disturbing you," she said.

Gabriela turned around to find Ripley fumbling around for some clothes. He was completely naked.

"No, we were just sleeping, I promise. Ripley, can you make yourself decent, please?"

The girls laughed.

"I'm trying to find my clothes," he whispered. "She can't see me anyway, it's too dark."

"Yes, I can," Fox teased him. "I can see well enough to know that Gabs is a lucky girl."

He found a pair of underpants just in time. His body had started to react to all the attention.

"What's the news?" Gabriela asked.

"We've found him."

"He knows?" she asked nervously.

"No, we just told him that you wanted to talk to him. He has no idea why. At first, he refused and said he was too ashamed, but I promised him you weren't angry and that it was really important."

"He didn't guess the reason?"

Fox shook her head.

247

"Are you ready, Rips?" Gabriela asked.

"Yes, I'm dressed."

"It's pretty cold out here," Fox told them.

"Yeah, I can tell," Gabriela replied. "Let me grab a jacket."

Once they were dressed warmly enough, Ripley climbed out through the window and helped Gabriela down.

"He's over there. Are you ready?" Fox asked, pointing towards the leafless frangipani tree across the street. Under it were two immediately recognisable forms.

"You showed him where we live?" There was apprehension in Gabriela's voice.

"Don't worry. He doesn't want to hurt you any longer. We've had a long discussion. He owes his life to Ripley, and, once you tell him who he is…"

Fox didn't know how to finish what she was saying, but Gabriela understood. They would be linked together for the rest of their lives. She had ceased to be an only child, and he had ceased to be an outsider with no blood ties. Everything was going to be different for both of them.

Fox took Gabriela by one hand, and Ripley took her by the other. The three of them walked across the street.

The look on Dart's face confirmed that he didn't have a clue what was going on.

"Hello, Dart," Gabriela said.

"Hello," he replied uncertainly.

"Let's go to the gazebo," Brand suggested.

They walked through the streets in silence, Dart trying to guess what was happening, and the others wondering what he remembered and how he would react.

The gazebo stood there in the chill calm of the night as though expecting them.

Brand led the way and ushered the others in. He sat Dart and Gabriela together.

She controlled her fear, reminding herself that the tunnel runner no longer posed a threat to her.

Fox sat to the left of Gabriela and again held her hand.

Brand and Ripley sat to the right of Dart.

They waited in silence, unsure who should speak first.

Brand looked encouragingly at Gabriela, but she didn't notice. She was staring at Dart's face.

Dart looked from Gabriela to Fox like a schoolboy being reprimanded by two headmistresses for a misdemeanour without knowing which of the many he had committed was in question.

It was Fox who broke the silence.

"Let me start by saying I'm really glad that, after everything we've been through, we're mature enough to be sitting here together. It has been a difficult time for all of us, but we have it in us to move on from here."

"It's a credit to us all," Ripley agreed, encouraged by Fox's forthrightness. "We're not here to talk about what has happened or to point fingers. We're here because we need to make peace and because..." he paused, not wanting to say too much, "well, because I think our lives will be much fuller together."

"You want to be my friend, after the way I've treated you?" Dart asked. "The reason I decided to live in the tunnels, like Brand and Fox, is because I despise the way society is on the surface. We came from unhappy families and had to struggle in a world where money and the drive to consume were valued more than love and equality. That's what we created for ourselves underground, a real community, and we're all afraid of losing that. My anger at discovering that you were in the tunnels was based on a mistaken assumption that *all* surface walkers were greedy and dishonourable. I was wrong. The reason you went into the tunnels in the first place was curiosity, Gabriela. And the reason you went after her was love, Ripley. They are two motivations that mean a lot to us in the tunnels. What went wrong, a long time ago, is that I let love for my community transform itself into hatred for all surface walkers. I recognise that now."

249

"That happens to us all sometimes," Fox said.

"Yes, but not to the same extent," he continued. "I wanted revenge on Ripley because I thought he was going to expose us. When the police came after me, I thought it was because he had told them. Yet, despite almost killing him and the woman he loves, he saved my life. He has more honour in him than any tunnel dweller I know."

Dart was fighting to hold back tears.

Gabriela put her arms around him.

He pulled away instinctively, but then relaxed.

"Thank you," he said. "Nobody has ever done that before."

She pulled back and stared at him in disbelief.

"You've never been hugged before?"

He shook his head.

"You've never had a girlfriend?"

"No, never. Sex, yes, but not tenderness."

Gabriela turned to Fox.

She nodded in confirmation.

"Tell me about your family, Dart," Gabriela asked.

"Family? What do you mean?"

"Before you became a tunnel dweller, you must have had a family on the surface."

"Of course, but I don't consider them family. The surface walkers who owned me are the reason I first came underground."

"Can you talk about them?"

"Why? It's torture."

"How do you know? Maybe it'll be therapy."

"Well, I was kicked out of home, if *home* is what you can call it, when I was eighteen. My father was an alcoholic and didn't have enough money to support me. My mother was a weak bitch who wouldn't stand up for me. I tried to save her from being abused and humiliated by the monster on numerous occasions, but, every time, I ended up getting the crap beaten out of me and locked in my room while she made him dinner

250

and then sucked him off while he watched TV."

Gabriela suppressed a gasp.

"I tried to get a job so I could move out, but I just couldn't find one. Nobody wants to employ a teenager without a decent education or upbringing. Nobody wants to provide a young man with training, because there's no profit to be made out of that, is there? And that's what the surface world is all about, making money out of people.

"Anyway, one night, when he was even more hammered than usual after being at a strip club – I could always smell the cheap perfume on him – he came home horny. I woke up to the sound of mum moaning, *I don't want to do that. Please, not that. It hurts*. I didn't even want to think about what she meant. I lost my temper and slammed on the bedroom wall and shouted something like, *Go to sleep, you walking pile of shit!* and, well, that was it – he went ballistic and..." Dart's voice trailed off. "I think you get the picture."

"That's horrible," Ripley said softly. "And that's when you joined the tunnel dwellers?"

"Not quite, I spent a few years crashing with mates and getting up to trouble. I tried to find work, but it was hard, so I mostly stole to survive. Eventually, I started sleeping in the tunnels, but I can't really remember why. Then, one day, I literally bumped into Cooper down there." A shadow crossed his face. "Now, I've ostracised myself from him and all the others."

"There has always been a bit of competition between Dart and Cooper," Brand explained.

Dart turned and frowned at Brand.

"Brand!" Fox warned him.

"No, he's right," Dart admitted. "I'm not entirely to blame for that, but he's right. I'm jealous of Cooper's ability and charisma, and that's unacceptable."

"Dart, I have a question. How did you know Ripley would be at the Haunted House?" Gabriela asked, even though she knew the answer.

"I didn't," he admitted, shaking his head.

"So, why were you there?"

"I'm not sure. I go there every year. I go to the Ekka, and I go to the Haunted House, but I never go inside it. I just stand there and stare at it, and I've never understood the reason why. I suppose I'm just insane."

"No," Gabriela assured him. "There's a cause. I'm no psychologist, but I believe you have a suppressed memory of the Haunted House. Do you remember going there as a child?"

"I don't remember. My parents never took me, but somehow I've always had a feeling I must have been there once."

"You don't have any brothers or sisters?"

"No, I'm an only child. My mother had some complications during my birth and couldn't have any other children."

"She told you that?"

Dart's brow creased.

"Why do you want to know all this? What's going on?"

"I think she was lying, Dart. I don't think she was ever able to have children."

"That doesn't make sense," he said, his face screwed up. "She had me."

"I think she kidnapped you from the Ekka, from outside the Haunted House, because she wanted a child. She went to the Ekka with the intention of kidnapping a child because she couldn't have one of her own."

Gabriela could no longer stop herself from crying.

"How do you know all this? What's going on?"

She wiped her tears away as best she could and cleared her throat.

"When I was little, my parents took me to the Ekka, and my little brother ran off into the Haunted House. We never saw him again."

Dart's face froze. He didn't speak. Nobody did. Only the sound of the chill breeze whistling through the gazebo could be heard. The silence was too much to bear.

252

Tears were now welling in Dart's eyes too.

"You think I'm your brother?" he asked eventually.

Gabriela nodded, wiping her tears away.

"We do look similar, even though you're more beautiful than me, and I never did look like either of my so-called parents. But we can't know for sure."

"There's another reason," she said. "When Ripley pulled you off the railway tracks, he saw a burn mark on your chest."

"That's from an iron. Mum said she accidentally dropped it on me when I was a baby. I've always wondered if she was covering for dad."

"She wasn't covering for him," Gabriela said. "She was covering for your real mother. My mum used to tell me about my little brother. She said he had a burn mark on his chest from where he pulled the iron onto himself."

Dart was speechless. There was no longer any doubt in his mind; the obsession with the Haunted House, the burn mark, the simple fact that he and Gabriela looked similar. There were tests that could confirm the blood tie conclusively, but he didn't want surface authorities to have his DNA on file.

"Where do you want to go from here?" he asked.

She pulled him close and held him.

"Let's go for a walk," Fox whispered to the others.

When they returned to the gazebo, there was only one figure sitting there, head buried in hands.

"Where's Dart?" Ripley asked, placing his arms around Gabriela's shoulders.

"He left," she whispered.

Fox sat beside her.

"What happened?"

"He doesn't want to meet his parents. He thinks it would be

more than he could stand, and that he'll never belong to the surface world."

"We'll try to change his mind," Fox assured her.

"I doubt it. He begged me not to come after him."

Gabriela raised her head and showed Fox what he'd given her before leaving. Hanging around her neck was a diamond necklace. The jewels gleamed like Gabriela's tears under the moonlight.

"He must have stolen it from some rich woman's home."

The gesture was touching, but it just went to show that Dart didn't know his sister at all. Despite what he had said, she was still just a stereotypical surface walker to him, obsessed with consumer products, glittering distractions, and meaningless status symbols.

Gabriela decided she would keep it as a souvenir of her brother, but she would never wear it again.

"He'll come back one day, Gabs. Once he realises how lucky he is to have a loving family waiting for him on the surface. You know that, don't you? He'll come back to you."

But he never did.

———◦◦◦———

The friendship between the two surface walkers and the two tunnel dwellers continued and strengthened. Although Ripley continued his morning exercise routine with Pete and the boys, their friendship was never quite the same again. He often went back into the tunnels, especially at those times when the shallow distractions of the surface world reached saturation point and he just needed to get away from it all for a while.

Gabriela refused to go back down, and she never told her parents about Dart.

Fox and Brand eventually convinced Dart to come back to the community, but they weren't able to convince him to visit his sister. They gave her news about how he was doing, and it was a great relief when she heard that he had fallen in love with a young woman down there, another disenchanted surface walker who had gone to ground.

To this very day, whenever Gabriela opens the simple wooden jewellery box in which she keeps Suzanne Klipsch's necklace, and every time she walks past a manhole cover, she spares a thought for the brother she never had, the Tunnel Runner.

For news, reviews, competitions, author interviews, and exclusive excerpts

Visit our website
blackbeaconbooks.com

Like us on Facebook
facebook.com/BlackBeaconBooks

Join us on X
@BlackBeacons

Follow us on Goodreads
goodreads.com/author/show/20231552

Enjoy the photos on Instagram
instagram.com/blackbeaconbooks

Subscribe on Patreon
patreon.com/blackbeaconbooks

www.ingramcontent.com/pod-product-compliance
Lightning Source LLC
Chambersburg PA
CBHW031714170626
46808CB00005B/1738